Dead Spaces

THE BIG UNEASY BOOK 2

PAULINE BAIRD JONES

Dead Spaces

Be careful what you dig for...

A forensic surgeon in the New Orleans Coroner's Center—and part of her dad's Baker's Dozen—Hannah Baker thought she knew where to dig, how and what to slice, and when to walk away.

But when her big brother gets her involved in the exhumation of a couple of old coffins, she realizes the past can't be ignored. Not when it's been simmering up a big pile of trouble for longer than Hannah's born days.

Only New Orleans could produce a "Baked" gumbo of the mob, shadowy figures from the past, annoying figures from the present, murders, attempted murders, and a really cute detective who is technically off limits on account of he's her big brother's partner.

Good thing NOPD Detective Logan Ferris doesn't know the meaning of "off limits," because once more the Big Easy is getting mighty uneasy.

———

CHAPTER 1

THE LAW FIRM OF *LEBLANC, Fontenot, Miller, Robinson, and Hendry* had a long and somewhat infamous advocacy history. The Leblanc family had founded the firm at the turn of century, forming an unholy alliance with Zafiro.

When Zafiro was helped out of existence by Afoniki, Calvino and St. Cyr, the founding Leblanc had added partners so as to keep the tangled threads of the various "wise" interests from crossing and causing him problems. That Leblanc's son, and then his son's son, had stayed at the center of this web, helped maintain the illusion of neutrality.

In their own way, the firm was honest. They held the affairs of their clients as a sacred trust. Of course, it helped keep them honest that their clients would have no hesitation in visiting swift vengeance on them if they strayed from their crooked path.

But beyond this incentive, each of them found a kind of virtue in honoring the trust reposed in them. Each partner was like a small country, with strict borders that protected their clients, and only old Leblanc knew all the threads and steered their company ship carefully between the varied—and often conflicting—interests.

Until the murder of Phineas St. Cyr.

This event that had caused him, the current senior Leblanc, to steer the firm deliberately into stormy waters.

He hadn't done it with malice, but there had been much forethought. In the years before St. Cyr's death, the lawyer in him had argued the case for and against this action—and the man could admit to hoping that the choice would not come in his lifetime.

Not that he wished it on his son. Mostly he'd hoped it would pass them by as not relevant. He'd not been quite sure which instinct would prevail until the moment arrived.

When it did, and he'd made the inevitable and unwelcome decision to honor that promise to his father and grandfather, he was left wondering what the cost would be to himself. To the firm. To the others in the firm.

Had they known, had he known—but the law, even his side of the law, was not about knowing. It was about fulfilling contractual obligations. It surprised him to discover that at heart he was a lawyer.

He'd acted as one, even if it might be against his own interests. He hoped that he wasn't burning his own house down. Perhaps it would turn out to be a remodel of the existing structure, or possibly a shedding of burdensome layers.

But it felt as if he'd set it aflame. Very like it. He shifted uneasily as he considered this. His new client had been most unhappy with the role the firm had played. Quite vocally unhappy.

Through the years, through his offices, had passed many of the most dangerous, most unprincipled, evil—he didn't like the word because there was judgment in it, but it was the truth.

Some of the evilest of evil had sat in the chair across from him. All these years, so many faces and he'd never, not even once, been afraid. Because in the evil he'd known there had also been reason. There'd been logic behind the evil.

Until now. This evil was not reasonable. Or logical. He was not certain it was…competent. And it had something to prove. He did not see how this could go well. And he'd unleashed it.

Not just on the firm, but on an…unsuspecting world. The main targets were, no question, not innocent, but there would be collateral damage.

Probably too much to expect God to have mercy on his soul. He'd sold it so long ago.

———

An exhumation didn't make a lot of bucket lists. Not that Hannah Baker dared write her bucket list down. Life with many siblings had taught her not to leave a paper trail if she could help it.

And she wasn't sure she wanted a bucket list. It didn't seem like a good idea to have a list of things to do before she died when she worked in one of the "dead spaces" of New Orleans—the Coroner's Center—as a forensic surgeon.

It might be more useful to make a list of things to do before she got laid off. Whatever ongoing budget crisis was being experienced by the various city departments, it was multiplied by a really big number inside the NOCC.

Which meant she wouldn't be paid for showing up on her day off. She didn't know whether to curse her curiosity or her "un-bucket" list. Her gaze drifted to one of the four men who'd followed the two coffins inside.

Or she could blame her hi-jacked day off on her big brother.

Of course Alex shouldn't be here, even if he was keeping behind the chalk line she'd drawn on the floor. This particular exhumation was a little too personal for her usually impersonal brother.

No way she'd let him contaminate the chain of evidence—assuming that the two coffins produced anything remotely evidential. After thirty years in their crypts—New Orleans' other dead space—that seemed unlikely.

It wasn't that unusual to have a couple of Bakers—in this instance, three of them—cluttering up a crime scene. It was a bit unusual to have them "Baking" the morgue—which was already hot, thank you faulty air conditioning.

Both Alex and Ingrid—the third Baker present—were on duty and getting paid. Not that Hannah was bitter. She'd left sibling rivalry behind when she turned thirty. She still needed to work on not whining though. It was a hard habit to break when you worked in a whine-one-one zone.

A couple of techs positioned the two coffins on her side of the chalk line, bits of debris still clinging to their surfaces, and set the brakes on the wheels. The coffins were in better shape than she'd have expected after so long. Maybe there would be something inside. Was it wrong of her to hope so?

Each tech picked a coffin and went to work on the latches. This gave Hannah time to study the non-dead people in the room. She was used to having Ingrid, who worked in the Crime Scene Unit, around now and again, and she was happy to have her sister on her side of the chalk line. A little girl power never hurt.

Alex showed up less often in Hannah's dead space. No one really wanted to be in the NOCC—which was currently located in the back of an old funeral home—even when they had to. His partner, Logan Ferris, lounged next to Alex.

An invisible line of suspicion and aggression divided the two cops from the two bad guys, also unfortunately present for the occasion.

The wise cousins were Guido Calvino and Claude St. Cyr.

Hannah knew their presence was a Family thing more than a family thing—the crypts from whence the coffins came were family owned.

At this point no one knew who was interred in the caskets. Or not interred in them. It was confusing enough to make her eye twitch. She suppressed the twitch, because movement of any kind made her sweat more.

Either family could have blocked the exhumation and she was surprised they hadn't. Apparently curiosity wasn't limited to the legal side of the situation.

Instead they had both countered with a demand for a family representative to be present when the coffins were opened. Alex would have said no and fought it all the way to the DA.

Truth was, the case was still open because no one could find the file. It was a loophole Alex had driven his new truck through. He hadn't expected the bad guys to come through it with him. Sucked to be him right now.

Of the two bad guys, Guido was definitely the eye candy. Rugged everything, bad boy heir to a criminal empire currently run by his great-uncle. Guido had a decent skull, his frontal nicely balanced with his mandible. Acceptable frame, clavicles wide enough to make his suit hang nicely, though he was a bit elegant for her tastes.

It might be the suit. She wouldn't mind seeing him in jeans. He had dark coloring, probably from his Italian heritage. His most likely way to die? Gunshot or explosion, though it would be a pity to blow him to bits.

It took her a few seconds to realize that, unlike a corpse, he could look back. And was. With a look of amusement in his dark eyes, his gaze met hers. She blinked, gave him an apologetic half smile, and turned her attention to Claude St. Cyr.

And wished she hadn't.

Claude looked like he could have crawled out of one of the coffins. The skin hung off a skull with a receding mandible and an occipital begging to be bashed in.

All his skeletal frame did was make his suit hang oddly. Hard to see him as the new, big bad boss of the St. Cyr crime family when he looked more like a creepy accountant.

There was a slight gleam of something in his pale gray eyes. Hannah couldn't tell if it was worry or anticipation. One sensed he had the potential for evil. Now that he was the boss, he might be ready to explore that part of himself.

Hannah shifted her attention back to the "good" side of the room and sighed.

Her brother's physical presence overshadowed the two bad guys, even the tallish Guido. He was a *big* big brother.

Before his shoulders got that broad, Alex had carried a lot of the parental weight of looking after his younger siblings when their dad buried his second wife.

Hannah, as oldest of the second wave of children, had some memories of her mom, but it was her big, dark-haired brother that she remembered making her lunches and telling her the facts of life. Pause for internal shudder at that memory.

As always, she felt a wave of love and frustration. It was not easy to keep him on the other side of any lines. It didn't matter that this was her space, not his. He was the oldest and stood in for their dad more often than not until Zach—they all called him Zach because Alex did—had retired.

She felt his frustration, saw it in his body language—which spoke the volumes his mouth did not—as the techs struggled with latches sealed over thirty years ago. If Alex could have gotten closer, they'd probably pop open at a look. As far as Hannah knew, only their dad could stand up to the Alex glare.

In stark contrast to Alex's crossed arms and intense glare was his very relaxed, almost-asleep-standing-up partner.

Ferris, with his slighter build, should be in Alex's shadow as well but somehow wasn't. Beneath the lazy droop of his lids, his gaze was sharp. His rangy frame might lack the brute force of Alex's, but Logan Ferris could move fast when he wanted—or needed—to.

He'd earned Alex's respect—not easy to do—and their good cop/bad cop was legendary within the NOPD.

Alex's friends, at least the ones who'd watched her grow up, still saw all of the Baker girls as his little sisters.

It didn't matter that Hannah was the oldest little sister. It also didn't matter how many letters she accumulated after her medical degree—nothing quite like being the geeky genius in the Baker family, she acknowledged a bit wryly.

If she'd accumulated them to prove something—well, she hadn't. She'd done it for herself—with maybe a little of trying-to-get-daddy's-attention in there—and because she couldn't help it if she vacuumed up knowledge.

Mostly it didn't bother her that Alex's friends couldn't see the grownup she'd become.

Ferris was, for a reason she declined to parse too closely, the exception. It wasn't that she liked him or anything. Not that she disliked him, but she didn't *like* him. Besides, he hadn't watched her grow up. And he was younger than her by at least three years.

That disqualified him from seeing her as Alex's baby sister. A pity he hadn't got that memo. He didn't seem to notice her not noticing him, so she felt free to direct a quick glare in his direction. Annoying *boy*.

He did appear to be noticing Ingrid, who was a younger, cuter version of Hannah, though also older than Ferris. If she hadn't moved on from sibling rivalry, that would have bothered her. Wasn't it a good thing she'd moved on.

"That should do it, Doc," said one of the techs, arching a brow and making a lifting motion with his hands.

She shook her head—she didn't want to pop the lids until the two techs left. Leaks were impossible to stop, but she still felt a need to try.

She thanked them, waiting until the two men left before nodding to Ingrid. They got on either end of one coffin and, after a brief struggle, forced the lid up. She wasn't sure what she'd expected, but it wasn't—she blinked—this.

She looked at her sister. Her eyes were wide, too.

As one, she and Ingrid moved to the second coffin and lifted its lid. And stared.

Hannah tried to think of something to say. These were not the bodies she usually dug through. That meant the coffins just became Ingrid's problem and she might get her day off back.

She gave her sister a "take it away" gesture, trying not to giggle.

Ingrid grabbed a camera, her lips twitching. Only then did Hannah look at her brother.

"Well?" Patience was not really in Alex's wheelhouse, though it should be. As the eldest, he'd had a choice. Be awesomely awesome at patience or totally suck at it. He'd opted for sucking. He didn't appear to regret it either.

She didn't rub her chin. One didn't when one worked in a morgue. But she wanted to.

Ingrid finished her photographs and moved to the second coffin. Even though it would have been entertaining to see their faces, she didn't invite them across the line. Another lesson learned in family trenches: you'll never get back given ground.

"You wanna start collecting the, um, evidence?" Ingrid looked up from her camera to ask. She gave a quick look at her watch.

Hannah opened her mouth to remind her that it was her day off and that she hadn't wanted to get sucked into this but ran into Ingrid's hopeful look.

Hannah gave a nod that had a sigh in it and a lot of reluctance. She'd prepped for what she'd assumed would be an autopsy, so she was geared up enough to grab the nearest item.

There was a faint ripping sound as rotted fabric gave way. The "corpse" had apparently been secured on purpose in its, um, interesting pose. She held it high so that the four men could see it. It stalled Alex's next question. Four jaws went slack.

Ferris recovered first. "What is it?"

She turned it one way, then another, studying it for at least a minute. "It's a doll. Possibly a Barbie doll." She rubbed the mildew off of the face with her thumb. "Malibu, I think."

It was a bit embarrassing she knew this, but she did have five sisters. And seven brothers. Yes, that was also embarrassing.

She flicked a glance at the slack jaws and hoped Ingrid would get a shot of that. Even their heads were angled the same direction. It felt a bit like they'd wandered into a *Saturday Night Live* sketch when one combined those looks with a naked doll that had been secured in a coffin in the mooning position.

As if he heard the thought—he'd developed a bit of parental psychic power growing up—Alex's jaw snapped closed. "What's in the other one?"

Hannah stepped over to it and tugged at one of its "corpses." More ripping sound before she held it up. "I'm gonna guess this is Ken. Three of them in this one."

Were the dolls significant or merely a curiously weird joke?

Hannah knew the story behind the coffins, knew what was supposed to have been buried in them.

Phillip St. Cyr and Antonia Calvino, two star-crossed lovers, slash, mob prince and princess, blown to bits by person or persons unknown nearly three decades ago.

Only they hadn't got blown up. They'd faked their own deaths and fled to Wyoming where they raised a daughter. That daughter, Nell Whitby, had come to live in New Orleans.

This wouldn't have mattered if she hadn't looked like the ghost of her grandmother, Ellie Calvino. This resemblance had launched an unfortunate series of events, including a couple of murders and some attempts on her life.

That Alex was dating Nell, the long-lost granddaughter of

two crime families, added another level of complication to a situation weird even by New Orleans standards.

It made Hannah's head hurt thinking about the wheels within wheels of the messy past—a past that seemed determined to take out her day off.

The girlfriend was the other reason for keeping Alex on the other side of that line. The sibs were divided on the wisdom of Alex dating someone related to two crime families—as in, divided on how bat crap crazy it was, that is.

Hannah thought he'd be in Wit-Sec by the end of the year. It made it hard to warm up to Nell.

"Kens?" Alex looked and sounded incredulous. "Kens?"

Hannah studied Ken. "Could be Malibu, too, I suppose." She glanced at the other two.

"This one might be Superstar Ken. Looks like he was dressed in a suit. Black. With some glitter." Ingrid held up some rotting black threads, a bit of dull sparkle along what could have been a lapel.

Hannah released the last Ken from his bonds and studied him. "Nothing left of his clothes but a tie. I think he's a ringer, a fake."

Ingrid blinked a bit. "Really?" She moved closer and studied the alleged ringer. "It's scary you know that."

"You're telling me," Hannah muttered, her gaze moving between the dolls. Someone had a dark sense of humor. She liked that. But then she worked in a morgue. She frowned. Was the dirt heavier—she rubbed at ringer Ken's temple. "This one's been—" what did one call a doll wound? "It's got a hole in the side of the head. His temple."

Did dolls have temples?

"So does this one." Ingrid exchanged a look with Hannah, then checked the last doll. "They all do. Except Barbie."

"But—" Ferris stopped, most likely because he didn't know what to say. Or didn't want to say it with the wise cousins still in the room.

It wasn't a crime to disfigure and bury four dolls, though the attempt to deceive might be. Hannah wasn't clear on that. She didn't have to be. No human remains, not her problem.

Obviously it had been a crime to fake the deaths, but since they hadn't killed anything but some dolls, she figured that the statute of limitations had to have passed a long time ago.

As had the two people who were supposed to have been buried in these caskets.

Had Nell's parents arranged this before disappearing into new lives?

She could make the case both for and against a couple of teenagers thinking it up, but not even a tiny one for them having the resources for this kind of hoax. Someone back then had helped them, but who? And why? She'd have thought there'd been enough to do just to keep from really dying.

Hannah looked at Claude, then Guido, mostly so she wouldn't look at Ferris looking at Ingrid.

Claude's pale gaze had widened a little.

Guido looked amused, possibly a bit relieved. The coffins predated him by a lot, so what did he have to be relieved about? Or was he proxy relieved for his big bad great uncle, Bettino Calvino?

He knew what wasn't in there, but what had he been afraid *would* be in the caskets? Or was that who?

"Dolls?" Alex rubbed his face.

You'd think a guy with six sisters could wrap his brain around the concept of a doll.

"Dolls." Ferris echoed the word, only without the question mark.

With some reluctance, Hannah glanced at him. Of course, he'd opted not to shave. That was usual. According to Alex, his unmade bed look attracted girls like flypaper.

The chin was probably rough when—okay, not a place to go when it was already too warm and she was draped in protective gear.

She and Ferris? Never going to happen. His type of gal didn't dig through brains and body parts. Besides, she usually made her bed. Not because she was a neat freak. She needed it to function as a couch during the day.

It was a pity there wasn't a real dead body to distract her from Ferris.

She didn't want to notice that he had good hair and teeth—dark everything including the beard shadow. Ferris' hair kind of reminded her of Malibu Ken's, which made her lips twitch.

She knew his sleepy gaze hid a decent brain that he didn't always use for good. She studied the line of his jaw, easy to do with the five o'clock shadow.

He'd make a pretty corpse but was much sexier breathing. A guy most likely to be shoved out a window by an irate lover, she decided.

The thin, firm line of his mouth parted, then closed. The look in his dangerous green eyes told her he'd had something to say but had opted—again—not to say it.

It didn't seem like anyone wanted to talk, so Hannah filled the silence in a way that would hopefully clear the room.

"Ingrid will process the dolls and the caskets, and she'll

make a list of the, er, contents." She gave Ingrid a "jump in here anytime" look. "She'll let you know when…if…what happens next."

Her best guess was the dolls would be added to the file. If someone found it. Then the DA would stamp it closed and move on to the hundreds of other cases sitting on his desk. No one ever said the Big Easy was actually easy.

"Will I receive a copy of the list?" Guido asked.

The guy did have a nice voice. And smile. It was a pity he was a piece of evil crap.

"That's for the lawyers and the DA to sort out," Hannah said. Another thing a gal learned growing up with twelve siblings, never promise anything. Ever.

"You can be assured my lawyer will be in touch," Claude said, his voice as thin and cold as his frame.

Hannah blinked. She hadn't really expected him to care.

Maybe he cared because Guido did? Still, he'd only recently ascended to head of the St. Cyr empire. And he'd had to wait a long time for someone to take out Phineas St. Cyr.

Hannah had done the autopsy. It had been yawningly uninteresting, considering he'd been one of the infamous three wise geezers, the third being Aleksi Afoniki.

A single shot to the temple was a boring way to die— Hannah blinked, her gloved thumb rubbing the wound in Ken's noggin.

Three wise guys. Three Kens. But only one dead wise guy, she reminded herself. She gave a mental shake and looked at her unwelcome guests.

She gave a pointed look at her watch. "Since we're done here…" She threw in her "I can autopsy you" look. That got them moving toward the door.

Alex and Ferris pretended to follow, then shut the door when they were on the other side.

"You'll search thoroughly?" Alex asked.

Ingrid looked at Hannah and rolled her eyes.

"No," Ingrid said. "I'd planned to do a crappy job. Jeez, Alex. Check the big brother crap at the door."

"Preferably the other side of the door," Hannah added.

Ferris laughed, his gaze admiring as it rested on Ingrid. Why didn't Ingrid get the little sister treatment? And how sad was it to feel—well, it wasn't jealousy because she wasn't, but something enough like it to be annoying.

To distract herself, Hannah set down the Ken, popped the Barbie's head off and looked inside. Empty as Hannah's love life. Not even a brain to dig through.

"This is a message," Alex insisted. "Just—"

"Go away, Alex," Hannah said. She didn't look at Ferris, but she knew he looked at her, and she wondered how she knew that and what he saw, then was glad she didn't know when she noticed out of the corner of her eye that he'd grinned.

It was a nice grin. A pity they couldn't be friends. That was probably a guy rule, right after: don't date a dude's sister.

"Come on, Alex." Ferris grabbed his arm. After a moment of resistance, Alex followed him out. Though he paused and looked back.

"Be careful."

Hannah held the Barbie up, bare tush out. "Kiss my—"

The door swung closed. Hannah laughed, then turned around and met Ingrid's gaze.

She looked at the headless doll in her hand, then the doll Ingrid held. Three Kens and one stark naked Barbie.

Her thoughts drifted back to the three wise guys. Hadn't Alex said something about the three wise geezers, well, they weren't geezers then, but the three of them competing for Ellie Calvino back in the day before she married Bettino Calvino?

And that possible coercion had been applied to get her to marry him? Hannah shivered at the thought of being forced to marry one of those creepy boys. Maybe there was an upside to digging through brains.

Even the bad guys steered a wide path around her.

"A message?" Ingrid cast her doll a dubious look.

"Could be a lot of things." Hannah sighed, then wished she hadn't when beads of sweat popped out along her upper lip. She tugged off one layer of protective gear.

"If it was a message, I wonder who it was meant for?"

Before Hannah could respond, Ingrid's phone went off. She pulled it out and looked at it.

"Gotta suspicious death in City Park. Outside in August. Jeez fricking Louise. They could at least do their killing inside where it's cool. Would you mind bagging and tagging the dolls for me? I'll get someone to collect all this crap later." She followed the question up with another one of the sister looks.

Which just went to show how good deeds got punished. Sometimes really fast.

She sighed, which Ingrid took for a yes.

"You're the best."

Ingrid stripped off her gloves and tossed them in the trash. She eased the door open, grinned back. "I'll email you the photos as a thank you. I got the best shot of them all with their jaws slack. It's epic."

Hannah had to grin then, though it still had some wry in it.

At least there didn't seem to be much in the coffins. How

sad was it that she was sorry there wasn't a moldy old body for her to puzzle over? Yeah, that would be why she spent most of her Friday nights at home streaming CSI shows.

It felt a bit weird to be alone with the coffins and the dolls. Were there any horror movies with killer dolls?

There was a good reason she didn't watch horror movies, she decided, glancing around the suddenly too quiet room.

She rubbed at the hole in the side of the doll head. Was this a message? Or a teenaged joke? They'd all been secured in place. The three Kens lined up like corpses.

And Barbie? That she'd been secured in the mooning position did seem like a message. Had they thought the coffins would be opened sooner? Or had it been meant as a private joke?

She lined the dolls up on the table usually reserved for human bodies, and began her search of the coffins' interiors. She bagged a few dead bugs and some of the dust. You never knew. Maybe someone would shake loose some money so they could parse the dirt, investigate this like they did on TV. Yeah, and Elvis was going to walk through the door any minute now.

The Ken coffin netted lots of dirt and a Ken loafer that she almost missed. Why was it always one shoe that went missing?

The surface under the lining was hard, even where a body usually lay. Maybe they didn't pad coffins. It's not like a corpse needed soft.

She lifted the rotting fabric as much as she could without ripping it more. It looked like there was some kind of stone under there, possibly to weight the coffins so they'd feel properly heavy.

Ingrid was going have a cow when she saw them if she had to catalog them all.

She shifted attention to the Barbie coffin. There were bricks under the lining, too, or so it seemed.

She felt along the sides until her hand bumped something hard.

She shifted the debris carefully aside. A ring had been tucked—or fallen?—between the side and the bottom.

She grabbed her cell phone and took a couple of shots, then extracted it.

She rubbed enough grime off to see that it looked to be a fairly cheap version of a high school class ring. She held it up to the light and felt a rising unease as the school initials became visible.

It was her dad's high school insignia, one of the smaller, private high schools in the area. She put it under a magnifying glass, and saw, barely legible through the dirt, some words engraved on the inside.

It was just a coincidence. It had to be. Was it possible to pull prints off it after all this time? She bumped up the magnification and gently blew off as much debris as she could.

Charles Evans Baker.

She leaned against the table to support knees that all the sudden felt weak. How had her Uncle Charlie's high school ring ended up in a coffin buried almost twenty years *after* he'd disappeared?

————

"Do you think it's some kind of message?" Alex said broodingly.

Ferris stopped next to Alex, just outside on the loading ramp, in the shadow of the big freezer trucks where the bodies were stored.

The air was hot and thick, but despite being an alley, it smelled better than inside the NOCC.

He glanced at his partner and resisted the urge to shake his head. Love was kicking Alex's rear. He was so far up the river of denial, he needed an airlift rescue. And if he wanted to get punched out, he'd tell Alex that.

Since he was constitutionally opposed to getting punched, Ferris considered Alex's question instead.

"Yeah, sure." It seemed to Ferris it was a pretty succinct message: kiss this, jerks. With maybe a touch of: your turn is coming. That made him frown a bit. If it was Karma, it had been a long time coming.

Those coffins had been interred a long time ago. Pretty private message. Or inside joke. Really inside joke.

"Three wise guys. One girl. What if Ellie Calvino helped her daughter and the St. Cyr kid get away and that's why…"

Ferris had heard bits of the story. Though Ellie Calvino had been listed as missing for thirty-some years, the conventional wisdom was that her loving husband had her put down quietly.

Bettino did have some experience in making inconvenient people go missing permanent-like. As did Aleksi Afoniki and the late, unlamented Phineas St. Cyr.

The way the story went, the three had competed for her hand, Bettino had won, then had buyer's remorse.

What Ferris found interesting is that one of the two losers hadn't killed Ellie quicker for the crime of not picking them.

Neither of them were what you'd call good losers. The

three wise geezers had been a huge, stinking pile of brown stuff before they became geezers. A pile that didn't seem that much smaller since St. Cyr got his well-deserved bullet to the brain last month.

If Ellie Calvino had survived, she'd be on his suspect list, but it was St. Cyr's widow who was out on bail for the hit on her husband. It sounded like they had a solid case, too, even if the hired shooter's brain had short circuited a bit after his arrest.

As he recalled, the sort of geeky Hannah had been the one to dig the bullet out of St. Cyr's skull. Why did he find that kind of sexy?

He'd had a thing for smart girls since high school. He liked it when she turned her analytical gaze on him. He just wished it stayed longer.

Holy Hannah.

It was a pity a partner's sisters were off limits. Especially when his partner had so many of them. All blonde and all easy on the eyes.

It was Hannah who tested his self-control, though. So far he'd managed to keep it. He didn't want to get punched. Alex had been wanting to punch someone since people started shooting at his girlfriend.

A pity Calvino or St. Cyr hadn't given him an opening. The dude needed to feel better, even if it wouldn't last.

While Nell did nothing for Ferris, he could see why she had Alex's wheels spinning. They both had that look couples got when love whacked them upside the head. He wasn't one to wish marriage on a bubba but dude, it was coming, with or without the wishing.

He'd wish Alex luck if Nell weren't related to two mob

families. Okay, he did wish him luck. The guy was going to need it.

Why, he wondered, did Alex care if Ellie Calvino helped them or not, other than her being Nell's grandmother. Man, the guy was up to his eyeballs in crap. He needed to step back and take a breath. Use his brain.

Ferris would have told him that—which brought him back full circle to not wanting to get punched. He looked speculatively at Alex. On the other hand, maybe he was distracted enough to not notice Ferris chatting up his little sister. If the other sister hadn't been in there, he might have made an excuse to stroll back in—

Alex's cell shrilled. He answered with a curt, "Baker." Then his eyes widened. He lowered his arm, a frown forming on his face.

"What?" Ferris knew that look. Someone had died, but a someone whose death made the world a better place.

Alex rubbed his face. "Someone popped Bettino Calvino." He made a gun with his hand and pointed at his temple, then added, "In City Park."

So why the frown— Ferris stopped. "Don't tell me we're Guido's alibi?"

Alex's frown deepened to a scowl. "One of these days, he's going to give me an excuse to hit him."

"Be better to arrest him," Ferris pointed out mildly. Ingrid Baker was on duty, so that meant she'd have to go to the scene, leaving Holy Hannah all alone…

"I need to talk to Nell, hopefully before this hits the news."

Ferris looked at his watch. "Lunch hour?" He cast a speculative glance back at the NOCC. "Why don't you pick me up back here?" Alex arched his brows. "The body's going to end up here. Maybe I'll hear something."

Alex nodded an okay. "Want me to bring you something?"

"I'll figure something out," Ferris said easily, pulling the door open as Alex headed for their wheels. He didn't rush retracing his steps. In the park with the gun. In the head, too. Like the Kens. Did that mean Afoniki was next in line to get his? A guy could hope.

And he could wonder why it had taken so long...

———

Guido Calvino found it easy to let Claude—*clod*—get ahead of him. Four bodyguards waiting outside? Claude probably thought it made him look powerful, not scared of his own shadow.

He'd waited too long for power. He should have taken the old man out years ago. It had been obvious to everyone that Phineas St. Cyr had neither feared nor respected the spare heir.

St. Cyr had liked to think of himself as the "gentleman" mafia king. Guido could admit to wondering why his Uncle Bettino hadn't moved on St. Cyr. He'd been the weakest of the three—his thoughts stalled.

This Ken is a fake, a ringer.

Another day, Guido might have been intrigued with the idea, but St. Cyr was dead. A clod was now in command of his empire. If—*if* there had been some sort of agreement between Bettino, Afoniki, and St. Cyr, it would be void, would it not?

Not that Guido was eager to kick up Afoniki's anthill by making an obvious move on the clod's stuff. Afoniki made

Uncle Bett—who saw himself as old school mafia—look like the family pet.

St. Cyr had been a polite killer and Uncle Bett a practical one, but Afoniki? He liked it, the power, the corrupting, and the killing.

Guido knew better than to let it show, but he'd been as uncomfortable at Afoniki's dinner party as his reluctant new cousin, Nell.

If Afoniki had hoped to turn the girl back to her roots, well, he'd failed and not just for now. Nell had been remarkably resilient, not to mention resistant to exploring her darker roots.

His cousin, Cinzia, had it right when she'd said her bedroom was probably cleaned by singing birds and mice.

He'd never been opposed to corrupting the innocent, but Alex Baker had made it clear, you messed with Nell, you messed with him. In this city, there was one truth even his side knew to respect.

You messed with one Baker, you messed with them all.

The hounds of hell would be easier to manage.

It was possible the ill-timed shooting at the dinner party had tipped the balance for Baker. He couldn't be steered, led, or warned off. No one had owned up to it, but then if someone did, it would be their last act in this life.

Nell's return to New Orleans had stirred up more than old dirt.

Guido paused in the hallway, watching as Claude's SUV halted long enough for him to scramble inside. Guido smiled. He would be lucky to survive to the end of the year.

Not that Guido wanted to ignite a turf war with Afoniki. Both the old man and his heir were most likely formulating their own plans for seizing what Phin had left so ill-protected.

The widow, she might have been able to keep it together, but Claude was weak. And Helene was old and under indictment. She would be of limited help to Claude. Always assuming he wanted her help. Or she wanted to give it. No love lost there.

If there was an agreement between the three old men, how very much he'd like to see the details. It must be powerful indeed to have kept three such men in check for so long.

And where did Nell Whitby fit in? What did uncle Bett fear from her? Was there a secret still waiting to ooze up out of the past? And was it a secret that would help—or damage— Guido's very bright future?

Guido flexed his hands, feeling his own readiness to assume control. He was fond of his great uncle, but that would not stop him if he saw a chance. It was, after all, what uncle Bett had done.

He glanced back, past his two bodyguards, to the door of the autopsy room, just in time to see Ingrid Baker leave. She didn't look his direction. Her phone held to her ear, she moved rapidly, though with commendable grace.

The Baker girls. The younger Baker boys weren't unappealing either. He shook his head a bit ruefully. There were times when it seemed a great pity they were all so very law abiding.

All were attractive, some rather interesting, even—his gaze went back to the closed door, still swinging slightly from the recent transit. It would be amusing to wind up Alex Baker. Amusing and easy. One just had to be careful not to push him too far. Big fists and a good shot, so Guido had heard. Still...

"Wait here," he said, striding toward the swing doors.

Hannah Baker might be as honest as her big brother, but she had a dark side to be able to work in this place.

He went in, letting the door swing closed behind him. She'd tossed the goggles and loosened the protective thing, so he could see her tee shirt and jeans. She didn't look at all like her big brother, though the frown—

She turned with a less than graceful jerk. And her startled eyes were quite remarkable. One hand clenched something. Something small. Her hand slid into her pocket. A secret?

He loved secrets. Could smell them in the air, knew how to nose them out. Secrets become leverage.

Her lips parted, but before he could speak, his cell shrilled an incoming text. He smiled, held up a finger. "A moment."

He looked down and the smile faded. Without speaking he turned and left. He would find out her secret later. She would keep. This—he smiled in deep satisfaction—would not.

———

Ferris checked at the sight of Guido Calvino shooting out of the autopsy room like someone let the dogs out. He watched him head down the hall, his cell to his ear. He'd only caught a glimpse of Guido's face, but he looked like a guy who'd just won the lottery. He must have got the news about Uncle Bettino.

Ferris hesitated outside the door, then pushed it open and slouched in, his grin on the side of deprecating. "What'd you do to Guido? He came out of here like his pants were on fire."

Hannah had been frowning as he entered, but the frown faded into a grin he'd call careful. A bit of wary in the eyes.

She half shrugged. "He got a call. He tried not to look

shocked." She thought for a minute. "Tried not to look pleased."

Her brows arched a tiny bit.

Holy Hannah.

He'd always wondered what a cool drink of water would look like. Which was kind of funny, because there was nothing cool about his thoughts. Blonde and curvy in the right places and those eyes. He'd like to get close enough to figure out what color they were.

He hesitated, not because it was a big secret, but because he didn't want to talk shop. Still, she'd find out when they brought the corpse in.

"Someone popped Bettino Calvino. Guido just won the bad guy lottery if he can hold onto it." The sharks were certainly circling Claude St. Cyr. Odds were against him holding on until the end of the year.

Her amazing eyes widened, improving his view into them, but he still wasn't sure about the color. He needed to get closer. Much closer. He halved the distance between them. Nope. Still not close enough.

"Really?" She started to morph into a forensic doc, instead of a girl with a guy. "Any news on how—"

"Bullet to the brain."

"Oh." She made a face. Caught his gaze and grinned. "It gets old digging bullets out of brains."

"Perps should be more creative with their killing," he agreed, watching the grin bloom into a smile. Almost he licked his lips.

Was it the forbidden? This wanting what he wasn't supposed to have? He'd been the new guy when he first met Alex's sisters.

He'd already been walking a line, trying to prove he could do the job. Then he'd had no inclination to mess with his new partner's sisters. Well, not much.

He wasn't new now. They were a solid team. There was mutual respect. He could tease Alex about almost anything. He knew him well enough to know the no-go list.

And he didn't want to mess with Holy Hannah, exactly. Just get to know her. Maybe kiss her on the mouth once or twice. He studied the mouth in question. He might need more than a couple of kisses to scratch his itch.

He'd keep it this side of serious, of course. She was Alex's sister. It might be okay to kiss a sister, but not okay to mess with her heart.

"So Bettino Calvino is dead." Her brows slanted together. "Didn't he have, like, bodyguards and crap?"

"Lots of crap." He grinned, saw the change in her eyes and liked it. "You have to do the autopsy?"

"I'm not here," she pointed out. "It's my day off."

"Alex?" Her nod had a grimace attached to it. "Must be a tough gig for all of you." He glanced at the coffin just off his elbow, decided it wasn't too grimy, and propped himself against it.

"Batons of parental-like power were supposedly passed on to the next sib in line as we each left for college. Maybe it's a brother thing, but I got the responsibility without the power. Alex is the worst. He claims to be hands-off but..." She shrugged. Her head tipped a bit. "Do you have siblings?"

"My parents kept it simple. Just me and some dogs." There was a bit of an edge to his tone, so he added a didn't-bother-me smile.

"Maddie brought a dog home once. It took one look at the lot of us and ran for its life. Smart pooch."

"You ever thought of leaving?" He didn't like the twinge in his chest from that thought.

She laughed at that. "Every day." She looked around. "Sometimes every hour."

"When you move to the new building, it should be good." It was kind of a question. He'd read in the paper that the new coroner had asked for everyone to resign and reapply. He wasn't sure that was a good plan. It didn't seem like there was a lot to incentivize the reapplication part with the reported state of his budget.

She made a face. Cute and sassy. He liked sassy. She made this place almost bearable. He crossed his arms over his chest. Holy Hannah. How had he missed this version of her?

"One lives in hope." Her gaze strayed to the row of dolls on the metal table, the one still missing its head. A hand slid into a pocket and clenched into a fist, bulging the fabric.

His gaze narrowed. Color scored the line of her very nice cheekbones. He straightened. "Did Calvino say something? Threaten you?"

No hitting on the pretty girl, he wondered a bit grimly, or Alex might not be the only one wanting to pop the wise guy.

Her gaze jerked to his. "He started to say something but he got the good news."

So why the frown pulling her brows together. Her gaze went back to its avoidance pattern and even white teeth gnawed the lower lip.

So if not Calvino, then what? He looked down at the coffin and sensed she stiffened and stole a look.

He thought she'd made a fist with that hand, but maybe it

was clutching, not clenched. Had she found something? She turned back to a tray where the dolls lay in a grimy row, and put Barbie's head back on. Her hand left her pocket, but a slight bulge remained.

She went down the row of Ken's popping heads off and staring inside each one.

"You lose your ride?"

Her tone was too casual. "Alex wanted to talk to Nell," he said.

The last Ken lost his head. "Oh."

He liked the profile, but he wanted her to look at him. "You don't like her?"

The brows arched. "I do like her, just not—"

"...her relatives." He strolled forward, casting a quick glance in the other coffin. Looked full of dust, too. She stiffened, so he stopped. "There's one less."

"Still a passel of nasty cousins."

She picked up a magnifying glass and a Ken head, subjected it to what looked like a minute scrutiny. But there was this pulse at her neck that beat a bit too hard.

"You find anything else in there?" He asked it casually. The color spread further across her face. She was a Baker. The inability to lie was probably imprinted in her DNA.

"I found one of Ken's loafers." She held up a tiny shoe and waved it at him.

With no more Kens to examine, her hand stole to her pocket again. If he were a betting man—which he sometimes was—he'd bet it wasn't a doll loafer in there.

If she'd found something, she'd have a good reason for hiding it.

Bakers, they always had good reasons for everything they

did. It was also part of their DNA. Though hiding evidence didn't usually make the list. Was it evidence though? Just some dolls in coffins—that some lawyers may or may not fight over. Of course, if there'd been human remains, no one would have claimed them.

She fiddled with the doll closest to her. Did it matter that the Kens didn't get their heads back. And did he really want to know the answer to that. Or what she'd found and was hiding?

Right now, he wasn't part of the hiding. He was in the clear —a good place to be in the NOPD. And with the mob—who might be interested or she wouldn't feel compelled to hide it. That made him frown.

What if Guido had picked up on her unease? She wasn't unprotected, but he'd bet a month's salary that she wouldn't tell her brothers unless she had to. Would she know when she had to? But if he pushed, if he found out, then he was in it with her. Keeping a secret from his partner, too. About his partner's sister.

Not the "in it" he'd been hoping for when he took his stroll this way. He didn't know Hannah that well, but he knew Alex like a brother. Which meant that Holy Hannah was—not a sister. His mind flinched from that, so far he almost fell over from the jerk. Neutral ground, that's where he'd be if he didn't ask. In it up to his neck if he did. Only it felt like the ground under his feet had already shifted. He might not know, but he knew something.

She glanced back at him, and it was the hint of anxiety in her eyes that did it. They were blue, really dark blue except around the pupils. Close to the pupils, her eyes were a softer, lighter blue. The effect was—he tugged at the neck of his shirt. Kind of like drowning, but in a good way.

"What did you find, Hannah?" He used her name on purpose, made it personal. Safe. He hoped. Her lips parted in protest, but he shook his head. "I can call Alex, but I don't think either of us want to do that. Alex, well, he's a wild card right now." He had a chilly thought, one that killed the warm caused by her eyes. "Did Guido see—" He didn't know what question to ask.

Her eyes widened some more. Yeah, blue, but more than blue. Her lips firmed. She didn't look at all like Alex. Until that. Now he could see a resemblance. The same stubborn set to her mouth. He waited her out. One thing he'd learned from partnering with Alex. How to wait.

The clash of gazes was prolonged. He enjoyed it. Wasn't sure she did. Her sigh signaled surrender before she pulled her hand out of her pocket and held it out to him.

A ring.

Not what he'd expected, though he wasn't sure what—just not that. Not even a nice one.

He moved in for a closer look at it. The first decent smell in the place was her. He took several deep ones while he examined it. School ring. Old school. He didn't get—she pulled the magnifying glass over for him. He used it, first on the outside, then on the inside—

Who was Charles Baker? He didn't remember hearing the name, but to tell the truth, he'd tuned out a lot. Alex had a reason to be interested in an old, cold case. Ferris…less reason. He lowered the glass, turning the ring with his fingers. He cleared his throat. "You wanna get some lunch?"

Her eyes widened again. He got a cautious nod.

He leaned close, took a deep breath of her, and his gaze holding hers, he pressed the ring back in her hand and closed her fingers over it. "Let's go."

He had the upper hand, would have kept it if he looked away while she stripped off her the rest of protective gear. Couldn't call it a tease—no sign she knew what she did to him —but *Holy* Hannah. When he didn't move, she looked down at her jeans.

"I usually wear scrubs, but I'm not working today," she said, half apologetically, half defensively.

"Well, let's get out of here before someone decides you are working," he said, a bit hoarsely. Holy *Hannah*.

CHAPTER 2

HANNAH LOOKED AROUND, because she was behind the wheel and she had to, but also with a strange sense of disconnect.

New Orleans looked the same. So why did it feel different? Seem different? Could it be because Logan Ferris was in her car with her? She felt like she'd wandered into an alternate reality, one where it was perfectly natural to be on her way to lunch with her big brother's partner. One where she'd over-shared with the same.

She didn't share that much with her sisters. And if she'd shared that much with her brothers? She might as well hire a billboard. That was the fast track to Zach finding out. The sisters only shared with each other. Sometimes that worked. Sometimes not.

The wheels in her head churned out a few thoughts—and some revisions—on the man lounging next to her in the front seat of her car.

He'd noticed more than she realized. That was a bit embarrassing.

She liked he hadn't asked to drive her car. Points there.

He didn't protest the drive-through order or heading to Audubon Park to eat. More points.

He wasn't looking at her like Alex's little sister. He might get points for that. She wasn't sure.

She was still processing that he'd become her partner in —what?

She'd left the ring in a desk drawer. Not with the dolls. She'd acted on instinct when Guido popped into the room. As far as she knew, Uncle Charlie was long dead, but finding his ring there? That might, just might rebound onto her dad.

Zach had always played his cards close to his chest, but they all knew that the stirring of the past from Nell's arrival troubled him—and not just because it had landed one of his oldest friends in jail for past and present crimes. Not to mention it left his kids wondering if Zach had known his friend was a dirty cop.

No Zach didn't need more trouble.

Hannah spotted an open parking spot, and after a moment of shock at the sight of it, pulled in quickly and a bit crookedly. Maybe it was the heat cutting down traffic to and through the park. The air was so thick, it took effort to walk to the second surprise: an empty bench. She sat with a sigh of relief—though not before she checked it for bird deposits. Heat didn't change avian elimination practices as far as she knew.

Ferris joined her, their shoulders almost close enough to brush together. He divided the contents of the paper bag, digging into his share without comment. That was not a surprise. Her brothers tended to eat first, talk later.

She opened her burger though with less focus than usual. It

was hard to be hungry with humidity sucking the life out of her.

The traffic flowed past on St. Charles, the streetcar rumbling through the middle of it. Distantly, she heard a ship blast a warning from the Mississippi.

Even the few joggers she spotted looked like they were phoning it in. She wasn't sure why, but the flowers smelled different in summer. Or maybe the air just moved slower, so the smell seemed richer? Mixed in with the usual bouquet of spicy scents that was New Orleans, was something she suspected was Ferris. Logan? He'd called her Hannah like they were already friends.

If she started calling him Logan out loud, her sisters would notice. And then want her to explain what she didn't know. Had there really been a time when she thought she had all the answers? She would have shook her head but didn't. Movement made her sweat more. But if they went inside now, that same sweat would freeze from the air conditioning. Like seriously freeze.

She wrapped up half her burger and shoved it back in the paper bag, then picked up her Coke and took a long, cold drink.

"Heat's killing my appetite," he said, finally breaking the long silence, as he added his unfinished food to the paper bag.

Hannah felt like she'd been holding her breath since that moment he'd handed the ring back. Of course she hadn't, but she had been holding her words which was almost as hard.

He hadn't said anything when she tossed the ring in the drawer of her desk. She wasn't sure why she felt like he needed to be the one to break the silence. She just did.

She stole a look at him and found him looking at her. She still couldn't parse his expression.

"Yeah." The sound of her voice was kind of a relief. She could still talk. "Why—" She stopped. Was that the right question?

"You wouldn't have done it without a good reason." Now question marks showed in his eyes.

"How much do you know of the old story?" she countered, while trying to figure out what to tell him, how to explain what she didn't understand.

He blinked. "Not much. Who is Charles Baker?"

"He's Zach's brother. His older brother. He disappeared not too long after he graduated high school." She tried to mentally edit the story, but that made her sweat. "I knew he had a brother who died, but we didn't know there was this big mystery until Nell came back."

Ferris blinked. The frown pulling his brows together was kind of…charming. She looked away. And then looked back. She found him still looking, his expression now deep in puzzled territory.

"What am I missing?"

"You weren't around when Nell and Alex met, were you?" She knew he'd been on vacation, but she wasn't willing to admit that. It felt almost stalker-ish for some reason. It wasn't like she'd been tracking his movements. She'd just noticed he wasn't around and managed to ask Alex without sounding like she cared. Not that hard to do with Alex. He was a guy.

Ferris shook his head.

"But he told you the basic story?"

Ferris hesitated. "Maybe refresh my memory? I might not have paid strict attention." He looked a little sheepish.

Hannah chuckled. "Alex does go on about it. I'd have tuned him out, too." Mostly she avoided him. She shifted so that she could see him. "What do you remember?"

"Three geezers before they were geezers decided not to kill each other. Killed Zafiro instead. Divided it all up. Two of them got married. Had kids. Kids fell in love." He hesitated, frowned. "Not sure why that got them blown up." His frown deepened. "Or not blown up."

Hannah opened her mouth, but he held up a hand. "Unless Afoniki didn't like the idea of the other two making a deal that didn't include him?"

"That was, I think, the theory at the time." They were all relying on the memories of old men, since the file had gone missing at some point.

"So where does Charles Baker fit in?"

"According to Zach, Charlie and Ellie Calvino were an item in high school. Nobody knows exactly what happened, but Charlie left for college, then went missing, and Ellie married Bettino Calvino."

Hannah felt her face tighten at the thought of why that might have happened.

"Zach was, well, not happy with her. He blamed her, I think, for Charlie leaving, though Zach doesn't say much." Massive understatement. "But I think he came to believe she was pressured into it."

"And when her daughter...died, she disappeared, too." Ferris looked thoughtful.

"And Charlie's ring ends up in one of the coffins they weren't buried in."

He stared straight ahead, but she had the feeling he didn't see the jogger doggedly moving past, his face glistening.

"I would guess that your dad tried to find him." He shifted, half turning to face her again. "Two high school kids could have disappeared. But they couldn't rig up the fake burials. They'd need help for that."

Hannah nodded. "I think Alex suspected Zach had helped them, for Ellie's sake. Possibly for Charlie."

"But—?"

"Zach wouldn't tell us if he had helped." Zach might not have been the perfect dad, but he did try to set a good example. It was her turn to stare ahead, not seeing. "Curly—William Gastonieau—who was Zach's partner at the time, sort of implied he did the helping, but then he tried to kill Nell. Alex has been mute on the subject. It feels like there is something— or someone—we are missing."

Could Zach be protecting someone else? If the dolls were a message, what was it? It was all old news now, wasn't it?

"I see your point." Ferris shifted again, resting his arm along the back of the bench, not touching her, so there was no reason for the spurt of heat along her shoulders. "You could ask your dad?"

"If I show him the ring," she shifted impatiently, "Zach will make me put it back in evidence."

"And if you do, then the wise families will know it—" he stopped, one brow lifted.

She knew the question he wasn't asking. What would they think about it? What would they do about it? Of course, there was only one geezer left to do something. Aleksi Afoniki hadn't been invited to the viewing, but he'd probably hear about it. He had eyes and ears everywhere. It's why he'd managed to get old. That and being über evil.

"What if Charlie," she hesitated, "isn't dead? What if—" She stopped.

Three dolls with holes in their heads. And two wise geezers with holes in their heads. What if Charlie had come looking for them? With a cane and a silenced weapon? There was a thought to make the eye twitch. A geezer-on-geezer crime?

"Ellie Calvino may have put that ring in there. If they were high school sweethearts, he would have given her his ring."

"That's something you give back when you break up," Hannah objected.

"Unless he disappeared before she could."

Hannah nodded. He had a point.

"You're wondering if Charlie came back for Ellie. But how would he know—"

Hannah couldn't help the worry she felt as she looked at him.

"You're afraid your dad was in touch with Charlie? That he told him? Helped them both?"

She didn't move, but she knew her eyes gave her away.

"It's a decent theory. But they're, well, geezers, too. If they are even still alive? Revenge after all this time?"

"Unless it's not revenge, or not completely. There's Nell."

His eyes widened. He looked away for several minutes, sighed, then looked at her again. "What do you want to do about it?"

Her lips twisted a bit. "I want to go back to this morning and have a do-over that doesn't involve an exhumation. There's a lesson in here about being careful what you wish for."

He chuckled and she sent him an inquiring look.

"You were wishing for an exhumation?"

She half grinned. "Maybe." She rubbed her face, then sighed. "I delve into bodies, not...secrets." Really, really old secrets. How could they still matter now? They wouldn't if Nell—

"You can let sleeping rings lie. If Guido didn't smell your secret?"

"If he did, what can he do about it?" She couldn't stop the chill running down her back, though.

"He's a bad guy. He can do what he wants. If he thinks you know something, he will try to find out what it is."

"I won't tell him." Her chin came up, then drifted down. She hated it, but she asked it. There was no one else to ask. And she trusted him, which surprised her but didn't dismay. Which was also a surprise. "What do you think I should do?"

"Maybe it's time for the secrets to come out. All of them. I had a mentor that used to tell me that only the truth makes you free."

"We don't know—besides, I'm a forensic pathologist, not a detective."

"Well, isn't this your lucky day. I'm a detective."

She fought back the relief. "This isn't your problem."

"Well, maybe I'm willing to make it my problem, if you'll call me Logan, and answer one question."

Her lips twitched. "And what's the question, *Logan*?" She could like this guy. A lot. Too much? She hoped not.

He leaned close, a slow smile turning up a sudden heat in his eyes, and igniting a quiver in her mid-section that her brain tried to discount...

"Is the age difference going to be a problem?"

Her eyes widened. Her heart sped up. It got hard to breathe. "With what?"

"This."

The arm along the back of the bench slid down to her shoulders and tightened, bringing her in close.

His eyes open, he moved in, holding her gaze as he very deliberately and with intent pressed his mouth to hers.

At first the pressure was light, but her lips parted involuntarily, surprised by the sweetness flowing from his touch—sweetness with a little fire in its core—and he increased the pressure. Not too much.

She didn't want to go up in flames in the park. In the summer. Her head tilted, her lids sliding down. His grip tightened then. That was nice, too. Maybe more than nice. It might have made her head spin a bit.

Then gently, slowly, he dialed it back, bringing them back to earth. And the bench. No thump though. His arm was still around her.

"Well?" he asked, his voice husky.

She cleared her throat. "No, the age difference won't be a problem."

The way the kiss had curled her toes and scrambled her brain? Yeah, that was a problem.

———

Claude expected Helenne St. Cyr to be pleased at the news of Bettino Calvino's death. That she was not surprised him. He knew the old story. Oh, not because she—or anyone else—had shared it with him. Everyone thought him dull and defeated, a pale imitation of Phineas St. Cyr. Even Phineas had failed to perceive the man he was beneath the dull.

It was—he'd learned early—much better to be underestimated than overestimated. Look at Phil. Phineas had such high hopes for his son's ascension to power. He had believed what he wanted to believe about his only son. He hadn't minded the love affair with the Calvino girl. He had minded Phil's honesty. Oh yes, he'd minded that. Enough to kill him? Claude was still not sure.

Claude might not be handsome and brilliant like Phil, but he wasn't honest. And he knew how to find out things. Knew how to adjust to the prevailing winds and alter course to stay out of the center of the turbulence. Even during the month since taking control of the St. Cyr business, he had managed to steer around the worst of the undercurrents. He knew everyone betted against him keeping control.

Let them.

They would find out that he could both have and hold. While they had been ignoring him, he had been watching them. He may not know where all their bodies were buried, but he knew what he needed to know about them. And he knew they wouldn't see him coming until it was much too late.

He studied Helenne, trying to imagine enough passion in her to nurse vengeance for so long. She was cold all the way through. Made it hard to believe she'd ever been warm. He had not pierced all the mists of the past, but he sensed that her long lost granddaughter was not the only secret trying to emerge into the present. Sensing currents was his specialty.

He didn't make the mistake of commenting on her lack of pleasure. Just studied her in that way he knew irritated her into dismissing him. She would not be around to do that for much longer, though the wheels of justice were not turning as swiftly as Claude might like.

She would either die or go to jail. He turned for one last

look before he closed the door and caught a look on her face that gave him internal pause. He made his way to the library, the place that had been Phineas' seat of power and now belonged to him. He sank into the chair behind the desk and considered that look.

He would never assume Helenne had been benched until it was done, but that look—there was something in that look. Something that said she had a card left to play? But why would Bettino's death give her a card? Was it because someone had beat her to it? Or something more? He considered what he knew of the three men. Afoniki, Calvino, and St. Cyr.

His research into their collective past had been most carefully conducted, so that no hint of it would reach them. All three had so many secrets. Interesting that all three could trace their past to the Zafiro organization, which had—back then—comprised the territory now divided between the three families.

There was much conjecture about the past, but there were some things that seemed certain. Zafiro had intended one of the three to take over his organization. But when he died, the three men had divided it up. Claude mentally corrected himself. When Zafiro was murdered. Everyone believed either one, or all three, had conspired to kill him. But there'd been no proof. And the three had formed an uneasy peace that had been broken once, when Phil and the Calvino girl were apparently murdered.

Only they hadn't died.

Claude considered that for several minutes. Who had helped them escape? They would have needed help. Phil had been eighteen. His thoughts moved forward once more, landing back in that room with the coffins. Dolls in coffins.

His thought circled, for some reason, on that doll that had been a fake. If it mattered then, it could not matter now. He was more troubled by the…prescience of the three "dead" Ken dolls. For some reason, those felt like they mattered.

He heard Helenne's light footsteps pass the closed door, tapping slowly up the stairs. He would need to keep a closer eye on Helenne. His instincts told him that, too.

———

"What are you thinking?" Ferris asked, curious when Holy Hannah didn't get out of the car after pulling into her parking spot outside the NOCC. He'd asked her to bring him back here.

That's where Alex expected to pick him up, so that's where he needed to be. Alex had a way of seeing what you didn't want him to, so it would be better not to be around Hannah until he could stop thinking "holy."

Only he didn't want to leave her just yet. That kiss had made him want to move in closer. And run for his life.

She glanced at him, almost as if she'd forgotten he was there, but then she smiled and the warmth in her eyes told him she hadn't forgotten the kiss either.

"What if—" she stopped, a cute frown pulling her brows together. She rubbed there, as if it annoyed her. "My head feels like a maze. Disconnected thoughts. St. Cyr's death—"

Funny how he usually didn't like it when a woman followed up a kiss with talk about feelings. So he should be thrilled right now. Nope, not thrilled.

"Now Calvino. Old…" She half turned in her seat. "What if *old* was the catalyst? Or part of it?"

It took him a minute. "Old what? The past coming back to get Calvino? Maybe." He frowned. "But the evidence against Helenne St. Cyr is pretty compelling."

She nodded slowly. "But what if St. Cyr's killing was…the trigger? The first person the police will suspect will be Helenne, or Guido. And time is running out. They say Afoniki hasn't got long. He's the oldest of them."

Ferris considered this. Though it was hard to wrap his brain around old killers— "You do realize what you're thinking?"

Her gaze turned wry. "That Uncle Charlie and Ellie Calvino are not only alive, but have returned to kill?" She gave a gusty sigh. "Yeah. It's an interesting mental exercise until that part." Her lashes drifted down, then slowly lifted. "You said the truth would set us free."

His turn to sigh. "I might have been wrong about that. It might just be opening a really old can of worms." The car had quickly turned stifling. He pushed open his door, but didn't get out. Not that the open door helped that much. For air to circulate, it needed to move.

Hannah—seemed that was the trick to removing the holy, focus on business—opened her door, too. Also not a big help, but better than not open.

"Not your case," she murmured. "Not my autopsy." She slid out then, but she turned to face him over the top of her car when he got out, too. "Just a lot of questions."

He had one. "What are you going to do about, you know?" It felt risky to mention it outside, even though they looked to be alone in the lot.

"Right now, it just looks like a personal keepsake. If anyone notices it, I might get teased about it."

So that's why she hadn't locked it up. By silent agreement, they both headed toward the rear of the NOCC. Ferris didn't see Alex's truck yet, so they'd probably beat him back. It was quiet inside. No sign that Calvino's body had arrived. Almost reluctantly, Hannah led him back to the coffins, her desk. She hesitated in the doorway, then stepped in.

"Did I forget something, Frank?"

Ferris moved past her, saw yet another of her brothers sitting at her desk examining one of the dolls. It was hard to not run into one of the Baker boys, he reminded himself.

Frank dropped it back with the others, rising to his feet with a smoothness that went well with his highly pressed exterior.

It was hard to believe he was Alex's little brother. Oh, the family resemblance was there, but a resemblance that had been airbrushed. Frank had better clothes, too. Maybe the FBI had a better dress code than the NOPD.

Frank's gaze rested on Ferris for several seconds, then tracked past as if he were looking for Alex. Ferris didn't answer the unasked question. Neither did Hannah. Frank's lips quirked slightly.

"I was curious about those." He nodded toward the open coffins. "Alex was supposed to call me."

"He wanted to talk to Nell, tell her about Calvino," Ferris said, lounging over to one side.

Hannah headed for her desk, forcing Frank to move aside. She sat, opening a lower drawer where she stowed her purse. Ferris felt her hesitation, felt her decide to wait. She turned in her chair.

"So far that's it. Disturbing, but so far lacking in clarity."

Frank stopped by the Barbie coffin and looked down. "Disturbing?"

"I guess you had to be here when they were opened. Ask Ingrid for the photos. Certainly a first for me."

Was there a hint of a question at the end there? Ferris wasn't sure. Frank turned and studied his sister. Then glanced at Ferris. No question he wished Ferris gone. Ferris looked at Hannah. If she wanted him gone—but she gave no sign, her gaze meeting her brother's for a long moment before her brows lifted.

"Was there something else?" Hannah asked.

Frank glanced at Ferris again. Either he wondered why Ferris was there or why he didn't leave.

"So that's it?" Frank glanced at the coffins again. "Just the dolls?"

"Was there something you were hoping I'd find?" she asked, not actually answering the question Ferris noted. He hesitated and she gave a frustrated sigh. "This isn't my job. I did a cursory search for Ingrid. She can dig under the lining—"

Ferris glanced down at the closest coffin. "You haven't searched beneath the lining?"

"I tore the lining when I removed the dolls," she said. "There are bricks or something under there."

"That's more than a tear." It was rent from end to end and then folded back.

Hannah joined him on one side, Frank on the other. "I didn't tear it that bad."

The base had been lined with bricks cut to match the shape of the coffin. Maybe so they wouldn't shift during transport. It had been a nice job for something that appeared—through the lens of time—to have been cobbled together last minute. Up near the right end of the coffin, one brick was missing. His gaze met Hannah's. As one they turned to the other coffin.

Same layout. Rent lining. Bricks, but none of them missing.

Ferris opened his mouth to ask who had access to the room, but closed it. Someone had known what to look for and had either bribed someone to get it or bribed someone to let them get it. Or just strolled in looking like they belonged.

Frank studied the gap for what seemed like a long time.

"What did you hope I'd find?" Hannah asked him.

When he didn't answer, Ferris thought he wouldn't, but he finally spoke.

"The material that was found by Nell—Miss Whitby—"

"In the music box?"

He nodded. "There was a gun and some papers. Maybe they meant something to someone at some time." He rubbed his face.

"Some kind of code?" Ferris asked.

"Maybe." He met their gazes. "It's not like this is a huge priority. On TV, they get to follow any lead. No worries about money."

"So no genius code breakers on staff." Hannah nodded.

She would know about budgetary limitations. Rumor was they had the smallest budget in the city. Possibly in the whole world.

He shook his head. "Old case. Beyond cold case. Might not even be a case. Only—" He stopped, then continued with obvious reluctance, "—maybe it's not so old and cold."

Hannah's gaze narrowed in a way that put the "holy" back in Ferris' thoughts. "Something's happened. Something new. And not just Calvino getting popped."

"It's gone…missing."

He hated admitting it. Ferris didn't blame him. Sucked.

"From?" Now she looked worried.

"Evidence locker." He sighed. "The ring is missing, too."

"Ring?" Hannah's eyes widened for a minute. She glanced at her desk, then at Ferris.

"The ring that St. Cyr gave Nell—Miss Whitby."

"Oh right. I'd forgotten about that," she said.

Frank must be really worried to miss Hannah's moment of panic, Ferris decided. A distraction seemed in order. "I wonder if Calvino was wearing his when he got popped?"

"Why would anyone care about the rings worn by some old wise guys?"

Holy Hannah shrugged and went back to her desk, tapping the top as if thinking, but Ferris noted her sidelong study of Frank. When he turned back to the coffin, she eased the top drawer open. She closed it, met his gaze with a slight shake of her head.

So Charlie Baker's ring was gone, too. Would have been nice if he could make a connection, have an *aha* moment. But the only conclusion he came up with was that someone knew exactly what they were looking for.

Which helped not at all.

———

Frank finally left, exuding federal frustration, which was more contained than local cop frustration, Hannah decided with an inward grin. She could remember a time when Alex used to blackmail Frank to get him to shower. Now he shone like a new penny.

At least Frank had made copies of the papers, so that was something. He agreed to send her a copy, though his lack of faith that she'd find something he hadn't was not surprising. Her brothers couldn't see past the little sister to the IQ. Of course, if they figured it out, they'd start having her do their taxes and stuff, but it still made her crazy. Which was crazy and made her head ache.

"I need to get out of here before Calvino's remains get here or I'll be stuck. Is Alex incoming? Do you have to stay?"

He shook his head. "It's taking too long, so I texted Alex and told him I found a ride." He arched a brow, making it something of a question.

Hannah, packing up her laptop, gave him a look over her shoulder, followed by a nod with possibly a hint of a smile. With everything that had happened, it seemed wrong to feel a spurt of happy at the thought of extending their—whatever it was. Her toes still quivered a bit from the kiss. She grabbed her purse and headed out, Ferris at her side. He didn't speak until they were in her car with the A/C on.

"So."

As an opening gambit it lacked focus.

"So." She shifted restlessly. "How do I report missing—or how do we investigate—something that didn't—technically—exist?" The missing brick would go in her report, and wouldn't that add clarity and get them to let someone investigate that missing brick? She put the car in gear. "And that no one but you and I knew about?"

"You, me—and whoever put it there," he reminded her. He frowned. "You're sure Guido didn't see it?"

She kept her foot on the brake while she considered this. It was all too easy to conjure up that bad guy. Why had he returned? What had he hoped to accomplish?

"He didn't see the ring, I'm sure of that. But," a chill ran down her back as she recalled the look in his eyes just before his cell rang, "he suspected something."

"Suspicion is in his wheelhouse," Ferris said, resting his arm on her shoulder for a comforting moment. "Bettino's death should keep his attention for a while at least."

Another upside to a dead wise guy? Almost she chuckled. This was so wrong on so many levels. But, for such an old crime, events were moving oddly fast. She considered that as she carefully backed out of her spot. Were events moving fast? Or was someone ramping up the pace? Growing up with a million siblings, one developed a fine sense of time. One had to if one ever wanted to use the bathroom.

"I wonder," she slowly accelerated toward the street, "how hard it would be to find photos of Ellie and Charlie?" She braked at the street edge and looked at Ferris.

"You're thinking of using aging software, see what they look like now?" Ferris looked thoughtful. "I can help with that. Think we need to do a…careful background check on both of them." He slanted her a look. "Chances are, they are both long dead."

"I know. But what about an unknown player?" Interesting that he'd followed her line of thought. Only—was Zach protecting someone else? She pulled out into traffic. That idea was unsettling, as was her next. "Or—"

"Or?"

"A family member?"

A pause. "You think Nell—"

"I don't want to think it, but this all started because of her.

She's been here for a couple of years. And only now do things start to happen?" She waited for a light. "Someone—or several someones—thought Nell knew something." She'd finally produced the papers that had gone missing. She'd claimed she hadn't known they were hidden in an old music box of her dad's. "It is stretching it a bit to think she just randomly came to New Orleans and, oops, finds a bunch of nasty relatives."

Ferris acknowledged her point with a nod. "Alex trusts her."

Hannah actually trusted Nell when she was around her but when she wasn't? When she lined up the facts? It got harder. Was Nell super good at hiding who she really was? Or just super good?

"Alex wants to believe her." She held up a hand. "But—you have a point. It's just a little easier to see her as—interesting— than believe that some geriatrics from the past have returned to wreak cold—old—vengeance."

Ferris grinned. "But much more interesting."

Hannah found she could chuckle. Because he was right. And it would be much better for all of them if Alex's girlfriend didn't turn into a mafia princess.

CHAPTER 3

HANNAH FELT a need to see Zach. Funny how that need surfaced when one's world went a bit askew. She resisted it, resolutely not steering her car in her dad's direction. Zach couldn't right her world and confession would not be good for her soul right now. And that's what would happen if she saw Zach while deep in the guilt trip.

It didn't seem right that he'd been MIA for much of her childhood, but he could reduce her to child status with a look. And there was the fact that she had Ferris with her, which would send his grizzled eyebrows up for sure.

Her next thought was that she'd like to talk Nell. "Do I need to connect you with Alex or…?"

"We should go talk to Nell."

She shot him a look in time to catch a wry grin. Had he read her mind?

"It seems like the next logical step."

"You think—"

"No. I don't think she's involved, but she might know something she doesn't know she knows." Perhaps she looked skeptical, because he added, "If this is something reaching out of the past, she's the only connection left of her parents."

That they knew about, she amended. "And how do we question her around Alex? About a case neither of us is actually on? A case that will probably be closed by the DA tomorrow?"

"I like a challenge." His gaze clashed with hers until the light change gave her a reason to look away.

Did he consider her a challenge? Hard to imagine, but a girl could hope. Even as she adjusted direction toward Nell's digs, she felt resistance. Was she ready to see Alex with her lips still tingling from contact with Ferris'?

She'd promised to call him Logan, she reminded herself. And because the name wasn't coming easy, she hadn't called him anything since that first time. Sad. So sad. Though—did she want to manage the name adjustment right before she faced Alex? He didn't have Zach's level of dad radar, but Alex did have an unsettling knack of noticing things just when one counted on him to be clueless. It was one of the more annoying things about her eldest brother.

She turned onto St. Charles and reflected—not for the first time—on the dichotomy that was New Orleans.

Enchanting, frustrating and in the end, clinging. She'd left at sixteen for college. Common sense said she'd make more money, be many degrees cooler, and find parking easier almost anywhere else. She knew what it meant to miss New Orleans. So she'd come home, and not just because of family and food.

There was something about her city that dug into the heart and refused to be rooted out, not even by a big old hurricane. Common sense, logic, even self-interest faded away in the face of good jazz, great food, and—she studied the street line with elegant houses from another time with the knowledge that just a few streets over the charm might fade to rundown—and sighed. The Big Easy. She wasn't always easy, but it didn't seem to matter to those who called her home. Impossible to explain the why and wherefore when she didn't understand it.

She spotted a parking spot and did the math on how far it was from the St. Charles mansion where Nell lived and worked. She decided it was close enough to grab, knew she'd probably see something closer—but only if she parked. Weird parking karma was one of those crazy, mystical things about New Orleans. As was being obsessed with parking.

She pulled in, stopped the engine, and looked at Ferris. He grinned.

"I'd have taken it, too."

They climbed out. The big oak trees flung their shade over them, the light filtering through the leaves in interesting patterns on the uneven sidewalk and giving them the illusion they were cooler. Even exhaust fumes couldn't completely cover the sweeter smell of grass, flowers and trees.

"Do you think the children tell you something about the parents?" she asked, as she stepped out of the way of a cluster of students.

Ferris arched his brows. "That's a loaded question."

"Nature versus nurture." She was quiet for several steps. "Heavily loaded, I guess. I could expound a bunch of theories, but most people think that if the kids are being what the parents want, then it's nurture, if not...Nell's parents seem to make the case for nature."

Nurture sure hadn't made them honest. She cast him a sidelong look, curious about his parents. She'd noticed the hint of something in his tone when he'd talked about being an only child.

It was a bit of a shock to realize just how little she knew about him, well, about his life before New Orleans. How had the daughter of a cop managed to totally not get the interrogation gene? She had no clue how to dig into his past—at least not while he was alive.

She also sucked at small talk. She tended to lose threads when stray comments sent her thoughts off in tangents. She could be dogged, as today proved, when the topic was of sufficient interest. Or when digging through a body. She'd managed to spend a couple of hours with Ferris and not once gotten lost in some stray, scientific thought path. Well, once she got past wondering about how he might die and what he'd look like dead. Did that count as losing the plot or not losing it?

"They certainly lived squeaky clean lives in Wyoming. Not even a traffic ticket. Well," he amended, "other than the whole fake identity issue."

"Shades of gray," Hannah murmured. Honestly living a fabricated life. Did that qualify as squeaky clean? How did Nell feel about it all, she wondered. What would she feel if she found Zach was not who she thought he was? That was hard to wrap her brain around. Zach was Zach—and yet, what if he had helped Nell's parents, or Ellie and Charlie, to hide? What did he know? Zach's past could still blow up in her face. And she couldn't imagine that or figure out how to get him to open up about it. Zach wasn't a real person. He was her dad.

Hannah had observed many dads, good, bad and indifferent. Zach, in her opinion, was a good one. But something, possibly her IQ, hampered their relationship in a way that none of the other siblings seemed to experience. Or maybe she just thought about it more than the others. And now they got to add possible secrets into the mix. Zach and secrets? Yeah, more not-real to make her eye twitch.

One block up, they reached the house. Hannah never knew whether to knock or go in, since the home was also Nell's roommate's business. The plaque by the imposing door informed the interested that *Blue Bayou Catering* could be found within. Ferris answered her unasked question, by rapping on the door, then opening it.

"Alex? Nell? Sarah?"

It seemed like he knew both women pretty well for first names. The thought formed and then she chided herself for it. Of course he knew them. And well enough for first names. This was New Orleans where strangers called you "baby" or "sugar." And if you were enough older, they tacked a mister or miss before your first name in the interests of being respectful.

Hannah assumed it was Sarah who poked her head out of her office. They hadn't actually met before. And she wasn't Nell, who Hannah had met. Did this count as a deduction?

"They're in the kitchen."

"She okay?" Ferris lounged forward, hands in his pockets.

"I'm not sure how to answer that," Sarah said, her gaze tracking past Ferris to Hannah.

Hannah felt immediately self-conscious. Hot from the walk and frumpy around the classically cool and stylishly dressed Sarah.

"You're...a sister," she stated, her gaze tracking down, then up.

"Hannah. Oldest sister," she added in a tone turned painfully prim.

"Wow. First girl after seven boys? No pressure there." Her smile was laden with an easy charm that was, to Hannah, so very Southern.

Hannah felt her mouth curve in response, even as she wondered how Ferris managed to notice her around Sarah. Blonde, beautiful, nicely shaped skull. Most likely to die of natural causes after a long and lovely life. Two of her brothers thought her interesting enough to mention, though they both claimed it was her cooking they liked. Her gaze flicked down the small-boned skeletal structure nicely padded in all the correct places. Yeah, obviously they *loved* her cooking.

Sarah's smile widened and Hannah realized she'd been giving her what her siblings called her "dissecting look." She tried to stop, managed a stiff smile that was softened by the kindness in Sarah's eyes. A bit unusual, in Hannah's experience, for a popular girl to be kind, at least to someone like her. One almost felt she could be friends with her, a shocking thought for the Baker family geek.

"You're the forensics specialist, aren't you?"

Hannah nodded, her smile turning into a grin. "Let me guess. One of them told you I dig through brains?"

Sarah laughed. "They might have mentioned it."

"I'm impressed you figured out what I actually do."

"I like CSI shows. And yes, I know they glam it up."

Hannah chuckled. "I like them, too," she admitted. "And I don't always pick them apart. Mostly I just wish for the cool equipment. And that I was paid enough to get the fun clothes Abby wears on *NCIS*."

"I love that show. Oh, TV budgets," Sarah said, with a chuckle.

"If only I didn't need to eat and pay my rent," Hannah

chuckled, though just a bit weakly. The end of the month was always interesting.

Sarah's grin faded to a speculative look. "I wouldn't want to insult you or anything, but I sometimes need extra hands with serving? Pay isn't great, but..."

Hannah straightened a bit, her ears perking up at the sound of extra pay. It's not like she could do off-duty security work since she couldn't secure stuff. "I'm really hard to insult. Seven big brothers made sure of that. And just by working at the NOCC I think I've indicated a willingness to work for peanuts."

Sarah grinned again. "Got a card? Or just a number?"

Hannah laughed, patting her pockets. She pulled out a bent card and handed it to her with a wry look. "Sorry."

"Hey, it's got your number."

"Is this a 'girls only' op?" Ferris asked.

To Hannah's amusement, they looked at him in almost perfect synch.

"I thought you cops all have after hours security gigs?" Sarah finally asked.

"Little harder to get them when your hours keep changing."

Thanks to Alex ticking off various politicians at regular intervals, they kept getting night shifts at random intervals. Hannah held back a grin.

Sarah held out her hand. "I don't discriminate."

A small silence formed after this second exchange of contact info, but not an uncomfortable one.

"Mind if we—" Ferris nodded toward the hallway.

"Be my guest," Sarah said easily. "Nice to meet you, Hannah. I'll call you?"

Hannah nodded, surprised to hope Sarah would call and not just for work. As they started down the hall, a chime and a creak announced the opening of the front door.

"Afternoon, Miz Gladys." Sarah said, her tone businesslike-warm rather than "I know you" warm. "Hope you and yours are well?"

"Fine thank you, Sarah, how are you?" The new arrival responded with the weirdly sweet tone of someone who talked to kids so much she forgot to change it up for adults. There was also a tiny hint of lady of the manor to the serf.

Hannah bet she'd smell like cookies, expensive ones, then she felt an immediate need for something salty, as if the sugar had reached out and coated her tongue.

Hannah glanced back, curious to see the face that went with that voice. Framed in the doorway, with the light behind, she cast a long shadow with a body that was plumply round and on the short side, like a character from a children's book or a movie about one. Then she turned to close the door, presenting her profile. Skull was delineated, thanks to her classic bun.

A bit Slavic, Hannah decided. A nicely shaped skull. She wouldn't have minded a closer look, though Hannah didn't expect to get it in her professional capacity.

She didn't look like someone likely to be murdered unless she withheld the cookies. She had a nice zygomatic and her mandible might have been elegant without the jowls.

Her pearls were a cliche that sat uneasily just below the jowls. Hannah mentally dubbed her Miz Cookie, because of the extreme sugar vibe, noting she held her chin high to mini-mize said jowls, and that the makeup was expertly applied.

Hannah could tell gravity was winning. It usually did.

"Coming?" Ferris spoke behind her, not impatiently, but a bit curiously. She caught him flicking the woman a look that wasn't exactly a recoil, but close.

"Yes," she said, suiting action to word. Not sure why, Hannah glanced back just before rounding a corner and caught Miz Cookie looking at her. Hannah gave the woman an uneasy half smile, as color warmed her cheekbones. She received an amused, rather motherly smile in return. Hannah took the corner, the smile lingering. From the mists of memory, she sort of remembered getting looks something like that from her mother. She looked at Ferris' back—a not unpleasant exercise —and wondered what it would have been like to have more than the memory of a mother.

Ferris called out before they reached the door. Very tactful. And necessary, she suspected. Both Alex and Nell looked a bit flushed—and like they'd just opened the distance between them. Nell's gaze was distinctly wary when it met Hannah's. Not a surprise, Hannah conceded. They'd all been polite, but it was hard to be happy about the relationship. Now, with mom thoughts swirling inside her head, Hannah conceded that Nell had put a lift in Alex's step. If she made him happy—

And on the heels of this concession she could admit, at least to herself, that it was hard to believe Nell was involved in anything criminal when one looked her in the eyes. If she was faking it, she was an actress of epic proportions. She made the persona of Miz Cookie seem incredibly devious in comparison. Maybe it was the carryover from Sarah—who also trusted Nell enough to bring her into her home and keep her there after the past came spilling out—but Hannah felt like her smile and greeting were warmer than was her wont. It showed at once in a slight softening in Nell's posture.

"Not sure whether to offer condolences or congrats," Ferris said, going where Hannah had only dared to think.

Nell laughed—a first in Hannah's presence—giving her a glimpse into what Alex saw in her.

"You're not doing the autopsy?" Alex asked.

"I think I mentioned it was my day off? Like fifty times?" Not a surprise Alex did not remember what she told him. She spoke and he heard, *blah, blah, blah*. She rolled her eyes and caught Nell's grin out of the corner of her eyes.

"Never stopped them before," he pointed out.

"True, but I managed to get clear in time." That sounded nicer than "before the body arrived." The senior Calvino was a stinking pile of poo, but he was Nell's grandfather. Not that Nell looked like him or her cousin, Guido. Ellie had had a fairly aggressive gene pool, which was kind of funny. She glanced at Ferris, wondering if he had a plan. Because she didn't. Seeing Nell wasn't a plan. Plans had goals, things to check off. Targets to be met. Specifics. Hannah liked specifics.

"Did you finish searching the coffins?" Alex asked.

She should have realized that would be his first question. "Not exactly," she admitted, propping a hip against the wood table so she wouldn't shuffle her feet. "And I would like to point out that searching the coffins is technically Ingrid's job. I dig through bodies."

"Ingrid got called out, so we popped out to get some lunch, and while we were gone, someone visited the morgue," Ferris said, as if neither event was that unusual.

Alex's brows shot up, but his attention went to the unauthorized visitor. *Nice move, Ferris.*

"There were bricks under the lining," Hannah said, "precision-cut bricks. And someone pried one out and took it."

"They stole a brick?"

"Well, they stole something from a brick-shaped space," she amended.

"What could someone hide in a coffin that would matter now?" Nell asked.

"That is a very good question," Hannah said. "I wish I had a good answer." Hannah looked at Nell and found, now that she'd met two of her cousins, she could see faint, very faint traces of both families in her bones, but Ellie mainly ruled there. Nell grinned and Hannah blinked. Not a good time to lose the plot. Hannah gave her a sheepish smile, then glanced at Alex. "Did Frank call you?"

Alex's gaze bored her direction. "He told you?"

"Shouldn't he have?" she countered, with a spurt of annoyance.

"It's not your case."

"Or yours." Hannah caught a glimpse of Nell biting back a grin.

"Not anyone's case yet," Ferris put in, possibly in hopes it would put oil on troubled waters.

Yeah, he didn't have siblings.

Nell gave Hannah an anxious look. "I thought," she stopped. She looked wry. "I didn't ask. I thought I didn't want to know." She turned to Alex.

It was interesting to see how her look got to Alex. He was too tough to cave, but his shields must have went offline or something because a crease formed between his brows. That was totally breaking out in expression for her brother. Hannah had to repress an urge to giggle. It was not a side of her brother she typically saw—and one he took care to tamp down when he'd brought Nell with him to family events. She didn't blame him. With so many siblings, sometimes the only privacy any of them got was inside their own heads.

"Do I want to know?" Nell asked.

Hannah watched with interest, curious to see how Alex would respond. He was a cop, so he always wanted to know, but he was a cop, so protective was his go-to place. Uncomfortable opposites that made him almost squirm now. It was possibly a character flaw that she enjoyed watching him almost squirming.

"The papers you found in the music box," he finally admitted, "lacked clarity."

Nell looked to Hannah.

"They were written in some kind of code," she explained.

"Code?" Nell did shocked like she really was shocked. Which she probably was.

"And now they're missing," Ferris added, possibly to see her reaction.

"I take it you never saw your…dad playing with codes?" Hannah asked the question carefully, keeping a weather eye on Alex. If he thought the question verged on interrogation, he'd shut her down fast.

Nell shook her head. "My dad—the man I knew was a garage mechanic. The music boxes were his most exciting hobby. And he kind of sucked at that." Her half smile rueful, before fading into worry. "Surely there are code people, though?"

"Code people cost money," Hannah had to point out. Life was so much more fun on television.

"Oh. Old case."

"Cold case," Ferris agreed.

"And the people in charge of the money didn't think there

was a case," Hannah finished. "Frank was massaging some contacts, so he had copies made, but the originals seem to have disappeared. The theft might change that." Sadly it was not a given.

Nell grimaced. "It's so hard to believe that long ago events could matter now. Almost impossible to believe it about my parents...even if I could wrap my brain around their past—they were kids when all this happened." She half grinned. "I could imagine them doing the doll setup, but why? And why bricks?"

"To make the weight seem right," Hannah said. But why the precise cuts? That argued preplanning?

"Oh, right. I should have thought of that." She frowned. "But to fake their own deaths? Set up alternate identities? And codes? Someone helped them. They had to have."

A small silence, then, "You think there's a connection between your missing brick and the missing papers?" Nell asked.

"Well," Hannah temporized, looking to Ferris for help. He rocked at tact so far.

"Let's say that your parents are the only other common connection," Ferris said, managing the tact pretty well, though Alex didn't look happy. "So far. I know you've probably been asked this, but can you think of anyone from the past? An older friend of your parents? Even an overheard name? In theory, they cut off all contact, but in real life? I would think that would be hard to maintain."

"A name connected with a feeling of unease perhaps?" Hannah added when Nell frowned and shook her head.

"Everyone in my life was there, where we lived, but I'll give it some thought. It's like I have memories of what I thought was real and the adjustment, well, it's challenging." Nell sighed, then looked up. "So they just took the papers? Not the gun?"

She'd forgotten there was a handgun found with the papers. Hannah hesitated. "The ring is also missing."

"The ring? My—St. Cyr's mob ring?" Once again her shock looked real.

"That's crazy. It's not the One Ring, for Pete's sake. It was just an ugly symbol of his nasty power," Nell protested.

Was it? There didn't seem to be any connection between her uncle's school ring and the mob ring of power, except that both had been worth stealing. Hannah felt guilty withholding that bit of information, until she reminded herself—again— that none of them were on the case. And she hadn't logged the ring. Her insides twisted uncomfortably. She felt Ferris' gaze on her, a hint of warning in it. It was done. She had to live with knowing she did it.

And that whoever stole it knew it, too.

————

Guido stood staring down at his uncle's body. How small he looked. How dead. He'd wondered how he'd feel in this moment, when the waiting was finally over. When he got it all. It was something of a surprise to realize he would miss Bett. A little. They'd trusted each other as much as was possible. Bett had raised Guido to want his power and had used his power to keep Guido in check. They'd both lived their lives watching their backs. Knowing that the other did not have their back.

No one could be trusted.

Ever.

He looked at the morgue attendant. "There is a list of my uncle's personal effects?" He'd seen the ring on Bett's hand this morning. Had not found it in his desk, so he must have been wearing it when he left the house. He wouldn't be able to get it until they released the body, he supposed—

The attendant handed him the list. He perused it quickly. His lips tightened. If someone had liberated it at the scene, he'd find out soon enough and make them regret it. Wouldn't be a shock if someone picked his pockets after the hit. But— Bett's wallet hadn't been taken. Why just the ring gone?

"When I go, Guido, make sure you secure the ring," Bett had insisted, more than once while twisting the ring on his finger—something he did often.

Guido had assumed his uncle did it as an act of pleasure. It was symbol of his power. Had it been something, meant something more? Had Bett believed it meant more? Or was his obsession with it a sign he was losing his grip? Guido did not spend too much time thinking about his uncle's past, about how he, St. Cyr and Afoniki had obtained their "inheritances" from Zafiro. It was all so long ago. How could it matter now?

Secrets had always swirled around Bett, but the flow had felt tidal since Nell Whitby was revealed as Bett's blood granddaughter. There were signs Bett had considered promoting a marriage between Guido and Nell—until he met her. In the end, he had not been convinced Nell was blood of his blood. Guido had not opposed the idea of marriage.

He would need an heir, of course. Luckily women did not repulse him. It would not do—he'd looked at his uncle and wondered if he'd ever suspected the broad-ranging nature of Guido's preferences. It didn't seem likely. There were other cousins he could have groomed to take over. And Guido had been careful. Very careful. Even now he could hear his uncle on the subject of Nell.

"She's too honest to have come from me," he'd scoffed. "Let Afoniki play his games. Plots and schemes were always his mother's milk. It will make his final hours interesting."

Had Bett believed that Afoniki would be the next to go? Unless his body lay undiscovered, Bett had preceded his old— friend? enemy?—to the grave. Or rather, he looked around, the morgue.

In his line of business, this place was certain to be a stop on the way to the grave. He repressed a shudder. Without Hannah Baker to distract, this place had lost its appeal.

He turned to leave, flanked by his men, considering how to approach the problem of the ring. And Hannah Baker. His thoughts paused. Had she—no, there'd been no time for her to secure the ring.

She'd left well before they brought in his uncle's body. He hesitated, then recalled the feeling he'd had that she knew something. He flexed his fingers, feeling the surge of new power flowing through them, through him.

Nell Whitby.

Hannah Baker.

They both interested him, though he tended to agree with his uncle that Nell was too honest to be that interesting. His concern was more about how Afoniki might try to use her for his ends, and that was slight. Her connection to Alex Baker— that might have potential for something. He could not decide if that something would help or hinder.

Uncle Bett had believed she knew more than had been revealed. News had filtered out—or been allowed to filter out—

that she'd found some old papers of her father's which had been handed over to the FBI. Interesting that there'd been no follow-up on that. It was most unlike the FBI. He made another note to chat with his uncle's—no, *his* contact there. His thoughts paused. Had Uncle Bett already gotten an answer to that question?

Threads, so many threads, with power flowing to and away from him. This was what Uncle Bett had kept from him by living so long.

Perhaps he did not miss him so very much after all.

————

"How do you feel?"

His voice broke into her thoughts. And she was not sorry, she could admit, though only to herself. She looked up, met his worried gaze and smiled.

"How should I feel?" she countered.

"However you'd like."

Oh that man. That man. Thirty years was not enough to spend with a man this wise in the ways of a woman. His woman, she amended. And he had not always been wise. Wisdom took time, she reminded herself. And courage. Both had needed to find their courage. So much time lost—and more than time. But if she let her thoughts go there, he'd know and feel her pain. He'd felt enough pain for a lifetime.

"I feel lighter," she said, after giving the question serious consideration. "And younger." She stopped there, lest she voice the wish. She knew he thought her loss the greatest, and it had been an almost mortal blow, but he—what he'd given up for her. And what he'd done since. The nights he held her when the nightmares came. Was it over? Or was it the beginning of over? "Did you find it?"

"Of course."

"Still in the coffin?"

He shook his head. "In a desk drawer."

"Really?" He nodded, his gaze meeting hers for a long moment. "Interesting."

"Didn't think the gal had it in her," he admitted.

There was something in his voice, something under the humor. Her gaze narrowed. "What?"

He hesitated, then shrugged. "I thought I saw a ghost."

Her brows rose as she tried to parse his tone and the look in his eyes. "A ghost?"

"Ah, my love, I am an old man."

"They say you are only as old as you feel." He knew better than to keep secrets, but he was also one to ponder long before bringing her into his worries.

He chuckled. "Then I am a very old man." He clasped her hand in his and gripped it. "A very old man who is, perhaps, seeing things that are not there."

She returned his grip. The guilt came more often these days, as the past bled through into their now. For so long they'd kept it at bay by not talking or thinking about it. By simply living. But perhaps it was time to face their past. Deal with it. Even as the thought formed, her heart rebelled. Just a little more time. Just keep the world at bay a tiny bit longer.

Thirty years was not long enough.

She studied his face, noting faint signs of lingering worry. "So tell me about this ghost."

———

The brick was where it had been left, sitting on the window ledge. Such an ordinary thing to cause such a stir. Sometimes the universe delivered to those who were ready to receive.

Not visible were the two rings and—bonus—the papers. Two rings down. One to go. Was the last old man afraid? He should be.

What was that saying about some being great and some having greatness thrust upon them? And then there were those —those select few—who were great and clever enough to take it from those who didn't deserve it.

Speaking of which…

The list was not in the open, but secured in a drawer with a lock. Harold might not understand it, so she hid it, but now she extracted it.

Such a pleasure to put a line through Bettino Calvino's name.

The question mark next to Nell Whitby's name would remain, clarity still elusive as to her status as useful or not.

A new name was added to the bottom, though really, it encompassed a family.

Baker. Would they be a problem? The enemy of my enemy should be a friend, but the Bakers were loyal to the law first, and then each other. Could that be used? Further reflection required, before stirring things up.

A sigh slid out breaking the silence.

This could be done. It would be done. But it was annoying. Why make the timeline so tight? It felt like she'd been setup to fail. Again. Her lips tightened as she remembered all the years, all the women's clubs, the slow rise through the leadership dealing with all those bitter, clueless cats and witches, and then—well, they hadn't appreciated her. Hadn't deserved her time and attention. She was meant to lead. To be on top. But she did hate the rushing. It was so messy.

A stray beam of light highlighted some dust that must be rubbed away from the sill. A metaphor perhaps? That order—the order of her life as it was meant to be—could be restored? *Would* be restored. Must be restored.

A final swipe and the sill gleamed. All clean. Just like that.

————

"It's frustrating," Hannah said.

Ferris glanced at her across the top of her car. He arched his brows because he didn't know which particular part of the huge ball of frustrating she meant.

She hit the unlock and waited until they were both inside—and the car turned on so that the A/C could begin trying to cool stifling to bearable. She stared straight ahead for several seconds, then looked at him.

"Do you ever get a sense of pace when you're working a case? Like a clock ticking in your head?"

"All the time." He considered this one, letting the facts—few as they were—slide into the background.

A cop did many things by instinct, followed clues, questioned suspects, asked questions. But yeah, the pace had been fast for one short day—and for such an old, cold case. Only few hours since the coffins had been opened.

He glanced at his watch. Three, maybe four. His thoughts jumped over lunch and the kiss. He couldn't afford the distraction. He needed mental clarity around Hannah, which was ironic because she tended to shut that down.

It was interesting that she felt the clock ticking, considering that she worked with the dead. The not moving. He didn't mention it though. The part of a crime puzzle that concerned her did have urgency, so that his side would have the facts they needed for the hunt. They were a team, even if a disconnected one at times.

"What are you," he hesitated, "sensing?"

She made a face. "I'm not sure." She rubbed her face, fiddled with the temperature knob, even though it was maxed out. The hot rush of air from the vents turned tepidly cool. "You were gone when St. Cyr died. It was a boring headshot, but then a flurry of action and counteraction."

Ferris had picked the wrong time to be out of town. Or the right time. "It was fast."

"And then...not much."

"There was the dinner party," Ferris pointed out. "Someone shot up the main course."

She smiled. "Nobody died," she said. "So I only got the family point of view. Weird, but in the end, more sound than fury."

"True. And today has been lacking in both sound and fury." And yet...he knew what she meant. It felt like something was happening out in the sultry underbelly of their city. The Big Easy was usually uneasy.

"I keep thinking about the brick. Why bury something important and then not do anything about it? Coffins aren't safe deposit boxes. If it was Uncle Charlie, and he had proof of something, why not use it then?"

She had a point.

"Old...cold...only it doesn't feel cold. It feels...wrong."

"What about the missing papers?" Her reaction interested him, though he didn't know how relevant it was. Didn't know much of anything so how could he know what was relevant? Well, he'd like to kiss her again. He did know that. But it didn't look like that would happen anytime soon. Other than the lack of kissing, this Hannah interested him. She was scary smart—if a guy were afraid of smart. If he wasn't. Holy Hannah.

"The ring was taken, too," she said, almost absently. She glanced at him. "What if the papers were the afterthought, not the ring?"

"Okay. Why?"

She looked rueful. "I don't know. Why would some old ring matter? This isn't Mordor."

He had a thought, might even have beat her to it, which would be a shock. "I wonder where Calvino's ring is right now?"

She looked at him. "I can get a look at the list of personal effects on the body. It would be interesting if it is missing, too. It would still be puzzling and inexplicable, but interesting."

Puzzling, inexplicable, interesting. Both the case and the woman. "Yeah," he said.

CHAPTER 4

TWO DAYS OF NOTHING NEW—ALWAYS with the clock ticking in her head, though Frank did email her the copies of the missing papers. She didn't have time to do more than glance at them. A sudden spate of drive-by shootings meant long hours for everyone at the NOCC. No sight, sound, or contact with Logan Ferris, which allowed doubts to set in about the kiss, about what he'd meant about their age difference. About everything.

Heat built into the city, which didn't seem possible but somehow was, while that clock kept ticking inside her head. Other than the shootings, nothing seemed to be happening with their non-case. Nothing from Sarah either. She did catch an occasional glimpse of Ingrid coming from, or heading to, a new crime scene. The rest of her family was as MIA as Logan Ferris, though that wasn't unusual since she lived alone in a microscopic apartment off Magazine. Her family scoffed at it, but at least she never had to wait for the shower—just the hot water and then only when it was cold. This time of the year she could use a little more cold in her shower.

After two days of digging bullets out of bodies—was it bad to wish for a nice, complicated poisoning or even a stabbing that would at least be a change of pace? She paused, the stomach still over the body cavity she'd just extracted it from. Was professional boredom the reason for her interest in the cold case? She sighed and quickly finished. Then nodded to the attendant, who wheeled the body out.

She stripped off blood splattered gear, grateful when another body didn't appear. She checked the time, tiredness hitting her like a rogue wave. She couldn't remember the last time she'd ate.

She washed up, made minimal repairs to her face and tried to figure out if she had the energy to pursue food. As she turned to dry her hands, the door swished open. Almost she cursed, but when she turned it wasn't another corpse. Guido Calvino stood framed in the doorway. Well, not a corpse yet, she amended a bit wryly, though thankfully not out loud.

She didn't have a dramatic start in her. An unexpected upside to tired-to-her-toenails. From her side of exhausted, she knew she should be worried, if not actually afraid. He wasn't just a bad man. He was the just anointed king of evil.

"Dr. Baker." He had a pleasant look papered over evil. He studied her but kept his conclusions to himself.

Hannah didn't need him to conclude anything. She wasn't at her best. Her make-up repairs were just enough to keep her from being mistaken for a corpse and her scrubs were pretty nasty. She didn't sniff her armpits, even though that would have cleared the fog some. It might by why he didn't come any closer. She summoned up enough energy to arch her brows.

"I was hoping you'd join me for a coffee or perhaps something to eat?"

She blinked. So he did think she knew something. It kind of surprised her this did not worry her more. She was that tired, but a girl couldn't grow up with seven older brothers and not know how to take care of herself. Even if Guido had a couple of bodyguards with him, she could take three without breaking a sweat. They wouldn't see it coming. Her brothers never did, and they knew her a lot better.

"Dr. Baker?"

She blinked again. "Sorry, I think I dosed off for a minute."

"I presume you do eat?" he said, bringing a lot of charm to the smile that followed the question.

It was wasted effort. She couldn't even appreciate what didn't suck about him, but he couldn't know that. She considered the real problem. He wanted to find out what he thought she knew. She knew that what she knew wasn't that interesting to him, but it could result in unwelcome attention for Zach.

So if she blew him off now, he'd be back until he concluded she didn't actually know anything. If she could get him to believe that. But the more she put him off, the harder that would be. She balanced the risks. Tired might help in this case. He'd expect her to lie to him, so he would be looking at her reactions more than listening to her words. She had few of either left in her. And she did need food. If he was going to be a pain in her backside, he might as well feed her.

"I do eat." Though not nearly often enough when they were busy. She was aware she needed to add something to that. "Thank you." Okay that felt wrong. Even though it was polite. Was one required to be polite to pond scum? Had Emily Post ever had that problem?

"Is that a yes?"

It was more of a "whatever," but she nodded. She grabbed her purse, checked that her computer was off and walked toward him. He backed into the hall without touching her, which was good. Or maybe he'd caught a whiff of her. She started toward the back entrance and her car. He headed for the front. They both stopped.

"Where can we meet?" she asked, hoping it wouldn't be too complicated. She wasn't sure she could manage complicated.

He named a place a couple of streets over. If she'd had the energy she'd have grinned. It was pretty low brow for him. It suited her present ensemble, however.

"If parking will present a problem, we could walk?" he suggested. "Or my car is out front…"

She wasn't sure she could walk two feet but didn't want to get into his car. She wasn't that tired, had never been that stupid.

"Walk it is," she said, not surprised when two bodyguards met them outside. She studied them while they assessed her and dismissed her as a threat. Yeah, she could take them.

"I wanted to thank you for the list of contents from the two coffins," he said, as they turned and started down the street. "I will admit it was not expected."

What had he expected, she wondered? "It wasn't me. No body, not my job."

He paused at a light, directing his gaze down at her. Hannah met his gaze blandly. Or possibly indifferently.

"I received the impression that my return the other day startled you."

"Did you?" The walk light flashed and she stepped down

onto the street. She internally debated the wisdom of leaving it or— "I thought it was my brother coming back." She looked at him then, caught a narrowed, considering look. He wasn't going to leave it alone.

He smiled, but his eyes didn't warm. "Your brother does not like me."

"No," she agreed, stepping up onto the sidewalk again.

He chuckled, a hint of surprise, and something more in the sound. But real humor as well. She'd never considered it before, but it was possible pond scum could have a sense of humor.

"And you, Dr. Baker? Do you like me?"

She stopped and a bodyguard almost bumped into her. She arched her brows. "Why should I?"

That surprised him. He didn't seem to mind though. Which was probably good. It was a public street, but one not exactly teeming with people.

"I am not so very bad."

She gave him a skeptical look and started walking again. She was tired enough that the street had a kind of wavering quality.

Perhaps that's why, when the van turned onto the street it didn't startle her, even though its tires shrieked. It did cause the bodyguards to leap into action.

Hannah wasn't sure if they knocked Guido down or just dived onto his diving body. They knocked her down, which was a surprise. Unless they hit her in their scramble to protect Guido.

Whatever the intention, she was where she needed to be when the shooting started….

———

Ferris found himself unexpectedly alone with Zach Baker, father of the thirteen Baker siblings—including the one he'd kissed a couple of days ago.

How did fathers feel about men who kissed their daughters, he wondered, then wished he hadn't when Zach's shrewd gaze narrowed. No wonder his children tended to toe the line. He managed to not shift guiltily in the suddenly hard chair, held the gaze by reminding himself he'd faced down bad guys.

Old guys who were dads, he conceded, might be tougher than bad guys. He searched for something to say that wouldn't be revealing or stupid. The silence stretched long enough to tighten his tie. He didn't tug on it. But the fight not to tug helped, kept his focus on something besides those eyes boring into his head and trying to mess with it.

In the end, his sense of humor saved him. If his dad had been this tough or this interested—he cut that thought off. Zach's gaze eased, as if he'd caught that thought. If the old man was psychic, Ferris was in trouble. He glanced at the clock hanging over the kitchen sink.

"Alex okay?" Wasn't like him to not be waiting when Ferris arrived.

Zach snorted, his fingers tapping the newspaper spread out on the battered tabletop. "What's okay?"

Not dead. Or sick. Off his game. Not in love with the grandniece of two wise geezers. Ferris looked up with relief at Alex's appearance in the arched doorway. Zach's gaze found him again. Part two of laser look was a bit easier to take, only because it was shared with Alex.

"You got a bur under your saddle, Zach?"

"Got no burs, no beef with a son who thinks his old man can't be trusted."

Ferris stood up so fast he almost tipped the chair over. He managed to grab it in time and eased it back under the table.

"You mean a son who learned from his old man to keep his trap closed?" Alex shot back.

Zach didn't speak until they were at the door. Ferris felt for the knob, fumbled it open.

"Gonna play with dolls again today?"

Alex glared at his dad. "Who—"

"What? You think I don't have friends still in the force? Friends who just might know more than a—" Zach stopped, his grin sardonic. "Well, more than someone else."

Alex looked fit to explode, but Ferris? He was curious. Did the old man know something? Zach seemed to have two expressions. Glare and not-glare. When he wasn't glaring, he looked like the first cousin to a Sphinx. How did they—he and Holy Hannah—find out what he knew?

Zach's gaze shot to him again, as if he'd heard that holy and didn't like it. Ferris almost tripped on the step in his haste to get gone. He made a mental note to can the holy around Zach. His dad-dar was the best Ferris had ever seen.

He clambered behind the wheel with a silent prayer of thanks—that lasted until Alex's cell shrilled from multiple texts. Alex looked down and cussed.

"Hannah's been involved in some sort of drive-by shooting incident with Guido Calvino."

"Is she—" His heart jerked in his chest, like it had been punched.

"She's fine, but what was she doing with Calvino?"

Ferris knew but he wasn't stupid enough to say so.

Texts kept arriving as Alex jerked his seatbelt across and shoved it home.

Ferris put the car in motion with the feeling the scene was about to get Baked like no scene ever got Baked before.

———————

Hannah sat in the back of a NOPD patrol car, her feet propped on the edge of the opening while she sipped water from a bottle someone had brought her. Every few minutes a legal someone or other stopped and asked her if she was okay. At least they'd quit asking if she wanted to press charges against Guido. She wondered which one of them had ratted her out to her big brother and how long it would take for Alex to get there.

Guido and his goons did not appear to be getting the same level of concern she was, which did not seem to bother him or them. In fact, she thought she spied some thoughtful lurking at the back of his impassive expression. Thoughtful was not the usual go-to expression for someone who'd been shot at, but perhaps he was used to it.

It was not a huge surprise when Ben showed up, since he belonged to the Organized Crime Unit of the NOPD. He strode toward her, mainlining big brother almost as well as Alex. Well, he was the second oldest. And apparently, he was the closest. Based on the texts hitting her phone, the sibs were either incoming or pissed they weren't incoming.

She rose as he halted in front of her. "I'm fine. A few scrapes from hitting the turf."

His mouth worked a few times, which was kind of interesting. Ben was typically more easygoing than Alex.

"What the—" He stopped and glanced around. Lowered his voice. "What were you doing with that—" His mouth worked some more as he tried to find a sister-friendly word for Calvino.

"He offered to buy me lunch. On my salary..." she trailed off, aware the words were provocative, even though she didn't mean them that way. Tired had been displaced by adrenalin, but that was fading. It did give her a bit of a buffer as he processed her words without visible pleasure. A distraction seemed in order, particularly since she might lose the ability to form words before long. "No one's taken my statement yet."

A certain level of sentience returned to his gaze as cop began to take over from big brother. "So what happened?"

"We were walking along when this van came around the corner and started shooting."

Her gaze tracked to the line of shots where the shooting had started and stopped. Why had the shooter stopped before it reached them? She had some minor scratches from flying glass and had scraped her knees and elbows when she hit the pavement. The two goons had done more damage to them both while trying to protect Guido.

Someone had marked their positions on the pavement, all of them well clear of the line of bullet holes.

Ben grunted and started to leave.

"I wrote down the license plate number." She held out the paper.

He took it but still didn't ask her if she'd seen anything else.

"The shooters were young. Excited. Might be why they missed." But they had been dead on with their shooting until they stopped. Why had they stopped?

"Maybe it's another message for Calvino." His tone said to leave the detecting to the detectives.

She'd said the same thing to Ferris the other day, but this annoyed her. Maybe because it felt big brother rather than one kind of professional to another.

It had happened so fast, and it was her first drive-by shooting. She was surprised at how much she remembered, how crisp and clear the memories were. She'd rather expected to be like most witnesses, long on shock and short on details.

"I can probably come up with a couple of sketches of the two kids I saw," she said, even though he hadn't asked, "if you send over your sketch...person." Clarity faded as tired moved in. Or rather, clarity moved to a different part of her brain, one without access to her speech centers. "But let me get some sleep first."

"I'll get someone to run you home." Big brother took the top spot, mixed with concern. "Been a busy few days."

She nodded, managed a wan smile, then groaned as Bakers began flooding the scene from multiple directions. Maybe she should have taken the ambulance ride when it was offered.

————

Hannah wasn't sure how Logan Ferris managed to cut her out of the crowd of siblings. She was just grateful he had.

He drove her home—his route taking them through a fast food lane. She finished her burger before he pulled out into traffic again. At her place, he settled down, obviously planning to wait while she showered and changed. It was not a comfortable feeling, knowing he was on the other side of the door, but discomfort warred with relief that he didn't seem inclined to leave.

She'd missed him.

That thought left her feeling vulnerable and, had she not been so whacked, she'd have defaulted to stiffly self-conscious when she finally joined him in the living room that was also her bedroom. There were advantages to being well beyond tired.

"Got enough in you to talk for a minute, or do you want me to tuck you in and go?"

For a couple of seconds she wondered what "tuck you in" meant, then decided it couldn't mean much. Not when followed by "and go."

"I got my second wind, though it probably won't last long." She hoped he hadn't noticed her brief hesitation before settling on her couch. She was pleased when he sat next to her, his body angled so he could see her. Wished he'd tucked in a bit closer. His shoulder looked very inviting.

"So, what happened?"

She told him about Guido's sudden appearance at the morgue. He gave her a look when she told him about the lunch invite, but she didn't have the energy to connect the dots that got her to go with him. "I was hungry, and it's the end of the month."

He grinned, but his eyes looked worried. "If you'd blown him off, he'd have found another way."

"That's what I thought." She rested her head on the couch back. "And he only had two guys with him." Ferris' brows rose. "I only have trouble when the opposition gets to seven."

He laughed.

She managed a chuckle. "They used to tell me they were

doing it for my good and then they treat me like a puff of air will knock me down. They like it when I leave the thinking to them, too."

"The shooting?"

She nodded.

"That was a big miss."

"Could they really be that bad? Looked to me like the kid held the firing line for a few yards. Only moved an inch or so up or down. Then it just stopped."

"I saw that." Ferris frowned. "Hard to imagine someone having a clear shot and not taking it."

"Unless that was the plan? I wondered if someone was trying to kick the anthill? Stir things up? I've had a ton of drive-by shootings this week."

"It's been a particularly messy few days," Ferris said slowly. "Be interesting to see the stats on the various shootings."

"Vics have been from all three organizations," Hannah said. "At least, based on their body ink. You heard anything about the wise fams ramping things up? With Afoniki about to kick it and the two new guys…"

Ferris shook his head. "What we've been hearing is that frontline troops are being told to keep it cool. Of course, they would say it wasn't them, but it's interesting they don't seem to be interested in heating it up."

Hannah settled deeper into the couch, lifting her feet onto the small ottoman that doubled as a coffee table. "If I was going to make a move on another org, don't think I'd start with the small fry. Like, you know, actually shoot the top guy?"

"It does seem like taking the long way round," Ferris

agreed. "Before I forget, here's what I've been able to dig up on your Uncle Charlie—which is not a lot." With a wry look, he handed her a folder. "Also on Ellie Calvino and the wise kids."

Hannah took the folder, curiosity trumping sleepy. She flipped it open. On top was a grainy photo of a face vaguely like Alex's. Baker genes were dominant in the boys, that was for sure.

"His disappearance never made the news," Ferris said.

"He was away at college when it happened," Hannah murmured.

"Found that pic on Facebook. One of his classmates posted it. When I get time, I'm going to check out the high school yearbooks for the years he was in school."

Zach might have Charlie's old yearbooks. He'd gotten a lot of stuff from his parents when they passed.

"That's a good idea," she murmured, moving on. The news stories on Ellie and Nell's parents had come from microfiche and were hard to read, but she could probably track down better copies or clean them up on her computer. "Amazing how much Nell looks like Ellie. No wonder it freaked people out. Like a ghost or the dead coming back to life."

If Bettino Calvino had had Ellie killed, Nell must have given him quite the shock.

"Yeah." He eased closer, probably to study the contents with her, but succeeded in creating an element of distraction that tired couldn't completely contain. His aftershave was nice, not too spicy, not too bland. Her nose twitched, not opposed to smelling something not morgue related.

She stopped at one news item, lifting it to study through sleep hazed eyes. "Who's that?"

"That is Zafiro. It popped up and I was curious," he admitted. "Thought you might like a gander at him."

The waves were hitting now, and the image was beyond grainy, but something in the very back of her brain twitched. She studied a couple of seconds longer, then put it down and closed the folder, giving a big yawn that her hand could barely cover. She gave him a rueful look. "Sorry."

He grinned. "No worries. I'm surprised you made it as long as you did."

The room began to waver, and her eyes burned so she closed them. She was sort of aware of someone lifting her legs up onto the couch. A pillow appearing under her lowering head and a soft blanket sliding up her body. Then, so lightly she muttered a protest, lips pressed against hers…lingered… and then darkness swallowed her up….

While he was sorry that the shooters missed, Claude St. Cyr found the incident curious, but not terribly interesting, until the very end. There'd been nothing on the news about Calvino's female companion, but it seemed that at least one of his informants knew why the scene had been so heavily "Baked."

Dr. Hannah Baker had been with Guido Calvino.

What was Calvino's interest in her? It couldn't be personal. Not with her family baggage. And if it wasn't personal? There was her family baggage. One stepped lightly around the Bakers. There were so many of them.

Which brought him back to why?

Had he received the same list of contents as Calvino? Was the doctor setting up a side business for herself? It seemed unlike a Baker, but all the apples couldn't fall that close to the tree, could they?

Calvino had a knack for sniffing out what he wasn't supposed to know. He'd seen the way Calvino looked at the doctor. And the way the doctor looked at Calvino. He moved quickly past how she'd looked at him. He preferred to be overlooked. It was safer for him. Look what getting involved with a woman had done to Phineas. Business was what mattered. Everything else was a distraction—

Had Guido set up the shooting for that purpose?

Claude leaned back in the huge chair, shifting in satisfaction, knowing Phineas would never again sit in it again. At long last, the shadow of the past was gone, well, almost gone. He'd have to do something about Helenne if the law didn't take care of her.

He steepled his hands, resting his chin on his thumbs and considered the problem of Guido Calvino and Hannah Baker. It was possible that the meeting had been more about Bettino's ring than the coffins. His mouth tightened. It galled him beyond words that his ring was being held as evidence. That Phineas had tried to keep it from him—it didn't matter. Rings were symbols. Irrelevant in the end. What mattered was this. He gazed around the opulent office and remembered the power, the people he now controlled. The ring was—something, he admitted, or Phineas wouldn't have tried to keep it from him. But it wasn't everything.

He frowned suddenly. Could Bettino have been more forthcoming with his heir? Did Guido Calvino know something, either about the rings or the coffins, that Claude did not?

It made more sense than the doctor asking for money or

Guido getting a crush on a Baker. Had he learned anything before the bullets started flying?

No way to find out, unless…

His thin mouth curled up. There were other ways to find out what one needed to know. A dossier and, yes, perhaps a discreet surveillance was in order. And if the doctor noticed? Then it was a sign she was not as innocent as she appeared to be.

CHAPTER 5

HANNAH CARVED slices of beautifully cooked prime rib and ported them neatly to the extended plate, suppressing comparisons of doing the same with some bullet-ridden kidneys less than twenty-four hours previously.

The guests of Sarah's client wouldn't appreciate the distinction of having their meat carved by a morgue cutter. Her siblings sure didn't like her doing any carving at the family gatherings. It tended to kill their appetites.

Sarah appreciated her cutting skills. Hannah liked that. It helped being able to stay somewhat in her comfort zone—though it made her blink to think of the morgue as a comfort zone.

Hannah hadn't been sure what kind of server she'd be. Her brains had netted her scholarships, so she hadn't had to wait tables to get through school. So far, she'd label herself as not bad, though she hadn't had to tote trays of food or drinks, at least not in front of the guests. She'd helped unload the truck, of course.

It had been a bit of a surprise to find this rather posh party was being given by the very same Miz Gladys who she'd dubbed Miz Cookie that day at Sarah's place.

Miz Cookie's house was like her. Perfectly sweet and trying to be more. It fell short, though it was hard to pinpoint exactly how. Hannah didn't run in the kind of circles that Miz Cookie clearly aspired to join. If Hannah ran into rich and connected—and she tried not to—it was when they weren't at their best.

Miz Cookie's motherly smile—understandably MIA this night—kind of haunted Hannah. From what she could tell, peer pressure only got worse as the income went up. But it wasn't her place to tell Miz Cookie that these people would never be her friends, had Hannah had the chance. Hers was to keep her mouth shut, and to slice and dice.

Hannah was used to fading into backgrounds—something easy to do in her sprawling family—but this was a different kind of fading into a very different background. In fact, it was about as far from her middle class, beat-up-furniture back-ground as she could be. She was pretty sure none of the people holding out plates had given her more than the most cursory glance as they passed. The focus on the cutting had kept Hannah from doing much cranial study from her side of the table, which was good, since that made her lose focus. If she hadn't been so busy, though, she could have assigned some very creative deaths to this crowd.

Seeing Miz Cookie with her guests was a bit like watching a guppy in a shark tank. Hannah could only suppose the poor lady's extreme innocence protected her from the barbed comments about their hostess and her home that Hannah had heard murmured as guests passed along the buffet table. At least they liked the food.

Sarah drifted up behind her. "You doing all right?"

"So far." Hannah didn't miss a slice.

"You're a wizard with a carving knife," Sarah whispered, with a hint of a laugh in her voice, "and you haven't dropped one slice."

"Well, it's kind of frowned on." Hannah managed a quick grin over her shoulder, as the line began to slow. The table looked vaguely post-mortem, or perhaps ravaged was a better description. Sarah busied herself fixing that. Removing trays, replacing them with full ones.

A small lull in the chatter came about the same time as a late arrival. Hannah had a feeling she should recognize the woman. Perhaps from the cover of something or other? Hannah was addicted to forensic magazines, but her youngest sister liked popular culture stuff and left her magazines lying around Zach's house even though she didn't live there. The man with her was quite striking—though his creepy vibe had Hannah adding a toe tag labeled "stabbed in the back" to his ensemble.

"Mr. Afoniki," Miz Cookie faltered, her polite not quite covering up her dismay at having a notorious mobster show up for her party. "Um, yes, well." She glanced back toward the buffet. "There's still some lovely…if you're hungry? It's quite good…at least…"

"I am a fan of Miss Sarah's cooking," he countered smoothly, just a hint of Russian in his voice. He moved forward, her guests parting for him and not completely closing behind him. With a true shark in their midst, her guests now looked more like guppies, too, in a pond they wished they could flee.

"Miz Cookie is a bit out of her depth," Hannah muttered.

"Miz—oh." A pause. "Why do you call her that?"

"She's so sweet. Like a sugar cookie with sprinkles. Tons of sprinkles. So many sprinkles." Saying it made her tongue feel coated again. When Sarah didn't respond, Hannah turned, catching a very thoughtful expression on Sarah's face.

"Do you think she's sweet?" Sarah finally asked, then moved toward another tray that needed replaced without waiting for an answer.

Hannah turned her attention back to Miz Cookie and caught her watching Dimitri Afoniki—it had to be him, the nephew of the last surviving wise geezer—as he greeted Sarah with an interest not at all kind to his date. Miz Cookie's looked the same, the sweet expression firmly in place, with just a tiny frown of worry between her carefully plucked brows. Were there depths beneath the sugar?

Expressions were usually gone by the time she was brought on scene, so she hadn't spent a lot of time training to parse them. If she was going to step out of her comfort zone, she might need to bone up.

"I would so very much like some of the prime rib," the smooth, somewhat amused tone broke into her thoughts.

Hannah was annoyed with herself for losing track of the wise nephew, especially over Miz Cookie. She'd wanted to stay focused, do this gig right.

She gave him an apologetic smile and swiftly compiled with his request. When Dimitri Afoniki didn't move away, Hannah looked up to find a slight frown between his well-marked brows.

He was tall, blond, so handsome it was almost fake, like he'd been air brushed. One could imagine the skull had been fashioned by a master sculptor, rather than formed by nature. It was that good. She suppressed the urge to add a bullet hole to the temple. Charm appeared with a smile. His gaze flicked up, then down to the half-carved hunk of meat, then back to her face. The smile deepened.

"A most intriguing place to find you, Dr. Baker," he murmured, as if he knew she didn't want to be outed and he'd keep it their little secret. Because he was that kind of guy.

Hannah revised his possible death to something frontal with a knife. Multiples. She managed to keep her grip light on the knife in her right hand and gave him a puzzled look. "Have we met?"

"To my great regret, no, we have not. Something that needs to remedied and soon."

The charm was there, in spades even, but Hannah was immune to charm floating atop pond scum. He moved away, which was a good thing, because her hand did tighten on the knife this time. She really didn't want to expand her wise guy acquaintances any further than she already had, as it was sure to kick Alex into Big Brother, high alert status. And that might get in the way of whatever was going on between her and Ferris. If something was. Which it probably wasn't.

His companion seemed untroubled by her date flirting—was it flirting? Hannah wasn't sure if she'd been flirted with or warned. His date passed on the meat, her plate showing signs of tepid veganism. And possibly some gluten issues. She didn't look like someone who liked to live dangerously, but it was possible she didn't know her date was a black-hearted scumbag who probably ate raw meat in the privacy of his mansion.

The small interchange had not gone unnoticed by Miz Cookie, who popped up in front of Hannah with her most motherly smile and deepening signs of worry creasing her brows. Was she afraid Afoniki had hit on her?

"Would you like some, ma'am?" Hannah asked, indicating the prime rib in hopes of forestalling any mother-like questions. She was a terrible liar.

There was a pause, while suddenly intent eyes studied her. Then a polite-ish smile, tamped down for the help, creased her face very briefly.

"Does the hostess ever get to eat at her own party? I'll have some later, dear." Her gaze lingered on Hannah for another long moment, then turned toward a guest lingering over the tray of tarts. "I knew *you'd* like the tarts, Clara dear."

Clara dear flushed and backed away from the tray.

Hannah's eyes widened at this outbreak of not so nice, then looked hastily down when Miz Cookie's gaze swung back her direction. In the silence, she finally had to look up, and this time she saw past the sweet. Hannah felt the hairs on her arms lift and had to work at keeping her expression that of an innocuous server.

Usually she didn't feel a need to fill silences. In her family, there weren't that many.

"Everyone seems to love the food, ma'am." Hannah's throat felt dry all of a sudden.

"The food is—" Her gaze flicked toward Sarah for a moment, "as advertised."

So might a cat sit on the hearth cleaning its claws one by one while it digested a songbird. And studied the next bird to go down. Almost Hannah thought she heard purring. Probably a good thing the lady's ambitions appeared confined to social advancement. Miz Cookie's gaze slanted her direction and Hannah wondered how she'd ever thought her nice. With some surprise at how steady her hands were, she produced several slices for a guest, feeling her tension ease as the Miz Cookie closed in on a bird-er-guest. Hannah lowered knife and fork and flexed her fingers with an inconvenient tremble.

Hannah was tired again, but pleasantly tired this time. Sometimes a change was as good as a rest. Her sense that Sarah was good people had been confirmed, as well as her excellent intuition. She owed her for the warning about Miz Cookie. She probably wasn't Afoniki and Calvino evil, but she was the poisonous type who would smile as she stabbed you in the back.

Hannah felt distinctly sticky after an evening in her home.

As if she heard that thought, Sarah reached down and snagged a bag of pretzels. "These help."

Hannah chuckled. If Sarah was good stuff—which she was —didn't that mean that Nell was probably good stuff, too? Following that thought line, Hannah said, or possibly asked, "You've known Nell a long time."

"We were roommates in college. Clicked from the first minute we met." Her smile was reminiscent. "Sisters of other mothers."

"Did you ever meet her parents?" Should she not ask? Tact wasn't always her strong suit.

"Oh yeah. Still can't quite believe it. You can't imagine how weird it is." She blinked and shook her head.

If it was that hard for Sarah... "Must be pretty challenging for Nell."

Sarah's gaze met hers, and Hannah was glad she meant it,

wasn't just saying it. Sarah nodded. "Nell's had many tough things to deal with, including losing her parents." She sighed. "Looking back, I can see it was really weird that they managed to never let her visit me here, but it all seemed so unavoidable and just, oh well. But parents, well, you believe them until you don't."

Hannah sensed something in that, something more than just growing up and finding out parents were human and fallible, but she'd never learned the art of being encouragingly noncommittal. A small silence fell, though not an uncomfortable one. Unconnected thoughts drifted through her head. Dissecting bodies was so much easier than sorting through family, history, life...

"Odd that Dimitri Afoniki showed up tonight," Sarah said, as if following her own drifting series of thoughts.

Hannah looked at her. "He's my third wise guy this week."

"You know him?"

Hannah shook her head. "But he knew me." That was odd. It's not like she ended up in the news. Even in the drive-by, her brothers made sure she was "and companion" to the reporters.

"And he still took the prime rib? Well, he is a tough guy." Her tone was light, but her eyes worried. "He keeps sniffing around my business. Not sure why."

Wasn't she? It had kind of seemed to Hannah that he was sniffing around Sarah—but then that could be a ruse to keep him in Nell's orbit. Sarah had sure as heck not returned his interest vibes. Hannah had a sudden desire to see Sarah around Frank or Ben. What would the vibes be like then? She couldn't imagine her going for either one of her brothers, but she might be too close. She loved her brothers but sure as heck wouldn't want to date them.

"So how long have you and Logan Ferris been an item?"

Sarah's question cut across Hannah's half sleepy thoughts. She jerked to attention. "There's not, I don't—you haven't said anything to—"

"To Nell? No chance. She'd spill it to Alex for sure."

"Who would go bat crap crazy." Hannah sagged back in the bucket seat of the van. "Alex has never noticed I'm in my thirties." She paused, then added as if they weren't connected. "Ferris is his partner. And younger than me."

"Age only seems to matter when you're really young or really old." She studied Hannah for several seconds. "You look good together."

"We're not really...together together." Unless kissing counted, which it kind of felt like it did. She bit her lip, acting on an atypical impulse. "I found something in the coffin that— I didn't tell anyone about and then it disappeared."

Sarah blinked a couple of times and Hannah knew why. A Baker. Inconceivable.

"What did you find?"

"It was a school ring." Hannah rubbed her finger where one would have been, if she'd had one. She'd graduated early, not with "her" class. "It was Charlie Baker's."

"Your dad's brother, Charlie?"

So she'd heard the story. She nodded.

"Wow. But, didn't he...isn't he...well, dead?" her voice trailed off. Hannah could almost see her doing the math.

"That's always been the story," Hannah admitted. "Zach, well, he is really good at stoic and need-to-know." And protective. Really protective.

"A class ring," Sarah murmured, "wasn't he supposed to be in love with Ellie? Maybe she—"

"I did wonder about that. I mean, it's not a stretch to believe she helped her daughter disappear. But then why put it in there?"

"Maybe it was an accident? Must have been a tense time."

Hannah nodded. "It wasn't part of the, er, arranged stuff."

"Wow. And then it disappeared? Same person as the brick?"

Hannah shrugged. "I would assume so." It's hard to imagine two people lurking around the morgue." She paused, then added, "Ferris, well, he kind of guessed I'd done something. I guess." She may have helped him with that by being nervous. "He's…helping me try to figure out…what to do…" Heat flushed her cheeks. She didn't really know what it was they were doing. Wasn't quite clear on what they weren't doing either.

Sarah was quiet, but her eyes showed thinking going on. Finally she shook her head. "Who would have thought the past could be so full of secrets that it could bother and perplex us now?"

"Indeed."

More silence.

"Do you think Charlie and Ellie…" Sarah stopped. "If they are still…" She grimaced, her eyes filled with worry.

"It's a puzzle," Hannah agreed.

More silence.

"I think Nell is hoping she is still…she'd like one relative that doesn't suck."

"Zach is hoping too, I think." Or she suspected. Zach liked to be enigmatic. "But not if he's come back gunning for the wise guys."

"Just one guy so far, right? They know who killed St. Cyr."

"What if Helenne St. Cyr only thinks she's the one who got her husband? What if someone beat her hit man to the punch?" Hannah was a bit surprised when that popped out. She hadn't known she'd been thinking it. Or been worried about it. "It's not like he'd admit he was late to the party."

"How delightfully devious you Bakers are." Sarah sounded amused now. "I wonder where one looks for a couple of geriatrics?"

"I don't—" Hannah stopped.

"What?"

"I don't know why I didn't think of it before..." It was so blindingly obvious where one looked for old people.

———

Tired as she was, Hannah found it hard to go to sleep. Eventually she gave up, and grabbed her laptop. She fired it up. It didn't take long to get a rough number of the places older people gathered.

It wasn't a huge number, but how did one go about scouring through retirement homes when one had no official capacity at all? One could try to narrow the field, of course. She frowned. Could one apply the scientific method?

She might not be a detective, but she was a Baker. Her frown deepened. Could she draw Bakerish conclusions when the Baker in question had been living away for so long?

She sighed. If she did come up with a way to find them, she needed to know what they looked like now.

It was, of course, possible that only one of them was still living. It was a rather romantic notion to believe that they not only lived, but had found each other after their trials and tribulations. Yes, she read romance novels, but she didn't usually mix them into her reality. Even her job at the nasty end of the evil that men did hadn't stamped out her hope for happy endings.

She and Ferris had talked about aging software, but was it really necessary, at least in the case of Charlie? If he looked as much like his brother as her brothers looked like each other…

She pulled up a photo of Zach and studied it, not as a daughter, but as a scientist, noting the formation of his skull, the shape of his mouth and set of his eyes. As for Ellie, didn't everyone keep insisting Nell was her ghost? She had a photo of her, too, from a family get together. It only took a couple of moments to cut her out of the crowd and pop the photo into the aging software.

She studied the result, tipping her head to one side, then the other. If Nell aged this well, Alex was a lucky man.…

Her cell shrilled a summons from the NOCC.

More bullets. More bodies. Maybe it was the tremor on the New Orleans "easy" force, or maybe it was the lack of sleep, but the sight of the body on her table didn't kick her into the cutting zone right away. Or possibly it was that stupid clock out there ticking down to trouble zero hour. It felt like it was ticking faster. Almost like it was taunting her. Or laughing at her.

She geared up with less than her usual briskness, then stepped up to her table and pulled the sheet off.

For several long seconds she—and that clock—froze.

"Anything wrong, doc?" her assistant asked with mild curiosity. He'd been dragged out of bed, too, she noted.

"No." She shook her head and picked up her knife. Nothing wrong. Just weird. And possibly unsettling that her first customer of this day was the shooter from her adventure with Guido Calvino the other day.

She worked her way through his autopsy. She didn't recognize the second body, but the third was the driver of the van. The last body might be familiar, a vague impression of a face behind the shooter.

Normally bullets to the brain bored her, but not this time. This time it felt personal with that clock tick, tick, ticking in the back of her head, its pace getting faster and faster....

———

Such a pity they'd had to die. Four pawns removed from play, though truly, they'd been sacrificed for her greater good. It was the function of pawns to be sacrificed for their queen.

Queen. Mafia queen. She liked the sound of that. So much better than president of this garden or that club. How puny it all seemed. No wonder it had failed to satisfy her. She'd been born for bigger, greater things.

She fingered a pawn. She'd miss her boys a little. They'd been rather cute killers. Well, attempted killers.

A frown formed between plucked brows. And in the end, not only ineffective but dangerous to her. But they were tiny bumps in her path to greatness and one couldn't afford to be sentimental when one had larger concerns. And a stupid, illogical time pressure.

She hated time pressure. She particularly hated other people's time pressures. One planned and plotted. One orchestrated—but always at one's own pace. That old man was lucky someone else had killed him. Plots and machinations from the grave? So melodramatic. So...one might call it...common. Bad enough that he'd hid her heritage from her so long—with excuses about danger from those three old men—but then he'd had the nerve to try and control her from the grave. Really. So like a man.

Why even twenty years ago, she'd have done more with a crime empire than all the current idiots drifting around the edges of their families. Twenty years ago, before Harold. If only—

Not that she didn't care very deeply for Harold. It distressed her very much that she was going to have to do something about Harold. He'd never understand this new calling. Because it was a call. A call to greatness.

Which was why she rather wished they'd never met. Because now she'd have to spare him the distress of finding out. And it really, it really wasn't that easy to get rid of one's husband. The wife was always the first to be suspected. She'd plotted his death several times—purely for the mental exercise. Not because she'd planned to kill him. Though if one did, one would like to get credit eventually. After one couldn't go to jail for it, of course.

In one way, the timing of this new calling was fortuitous. She'd seen the way Harold's personal assistant looked at him. And at her. Such frustrated hate from an impotent, silly fool. She was in love with Harold, of course. And there was a slight —very slight—possibility that Harold might be swayed into straying in his thoughts. And where the thoughts went, the body might follow....

That could not happen. Queens didn't get left. They did the leaving.

A widow might be a bit socially awkward, but there was a sympathy factor. And there was the money, soon to be augmented by more money and so much power? She shivered in delight. She'd seen how all her guests had looked at her while sucking up her food. They'd made sure she heard some of their remarks, too.

They'd be so sorry. So very sorry.

Sorrier than she was about poor Harold. But this was not the time to falter. She must show no weakness. Not even for poor dear Harold.

She'd have to make it quick. He shouldn't suffer...much. Just a tiny bit for possibly letting his thoughts stray. But this was not the time to draw any legal attention her direction. She'd been very careful, but she wasn't sure the boys had been. The young were not generally known for being careful.

Why look at how they'd botched the shooting. While she was happy they hadn't killed Guido—since that was her... high calling to kill him herself—they'd been so obvious about not killing him she'd had no choice but to remove them from play.

She looked down at Harold's chess board and very gently flicked over one pawn after another until four lay on their sides. The black king lay on his side as well. She picked up the black queen and studied it. Did she still exist? No one seemed to know, at least no one willing to talk about it. Was Ellie Calvino old—dead—news? Or a problem that would need to be solved? The memory of her had been useful in luring the old man into the trap. She was rather surprised at that. She fingered the black queen. Was it love or hate that had lured him to his doom? If Afoniki was as easy to dupe as Calvino, well, she should be firmly in control very soon.

Her gaze lighted on the other queen.

At least Aleksi didn't have a queen—though one could

make the case that Dimitri acted the Queen's role for the old man. But he was unlikely to sacrifice himself to protect his king. All of them—Claude, Guido and Dimitri—had to be so hungry for the power those old men had clung to for so very long. Hunger—when properly manipulated—could make fools of them all.

They deserved to lose it. Why hadn't they done anything? Why hadn't her gambit resulted in a gang war? It always worked in the movies and such. She'd watched *The Sopranos* and read every mob-related book she could get her hands on. One side started shooting and the other side shot back. It was like a wise guy rule or something. Her boys had drawn blood. It wasn't like Afoniki to turn the other cheek. Why were they being so patient? She didn't have time for things to settle and let the heirs secure their place. She needed chaos and quickly. They'd all been so patient, so much so they should be embarrassed about it. Were they the mob or mice?

They needed to get fighting, get killing each other, the more the better. She didn't have a bunch of family and goons at her beck and call. All she had was her brains, a mandate from dear old, dead great grandfather Zafiro and the very, very small carrot of a snitch in the NOPD. It was like some stupid test.

She frowned. Afoniki wasn't going to be lured out of his fastness by Ellie's voice from the past. But Dimitri had shown up at her party. She smiled at that memory. She'd pulled the strings and he'd come.

She picked up the white queen and studied it. If she were playing chess—but she wasn't. In her game, there was only one way to win. The board must be cleared, with one queen standing at the end.

Her.

She picked up the black queen and tapped it against white. Then dropped them on the board.

A gray queen? No. She'd hidden who she was, what she was, for all of her life. She'd tried so hard to fit in with bitter, jealous women's group after bitter, jealous women's group. Well no more. Forget black, white and gray.

She'd be the red queen. It was appropriate. She'd be riding into her kingdom on a sea of blood...

"Oh there you are, my dear," Harold said, dropping his sadly weak chin to look at her over his glasses.

She turned toward the doorway where he hovered, uncertain of his welcome.

Not that she'd wanted to be dominated by a man, she thought with a slight, inward smile, but she'd have respected him more if he'd shown just a little spirit.

"Were you looking for me?" She smiled, but he didn't notice. Instead, he moved toward the chess board and began setting the pieces back in their proper places. She stifled a sigh.

What she really needed was for someone else to kill Harold, but she was the only one who wanted him dead. Now that secretary of his would be more than happy if she were to die.

She handed Harold a pawn, her thoughts following this very promising line of murder plotting—no, she decided, with very real regret. To be an almost murdered wife was to appear weak. Harold's death needed to look natural. Quiet. Like he'd lived.

In this city, optics were everything, particularly when the coroner's office had so many bodies to deal with. At his age, there wouldn't even be an autopsy.

"I am glad to see you looking so happy, my dear," Harold

said. "You seemed so distressed after your party the other night."

"I'm feeling ever so much better after your good advice. You're so right. I worry much too much what other people think of me. If I'm true to myself, that is all that matters."

"Er, quite."

For just a second, she thought she saw something in his eyes, but that was ridiculous. Harold had no idea who and what she really was. She gave him the smile that had snared him in the first place. "I was thinking about how long since we've just had a quiet dinner out somewhere." She gave a wistful sigh. And then cast him a soulful look. "Do you remember how we used to be, Harold? How young and care-free? Where was that little place we used to eat when we could barely afford to eat out?"

As expected, he looked alarmed. He couldn't remember because there'd never been a "place" for them. She'd always disliked inferior food. He blinked. She pretended not to notice. "We should go back. I wonder if it's even still there? I think I'll," she paused to giggle. "Google it."

Relief appeared in his mild gaze. Harold was like a faithful old dog, without all the downsides of owning a pet. It really was a pity that she'd had to have him put down. But she'd make sure he got a really special headstone, even if he hadn't been quite faithful. She'd even inscribe it "beloved husband of…" And a jazz funeral. She's always wanted to be the widow in a jazz funeral.

She'd keep her temper, too. It was only right that his last days should be as pleasant as possible. She would mourn Harold for a very long time, she decided. It was only right. And black was so slimming.

———

It was getting harder to be content. It was not the fault of the office. Dimitri Afoniki had arranged for the design himself. It was flawless, tasteful and highly functional.

No, it was what it represented. Second place. Second in command. Not in charge.

When he, Guido and Claude all waited for power—he would not say he was content, but he was less restless.

Aleksi sensed it, of course. He was no fool. He'd isolated himself in his room. He was too ill for visitors, but well enough to shoot orders at Dimitri through texts and email, and occasionally, with direct calls.

Dimitri could not honestly say he wouldn't have taken the opportunity, if presented, to clear his path to power. It would be so easy to blame it on others right now. While the police still considered Helenne St. Cyr their target for Phineas' death, piecing together information—both official and unofficial—indicated they were baffled by Bettino's murder and wondered if the two deaths were, after all, connected.

Dimitri picked up a report about the disappearance of the St. Cyr ring. There were rumors that the Calvino ring was also missing. None of the reports explained why the rings mattered enough to be stolen. He'd think it was some twisted collector of curiosities, except...

As long as he'd known his uncle, the ring had been on the third finger of his left hand. When he was agitated or thinking, he'd twisted it around and around. It was as if having it on his finger wasn't enough. He must always have both hands on it. If Aleksi weren't the coldest, most practical man Dimitri had ever known, he'd think Aleksi feared the ring would vanish. And with it, all his power, all of this.

Which did nothing to explain the why of the rings. Oh, he knew of the old story, well, as much as he could find out on his own. Aleksi never spoke of Zafiro. Dimitri had been curious and looked him up. The photos were old, but—he could see why it took the three of them to take him out. The wonder of it was that they had never turned on each other. Oh, they'd had skirmishes, but not even the flare-up when Phil and Toni supposedly died had amounted to much.

Why?

Were the rings some part of the secret? Dimitri was not a superstitious man, but lately he could almost believe the ghost of Zafiro had risen to take his final revenge.

He shrugged the thought away. He was not a superstitious man, so there must be some human agency at work. He began to sift through the reports again, his hand stopping at one.

Why would Claude have Dr. Hannah Baker followed?

He set that report aside and sifted through—there it was. A possible reason. What was Guido up to? He considered the doctor, as seen at that dreadful party. She was attractive, though not really his taste.

It was perhaps redundant to put his own man on the doctor, too. A bribe might work with the current watcher—but anyone who could be bribed once, could be bribed again. Yes, he'd rather one of own people were on it. There were risks in messing with a Baker. Serious risks. If Guido or Claude were planning something there, it would be wise to ensure he wasn't implicated.

CHAPTER 6

IT WASN'T easy to shake off Alex, but Ferris finally managed it. Guy could turn into a burr sometimes. It was like he had some sixth sense of when to stick. Good thing his thinking was scrambled some. A woman could—Ferris stopped, considered this, and decided not to finish the thought as he went into the autopsy room.

That helped clear his thoughts, hypocritical and otherwise. Hannah was not a pretty sight up to her elbows in someone's guts. She looked up, a smile flickering briefly on her lips before she bent to her task once more. She lifted out a slimy mass of innards and set them in a pan her assistant held out, then stepped back with a nod that must have been permission for said assistant to finish because he set down the pan and stepped closer to the corpse.

Hannah stripped off her gloves and tossed them neatly in the bin, then lifted her face shield. "You got my text."

He nodded, even though it wasn't a question. "What's up?"

She beckoned him to her cluttered desk just outside. He

joined her, taking care not to look at her corpse. Weird that he had no problem at crime scenes and got queasy when they were on the table. She pulled a couple of folders toward him and flipped them open and extracted two photos. Then reached into a tray and extracted two others.

"These are the sketches from the shooting, that the sketch artist did from my description," she said, "and these two arrived on my slab today."

He didn't have to study them long to conclude that Hannah had a good memory. A very good memory. He scanned the discovery details. It looked like they'd been quietly put away. Then bagged and tagged for garbage pickup.

"Someone didn't know that indestructible garbage bags aren't always indestructible." He looked up. "All four shot in the back?"

Hannah nodded. "But not at the same time."

Put down, he concluded, but for what? The crime of not committing the crime they'd been told not to commit?

"Look at this," Hannah stepped back to the body and showed him the kid's ink. Before he could connect the gang dots, she said, "It's temporary. Fake. Not even a good fake. I've ordered some tests of what was used, but not sure I'll get them."

The assistant gave a tiny snort of agreement.

Hard to justify the money on a couple of very low-profile punks. She indicated the door, and he followed her out into the hall. They stopped when they were alone. He frowned. "So someone sent out a couple of fake perps to stir the wise guys' pot?"

"It's—" she stopped, and he arched an encouraging brow,

"like a bad episode of a lame cop show. They couldn't even fake a shooting."

"Doesn't seem like a plan conceived by Afoniki or Calvino. I don't think Claude St. Cyr is that naive either. Maybe a new guy trying to kick the fire anthill?"

"Even if it had worked, what would the new guy have accomplished? A lot of shooting by a bunch of low-level wise guys?" Hannah looked vaguely frustrated. She rubbed her forehead with the back of her hand. "Am I overthinking it? If it had worked and a gang war erupted, it wasn't likely to affect the guys at the top."

"I can't see the genius hiding in this plan either," Ferris said, propping his back against the wall. "Seems pretty dumb-A to me, but perps do dumb things. Makes our job easier." He flicked a look back down the hall as the tech rolled her body past them. "Sometimes. The rest of the time, it gets confusing." He grinned at her and was pleased when her lips curved up and the worry line between her brows softened.

"I hate it when things don't make sense," she admitted.

"How do you survive in this town with that crazy attitude?" he shot back, and that time got a throaty laugh out of her, one that made his toes feel weird. "You just starting or almost done?" He tried not to sound hopeful.

"Thankfully almost done. And I had this idea I'd like to run past you if you've got time."

"I've got time." Though when they were finally seated across a table from each other, he did wonder how she managed to eat her meat rare. Her face was interestingly angular, almost aesthetic, and her gaze gravitated to analytical without warning, but her appetites were very earthy. Rare meat and rich desserts when someone else picked up the tab.

Her enjoyment of that dessert caused him some serious concentration problems, but he managed to soldier through by adding a lot of ice to his cold drink, then pressing it to the side of his neck when she wasn't looking.

"Wow, I feel human again," she said, finally leaning back with a contented sigh. Her smile almost took his socks off. "Thank you. I'll pay you back when I get my check from Sarah."

"Oh?"

"Yeah, did my first wait gig last night. It wasn't bad." Her look turned mischievous. "She had me carving the prime rib."

"Twisted, but clever."

"She's no fool." She flicked him a look. "I told her what we're doing."

"Did you?" His brows arched, but not with alarm. Sarah was solid.

Hannah looked at him a bit doubtfully. Her gaze dropped to her plate, and she pushed some crumbs from one side to the other. "She misunderstood what we're doing. Together, I mean. You walk into a room next to someone and..." She shrugged.

Ferris felt...he wasn't sure. Feelings were for girls. He didn't like having them unless they were basic. Easy to figure out. So he should be glad she wasn't assuming feelings not present. Or not acknowledged to be present, his brain tacked on before he could stop it.

"Anyway," Hannah looked up with an air of moving on, "I got this idea while we were talking."

Ferris knew this feeling. He had just cause to be wary when a woman got an idea. "Yeah?"

"Nursing homes. Assisted living."

He blinked. "What?"

"Uncle Charlie and Ellie. It's the perfect hiding place." She frowned. "Though there are enough of both to make it challenging." She paused, her gaze getting distant and analytical again. Then she blinked and continued as if unaware of the pause, "So I spent some time trying to come up with photos. I took a picture of Nell and aged it, because everyone says she looks like Ellie. And I didn't really have to age Uncle Charlie. He must look like Zach. The brothers are variations on a Baker theme."

Apparently oblivious to Ferris' mental scramble, she pulled out her cell phone and pulled up a photo, turning it around for his scrutiny.

"I have the photos, but it's not like we can put out a BOLO on them."

"Not without a lot of explanations," Ferris agreed. "May I?" At her nod, he took the phone and studied the image, making the image bigger and moving around. "So that's how Nell will look as a little old lady."

It was weird to think of Alex as an old man like Zach. He never thought about getting old if he could help it. It's not like he didn't know he'd get old someday, but there was this part of him that didn't quite believe he'd get *old*. Old was for one's parents and their friends. And other people's parents.

"I've been reading through the background stuff." The frown reformed between her brows. "I have this feeling I'm missing something."

"We're probably missing a lot of something," Ferris pointed out, hooking his thumbs into his pockets so he wouldn't go crazy and try to smooth that frown away. "Lots of holes in what we know. Or what we think we know."

Her look of assent was as distracting as all her other looks.

"I wish I had minions," Hannah said, with a sigh.

Ferris blinked. "Minions?"

"Sherlock Holmes called them his Irregulars, but he probably had to tip them. I can't even afford tips." She leaned back with a resigned sigh. "If this was a body…"

"What would you do?"

"Dig around inside, of course."

Ferris laughed. "What I do is like that, except I dig around outside of the body."

Her smile was a bit perfunctory. "What do we do if we find them? I don't even have an end game. Zach always says you should know your end game before you start anything."

Ferris felt a stab that should have been relief. Was he really willing to pursue an unofficial investigation, just to stay close to a girl? He liked truth and justice as much as the next cop, but would truth mesh with justice in this old, cold mess of a— he wasn't even sure it could be called a case.

"What are you afraid of, Hannah?" he asked, not sure it was the right question, or if there was a right question.

"I want my family to be okay. I want Zach to be okay," she said finally. She looked up. "He's worried about something."

"You could ask him."

"I have. He played the dad card. He stopped short of patting me on the head." Her brows pulled together. "Logic says there's nothing to find. That whatever *was* isn't relevant *now*. Only—it doesn't feel like nothing." She gave him a wry look. "It's like one of those old westerns with horse hooves pounding in the distance but getting closer."

"What would you know about old westerns?" The question was mostly to give him time.

She chuckled. "I am beginning to believe that's the only channel that works on Zach's TV." She sobered, a question in her eyes.

Ferris thought he knew what answer she wanted from him. Reassurance it was okay to ignore the beating hooves. "As a guy, I fear female intuition. As a cop...well, we call it gut instinct. Totally different things, of course."

"Of course." Her tone might have been ironic. "And what is your gut instinct telling you?"

He sighed. "That old, cold cases can still put out a stink."

Her shoulders sagged a bit. "So what's our move?"

He took his time answering. She deserved a serious answer. And if he took his time, he might just come up with one. Finally, he offered slowly, "When we have a real b—tough case, we set up a situation room. Make a board. Get visual so we can see what we know, connect what can be connected. Home in on what we don't know."

Her worry visibly eased. "Maybe we'll see a pattern. It does all feel random and disconnected." Her smile was a bit self-mocking. "I like order, even if it's just the illusion of order."

"Then we go forward?" He met her gaze steadily.

This time she didn't hesitate. "We go forward."

He wondered if she had the same thought as him. *May God have mercy on them both.*

———

The place gave him the creeps. He wasn't sure why he'd come. It sure wasn't because he trusted the broad. He'd learned that lesson. Old Lady St. Cyr better watch her back. You stick a knife in Roger Dunstead's back and you don't twist 'til he's dead then he's coming for you, fer sure.

He wouldn't be here, but she'd paid his bail. Didn't mean she owned him, but he'd give her a listen. He owed her that and no more than that. A listen. Then he was outta here. He wasn't going to hang around. Either the needle or the nut house waited for him. On his way out, he'd settle it with the old lady.

"Mr. Dunstead?"

The sweet voice pulled him around to face the door. The dumpy figure stood mostly in shadow. He didn't usually let someone sneak up on him. He'd lost his edge inside. Despite his inner resolve, he pulled his cap off and nodded.

"Please, have a seat."

The broad moved into the light, gesturing with one, some-what chubby hand toward one of two wing-backed chairs. The refusal rose to his lips and died there at the sight of the placid, motherly gaze. He found himself moving toward, then drop-ping into the chair.

Her slight smile of approval shouldn't have mattered.

"Ma'am," he muttered. His hands tightened on the cap, and he shifted to ease the jab of the gun tucked in the back of his waistband.

"You might be more comfortable with that somewhere else," she said. "Hold it if it makes you feel more at ease."

"Ma'am?"

"Your gun? I presume you have one? At least, I hope you do?"

"Yes, ma'am." On some level, it bothered him, but he had a sense of humor. He pulled it out, holding it loosely in one hand.

"Better?" Dunstead nodded. "Good." She indicated a tray. "Would you like a cup of tea? A cookie perhaps?"

Tea? Not in this lifetime—he opened his mouth, but before he could speak, his head nodded up and then down. His reward was another smile of approval and a cup with a cookie tucked in on the saucer. He balanced cup and gun for several seconds, then gave it up and set the gun on the table at his elbow and took a bite of the cookie.

"It's good, thank you, ma'am."

"I've been told I should sell my cookies in a store. My late husband," a shadow crossed her face, "loved my cookies."

Maybe it was the sugar that helped his thinking. He finished the cookie and set the cup next to his gun. He thought about picking it up, but before he could decide, she spoke.

"I imagine you're wondering why I invited you here today."

"Yes, ma'am. I am wondering." He looked at his watch, trying to take back control. "Got some business to take care of—"

"I do like a man who cuts through the clutter and gets right to the point." Her gaze grabbed his, and he saw something at the back of her eyes that made him wish he'd picked up his gun. "Of course, at least, I hope it's of course," she smiled again, but this smile made him want to shift in his seat, "I want you to kill someone for me."

His eyes widened, though he tried to play it cool. "I don't —" her brows arched. "I mean, I have, but—who?"

"Well, now that is the problem, isn't it? And exactly why I picked *you* to help me."

She didn't call him a big, strong man, but his shoulders went back and his chin went up, and he thought that of course she'd picked *him* to help her. She was already a widow, so at least he wasn't getting set up to pop a husband this time. And she had to have a lot of something in the bank to pay for this place, even if it was on the creepy side.

"Another cookie?" She held out the plate.

He hesitated, because for just an instant, it felt like a trap, not a cookie. But she was just some harmless, crazy old lady with an itch she needed scratched. And it wasn't like he was going to get a new line of work now. So he took the cookie. And possibly the job. He could back out anytime he wanted.

"I can't tell you how much better I feel," she cooed. She set the tray down, delicately took a cookie and bit into it with her small, sharp, white teeth.

CHAPTER 7

IT WAS anticlimactic to resolve to move forward and then not move forward that much. There was real life. And their jobs. There was always a new day with a new body to dig through for Hannah. And it wasn't like she could use that time to mull the next step. Even the obvious autopsies required concentration. It was, thankfully, all too easy for Hannah to get lost in what one of her brothers like to call "the innards." After that last autopsy, she was glad she didn't drink or smoke.

She nodded for her guy to move the body out and tossed yet another pair of gloves into the bin. So far her "move forward" had been to set up a bulletin board. It was old school, but she'd tied it into one of those brainstorming apps. She added some photos from her phone, and it looked like "something" only it wasn't. Not yet.

She studied the output from her electronic brainstorming. Not much of a storm. She switched over to the photo she'd taken of the actual board at home. Maybe an old-school case needed old-school methods. The disparate pieces she'd pinned up made her eye hurt. She rubbed the brow over it. She was a cutter—what if she approached it like it was a body? She mentally drew a chalk line around her board. The human body had certain, predictable responses to events, like getting shot. Bleeding. Shock. Death. She wasn't as good with live people, but she was one, so that should give her enough data to create a hypothesis. That's what she did with bodies. She looked for out-of-the-norm, created a working theory, then tried to prove/disprove it. She even had a tiny budget.

Could she find the familiar in the unfamiliar?

Predictable.

Unpredictable.

Old and cold…

If Charlie and possibly Ellie had returned to New Orleans, well, Charlie was a Baker. He'd have done some research before he came back. These days you could do that over the internet. So they'd be looking at the same list of retirement homes. Could she figure out which ones he'd look at, maybe narrow the list a bit? Zach, he'd read the reviews, but he'd also reject anything that sounded old. Or too cute.

And the timing would matter. She could postulate a couple of triggers that might bring them back. Nell. Or St. Cyr's demise. If Charlie was still one of the good guys, then Nell would be the trigger. If he wasn't…

Revenge was a dish best served cold.

But this was really cold. Like arctic cold.

She'd keep an open mind, but—

"I've got someone out front that wants to speak with you, Dr. Baker."

Hannah looked at the receptionist hovering in the doorway. Was she the same person who'd let Guido Calvino waltz unaccompanied into her surgery? Hannah examined her thesis and realized the answer was in the question. Of course they let Calvino come back. He was scary. Unlikely to take no for an answer. Or wait for someone to be fetched. Unless he sent a goon to do the fetching. Ergo—had she actually used that inside her head?—this someone must be someone relatively normal who could be stopped by their new—again—receptionist.

She peered at the girl, but her ID had flipped so it couldn't be read. She rubbed her eyes with the back of her hand and asked, "Wants to see me? What about?"

"Harold White. His body came in a couple of days ago. She's his PA. Melinda or Belinda Harris. She's got some paperwork. Something about final disposition of the body?"

Hannah stared at her, trying to remember if she'd done the autopsy, assuming there'd been one. There was no way they could physically autopsy every body that came through. A death certificate didn't always require a full autopsy. At times all it took was a phone call.

"Was he on my list?"

Instead of answering that, she repeated, "She wants to speak with you."

Translation: she won't leave until someone more official than a receptionist speaks to her. Hannah noticed the girl held a file, presumably White's. She held out a hand, got it, and scanned it quickly. Looked like a heart attack. Nothing suspicious. He was in their morgue because he hadn't died while supervised by his doctor.

"Someone called his doctor," she noted. The doctor was surprised, but not surprised. The other vitals didn't mean much until an address caught her eye. She'd been there surely

—that's right. The catering gig with Sarah. Miz Cookie's house.

"Did this PA say why she needed to talk to me?" Hannah asked, still studying the details. It looked like he donated a few organs before arriving at the morgue.

"She wouldn't say."

"She wouldn't say or you don't want to tell me what she said?"

"She wouldn't say."

Hannah sighed. She hoped it wasn't another "cry murder." If someone wanted to get away with murder, pick a city with a high murder rate and an overworked, understaffed, and underfunded coroner. She didn't like to think of anyone getting away with it, but it was only on TV shows or in books that official types had the budget to pursue hunches and such. She considered Miz Cookie and her unsweet expression. Too bad she didn't have the time or the power to pull her chain a bit. She'd bet she had Harold's funeral all planned.

She reached up, tugging at the fasteners to her bloody cover. "Okay. I'll see her."

The girl looked relieved. "I don't think she'll leave until you do."

Hannah confirmed the girl's impression when she met Belinda Harris. Her name was a tad too whimsical for the sturdy, practical woman waiting doggedly for Hannah to appear. If parents could see—but of course they couldn't see the future, just the baby. The woman she'd become seemed too practical for the morgue. She would die tidily—Hannah blinked, pulling her thoughts firmly back to the present.

Belinda Harris was about Hannah's height with a bland mien mitigated by an alert and intelligent gaze. Probably was a very good PA, possibly too good for her own good. The eyes were red-rimmed from crying, boosting the "too good for her own good" impression.

Hannah gestured her to a seat, then took one opposite. "How can I help you, Ms. Harris?"

"Mr. White had special instructions in place for when—" her steady calm faltered, and she compromised by holding out some papers. "I wanted to make sure you received his paperwork so you can release the body." This time she managed it with only a slight hesitation.

Hannah took the sheets and studied. He wanted to donate his body for scientific study. "This is kind of out of my area, too, but I'll make sure this makes it into his file. We can copy this and get it back to you—"

"I suppose there's nothing—it was a heart attack?"

Hannah opened the file again, pretending to study it. Death had not been kind to a face that already trended toward bland. And yet he'd married Miz Cookie and inspired devotion in his PA. Interesting.

"Our office spoke with his personal physician," Hannah said vaguely and closed the file.

"So no autopsy?"

She looked again. "The coroner has not signed a death certificate yet."

"But you think he will?"

Hannah looked rueful. "I did not perform the assessment, Ms. Harris. If you have information—"

A look that was almost—fear flickered in her calm gaze, and she stood up abruptly. "No. Mr. White trusted me to make sure his last wishes were respected. And I've done that. I'd better go."

"Well, thank you for doing this. It's a valuable contribution. Do you want to wait for copies—"

Again, that sharp shake of her head. "I made them in the office. Thank you."

And she was gone in a silent, determined rush. Hannah delivered the paperwork and headed back, her thoughts turning slowly. How odd that Miz Cookie kept, well, not exactly turning up in Hannah's life, but intruding. She had other, more important things to mull, but her brain hung on while she found her purse and logged off her computer for the day.

Why hadn't Harold White trusted his wife to make sure his wishes were followed? The party had seemed like a bid for attention. If she was trying to break into a higher social scene, well, if one couldn't marry in—her thoughts stalled for a moment, but she scrubbed her brain free of Miz Cookie in a wedding dress—philanthropy was another way to do it. Donating the body was a nice first step. And a lack of body never stopped anyone from having a big funeral with lots of important guests commiserating with one.

It was hard on Belinda Harris, who looked to have been in love with the boss. Neither of them fit the stereotype for star-crossed lovers, but real people didn't. Hannah pulled up Harold's face from the file and wished she hadn't. She could imagine any man preferring the crisp and salty Belinda after a few years with sugar-and-no-spice, however. But that wasn't to say they were having an affair.

Divorced women were dangerous, while a widow is a sympathetic figure.

She couldn't remember where she'd heard that. Probably accompanied by a meow. Hannah shook her head really firmly this time. It was time to move on from the Whites. But one, final thought crept through.

Black would suit Miz Cookie and not just because it was so slimming.

———

Claude closed the big door to the home that didn't feel like home. It hadn't ever, wouldn't until Helenne left it. The chill of her presence cooled better than the A/C. Perhaps she kept the cooling bill lower, Claude thought caustically, so she served some purpose by not dying.

All the way he'd debated what to do. Did he tell her or not? If she found out, she'd know he knew and hadn't told her, but if Dunstead was looking for some payback, he truly hated being the one to put her on her guard.

That, of course, assumed she was ever off her guard.

As if she sensed his thoughts, she appeared in the doorway of the sitting room. Claude studied her with his usual, color-less dispassion. She'd been attractive, beautiful even, at one time. Life had trimmed back all that was soft or womanly, leaving all hard, cold lines and a bitter gaze.

According to the old stories, it was Bettino Calvino she'd wanted to marry. He couldn't see that it mattered. Both had done about the same with the wealth they'd taken from Zafiro. So why had she cared? Unless she hated to lose. He could understand that.

Had she finally gotten her revenge on Calvino? Claude could believe she'd kill Bettino while out on bail for the murder of her husband. He just couldn't believe Bettino would put himself in a position where she could kill him.

Her thin, hard brows arched. "Well?"

The decision, in the end, was obvious. "Roger Dunstead made bail today."

Her lashes flickered. She hadn't heard. That was interesting. Were her sources drying up?

"Will he be a problem?"

"No." That response was too quick. She knew it. Her lashes flickered again. "Thank you for the…information."

"Of course."

Her gaze met his, each striving to be the most indifferent. Then she turned back to the sitting room, and he headed for the stairs.

For a little longer, they'd pretend that each didn't want the other dead.

———

Ferris was pleased to see Hannah emerge from the NOCC. Repeated exposure had not diminished his dislike of the place, but his desire to see Hannah currently trumped that. She stopped abruptly, though he could tell she hadn't seen him.

"Ow." The exclamation was soft, but emphatic. She also rubbed her head.

"Headache?" he asked from the bottom of the loading dock.

She looked around, her gaze unfocused for several seconds. Then she smiled, taking her time with it.

"Painful thoughts," she said, inexplicably, but with an air of certainty that he'd understand.

Holy Hannah.

She came down the ramp, the angle emphasizing all the

stuff that made her "holy." The lowering sun had lost its harsh edge, softening the pale and the tired in her face and bringing something more to her gaze. A gaze that turned a guy's brain to…

"You all right?" The touch of her hand on his arm put some heat in the spot, but it brought his brain back online.

"Yeah." He rubbed his face. It gave him a chance to look away from her eyes. But the memory of them lingered. Innocent—how was that possible in a woman who cut open bodies on a regular basis?—mysterious, deep enough to get lost in. "I, um, tried to call…"

"Really?" She extracted her cell phone and tried to activate the screen. "Battery is flat as Zach's griddle cakes. I guess I forgot to plug in after I messed around with this brainstorming app last night."

"Brainstorming app?" Alarm did a chilly run down his back. There was an app for that?

"For our incident board. It's kind of small on my phone. Looks better on the desktop, though I am finding the board I made more helpful than the app. Isn't it interesting how sometimes old tech works best? I took a picture of that board, but the app lets me input more information than, well, the board would let me if I weren't so lazy. Do you find it painfully hard to use a pen these days?" She turned her hands over, studying them as if they were on her table instead of on the ends of her arms.

"Yeah," he said, even though he'd lost the thread when her mouth curved at the edges. How did she do that and talk? He realized she'd gone quiet and was looking at him expectantly. "You free?"

"Yeah, was just heading home."

Something in her expression told him he hadn't responded to what she asked, but he was not going to admit he didn't hear the question because of her smile. He smiled at her, hoping it would disarm her like hers had disarmed him.

"I was hoping. I had one of the guys drop me off…just in case you were free?"

"Well, you lucked out. I have wheels and I'm flush again. Sarah paid me. I can buy you dinner." She hesitated. "We could get take out and put our heads together?"

The hint of hesitant in her voice helped get his head straight. Well, mostly. "I was hoping we could put our heads together." He didn't mean for his gaze to drop to her mouth. It did it all on its own, sending a faint color into her cheeks.

Holy Hannah.

He took her arm before he lost control of his thinking again. "So, tell me about your day. Punks still shooting at punks?"

She laughed, her chin lifting, releasing a throaty sound. "The pace has slowed some."

"And the clock in your head?" he asked it lightly, but he was back to wondering what had caused the ouch on the loading dock.

"Still ticking. Louder and faster. If this was a movie—"

—he'd get to kiss the girl. For a frozen second he thought he'd said it out loud, but she kept walking. She did stop talking.

"If this was a movie, what would happen next?" He rushed to fill the silence.

"Oh well," she unlocked her car, and he opened her door, but she turned to face him instead of getting inside, "if this was a movie, then someone would die."

"A lot of someones die every day in this city," Ferris pointed out, a bit dryly as her expression started to turn dreamy again.

"So true. Wouldn't even know which death was *the* death…" she slid behind the wheel.

He trotted around and climbed in beside her. Both hands gripped the wheel, but she hadn't started the engine, just stared out the windshield. "What? Did something happen today?" She shook her head, but without conviction. "Hey, we're partners, aren't we?"

She looked at him for a second, but her lashes slid down before he could figure out her expression. If a guy could figure out a woman.

"This PA came in today to give me some paperwork about her boss's body. He's donating his body to science." She stopped.

"And?"

"I just got the feeling she…was hoping…for more, maybe even an autopsy, but she wasn't willing to stir the pot. Or—" She frowned, then huffed impatiently. "You'd think with twelve siblings I'd be better with people."

Ferris turned in the seat and studied her. Hannah might not realize it, but she had good instincts. She just hadn't learned to hone them properly where the living were concerned.

"Tell me more. Who's the vic?"

"An accountant, not a vic. Heart attack probably. His doctor didn't dispute it."

Ferris arched his brows, sensing there was more.

"I kind of know the widow," she added reluctantly. "That's probably coloring my impressions."

When she told him about the first meet, he shook his head. "No memory of her at all."

"Not surprised. Not your type." She grinned, then filled him in on the dinner and her chat with Sarah after.

"Sarah's got good instincts," he admitted. "But you're not going to get an autopsy on those."

"I don't—" her lips twisted wryly. "Wouldn't dare ask for one. Though it would be a welcome change from digging out bullets."

"See, there's your problem right there. You're bored. Let's get some food and work on our case."

"The old, cold case that probably isn't?"

"That's the one." He grinned at her. "And if we work really hard, then maybe I'll…" he stopped, waiting for her to look at him.

"You'll what?"

He trailed a finger down the side of her face and found his grin fading with the movement. "Kiss your troubles away."

Her smile faded and she took a shaky breath, then said with attempted lightness, "Promises, promises." She leaned forward and turned the key in the ignition, but she took another breath before she put the car in motion.

Ferris, well, he was just glad he didn't have to try to drive a car. He just scared himself to death with the notion that she was a girl he might, just might be willing to promise anything. If he could survive what her brothers might do when they found out. Seven guys and that tough old man asking you what are your intentions? He studied her profile. She might be worth even that grief.

CHAPTER 8

MAKE SURE OF MY RING.

How many times had Bett said some variation of these words in the last few months? No, not just the last few months, but since Bettino became aware of the existence of Nell Whitby.

What was the deal with the ring? Guido wrenched back the curtains and stared out into what used to be his uncle's garden.

His now. All of it. The house, the garden, the business. The power. All his.

Except the ring.

He would have cursed his uncle, but why waste the words? His final destination had been determined long before he died. It was a reunion Bett had not feared.

Why the ring? It was such a small thing, easily lost, at most a symbol of something old and long gone. It was a pity he couldn't talk it over with Claude or Afoniki. Oh yes, Afoniki would know what the ring meant. He probably knew both rings were missing. Might have them. Wouldn't put it past the old devil.

If Aleksi didn't have it, well, it would probably turn up in a pawn shop somewhere. But it was…odd that two of the three rings were missing. Did that mean they *were* important? Or that someone wanted him to think they were important?

If keeping the rings in their possession was so important, why had the men worn them? Why not a safe or placed with lawyers. No one cared about the rings but them. Except…it appeared that someone did care. *Appeared.*

In this world of shifting shadows and uncertain loyalties it was challenging to discern what mattered and what didn't. Was there anyone besides Aleksi who remembered that time? His lips twisted wryly. Of course there was, but he didn't think Zach Baker would cough up any information. Besides, he'd been on the other side. The legal side. Funny, he could hear Guido saying he and Zach would have been friends if only one of them had been completely different.

Ah, the Bakers. So very law abiding. His brows drew together. So why had he sensed something—off—from Hannah Baker that day in the morgue? He'd always had the gift for sensing when someone had a secret. There was, he'd learned, always a way to find out secrets.

There was something quite delectable about the possibly bad doctor, even if she was a woman. Interesting. He usually preferred his partners less cerebral, more earthy, and with less figure. Never had a yen for a smart woman—when he had to have one. The smart ones were dangerous for a man such as himself. How sweet would it be to pluck some of the so-good Baker fruit and make it into something…sinfully different?

Though if he had to pick just one, the youngest brother was also interesting.

It was risky, of course. Probably be safer to go after the last ring. Could he take it from Aleksi's cold, dead hand? Since the shooting, the old man had almost walled himself in. His uncle had been wary, too, but not wary enough? What—or who—had lured him to his death?

Guido couldn't be sorry it had happened, of course. Would be nice to know so he didn't step into the same trap. When he considered who might have fashioned it, only one name came up.

Aleksi Afoniki. But why now? It could have been self-protective, he supposed somewhat doubtfully. A reaction to St. Cyr's murder? It was possible, though…

Aleksi Afoniki was the original ice man. He liked power and pain in equal parts. That dinner party had been about stirring the pot and possibly a little curiosity. He might have wanted to see if he could marry Nell Whitby off to Dimitri in some strange, dynastic marriage that, in the real world, meant nothing. Guido controlled his uncle's empire, no matter who the girl eventually married.

Rings and old grudges wouldn't change legal paperwork, and he had the strength to hang on to what was his. He'd earned it and no one was going to take it away from him.

So why did it feel like he'd inherited his uncle's unease with everything else? Why this sense of trouble coming? And when he felt that, why did the look in Dr. Hannah Baker's eyes come back into his mind?

He'd tried the direct approach. That left the forceful approach. He frowned. That would stir up more trouble than it was probably worth—at least for now. There was another way that might bear fruit.

He pressed a button and his newly minted second-in-command came in.

"I want a watch placed on Dr. Hannah Baker. Daily reports of everywhere she goes, who she talks to. *Discreet*, Aldo."

"You're on to something there, sir," Aldo said, looking past Guido, a signal that the news incoming might be unwelcome.

"Am I?" Guido angled his head, his gaze sharpening.

"St. Cyr and Afoniki are both having her watched." His gaze flicked toward Guido then bounced off. "It's in your briefing."

Guido leaned back, letting the chair rock once. "Well, how interesting. I hate to be late to a parade, but glad we aren't missing it entirely."

There was an easing of tension in the line of Aldo's shoulders. "I'll get right on it."

Guido's gaze slitted. "And find out if we missed anything important. I'm sure the other watchers will be happy to share." He looked up, spearing Aldo with his gaze. "I do hate to miss the important."

———

"I'm surprised you managed to get clear of Alex," Hannah said, sliding her car into its spot and shutting down the engine. It wasn't just the age difference that felt like the elephant in the room whenever she saw Ferris. It was also her seven big brothers who'd want to "chat" with him if they found out.

Jeez, Zach, she wanted to say to him more than once, what

were you thinking? She didn't, of course. If he'd been thinking, she'd never have been born. And as much as they annoyed her on occasion, she couldn't figure out which one of her siblings she'd wished not born, even when they annoyed the crap out of her.

Not to mention that Zach still knew how to keep his brood in line. Had he had that look when he was a baby? She wished she had memories of Zach's parents, but they were long gone.

"Someone paid Roger Dunstead's bail." Ferris's voice recalled her wandering thoughts. "Alex headed over to Nell's from work."

Hannah exchanged a worried look with Ferris. "Be stupid for him to try again."

Ferris grunted agreement, but pointed out, "Man's not that bright."

Hannah made a face and pushed open her car door, letting in a rush of warm wet air and lots of evening scents—not all of them pleasant since the trash bin butted up against the small parking lot behind her place. At least it had some tenant parking, no matter that it was on the seedy side. The street was a parking nightmare in the evening when everyone got off work. She paid extra rent to have it and had been offered more than that for the spot. Tempting, but she'd resisted. Most nights she was too tired to hike very far. And this was New Orleans. She knew better than most what happened here at night.

"I think Helenne St. Cyr should be the most worried—I'll get the food if you could grab the box out of my trunk. Didn't she rat him out?" She popped the trunk and waited while he snagged it. "It's a box of family photos and crap," she explained, leading the way up the flight of metal stairs. "I waited until Zach went out," she didn't add 'on a date' because she didn't want to think about her dad dating—a problem she shared with her siblings based on their comments, "and snagged it for this idea I have."

She turned to wait for him to navigate the stairs with the box. Out of the corner of her eye, something flared in one of the dark cars parked along the street. After a second, the end of a cigarette glowed before dropping out of sight. Maybe it was because the car was tucked in between the other cars that it looked familiar. Headlights from a car moving down the street lit up the plates, and she made a mental note to write the number down, even as she chided herself for being paranoid.

"Something wrong?" Ferris asked, glancing down the street, then back at her.

"I sometimes forget that people still smoke," she said, with a wry grin and headed for her door.

"Okay." Ferris propped a shoulder against the wall while she dug for her keys.

"Sorry. I just saw someone light up down there. There are so many places people can't smoke, you forget they do."

"Not on my beat," Ferris said, with a grin. He shifted the box in his grip and then followed her inside. "I don't know about you, but I'm starving…"

————

"Oh my gosh, look at Zach in high school," Hannah said, tapping a photo in one of his school yearbooks. "Well, there it is. Proof positive he was young once." She grinned at Ferris as he bent to take a closer look.

"He had the Look way back then, I see."

Hannah arched her brows. "He's been using it on you?"

Ferris shrugged. "Maybe he just forgot to turn it off."

"Or his face froze like that." Hannah chuckled. "Alex used to trot that one out regularly."

"He still does," Ferris said, grinning. "He told a perp his face was gonna freeze like that, just the other day."

Hannah laughed and caught a flare of something in Ferris's eyes. Not ready for it, she turned a page. "If Charlie was anything like Zach—"

"Will that help or hinder?"

"That is a good question," Hannah admitted. Would the scientific method work on one's parent?

"Here's another one of Charlie," Ferris said, presenting his yearbook for her inspection. He lowered it and met her gaze. "What exactly is it we're looking for?"

"Charlie," Hannah said. "We're looking for Charlie." She leaned back against the couch, shifting to ease the pressure of the wood floor on her tush. The carpet got thinner with every ten minutes that passed. "I'm not a detective, and we don't have the resources of the department to help us. So I'm trying to treat this like an autopsy."

"This?"

"Our old, cold not-case." She lowered the yearbook to her lap, because she needed her hands to talk. "Pretend it's a body on the table. A body is just unified parts, but still parts."

"Interesting." He looked thoughtful. "You're dissecting his past."

"And where the past doesn't help, we use Zach to help fill in the gaps."

"Zach?"

"In an autopsy, I'd try to match sibling DNA, when they let me have money, which they mostly don't. But if I could, I would. There are common threads with brothers, or there can be."

Ferris half shrugged. "Your brothers all seem pretty distinct to me."

"You never had to use the same bathroom they did." Hannah grinned. "And my brothers actually give us more data to work with. The model will have variations, but there are common threads we can pull out to build a working theory on what Charlie did then, and what he is likely to do now. Then we test the theory."

"Okay." He looked a bit doubtful. "What do you want me to do?"

Kiss me. She dropped her eyes, lest he pick up on that thought. This was a working meeting. For now? Well, a girl could hope.

"Zach was the younger brother. You'll notice that he followed a lot of what Charlie did, choosing the same clubs, trying out for the same sports."

"Okay, we're doing a profile on Charlie. I get that. But—"

"We might be able to predict present behavior based on past behavior. Or at least, that's what I'm hoping."

"Behavior? You're trying to figure out if he's targeting the wise guys?"

Hannah blinked. "Nothing so complex yet. I'm just trying to see if I can figure out which retirement home he'd pick if he did come back."

"Oh." A pause. "What if Ellie came back alone? Or did the picking?"

"Then I'll be wrong. Unless—" Hannah frowned. "If I'd lost the love of my life, I might try to finish what he started?

Do what I believed he'd do? And she'd have a lot more data to work with, since she actually knew him."

"That's pretty romantic," Ferris said. "For a scientific theory."

She looked up and realized that's what he wanted. He was close, close enough for her to see the variations of color in his eyes. She'd have listed them if her thinking hadn't slowed to a crawl. And this sort of shiver hadn't run through her.

"Your brain is flat-out amazing," he said, his voice husky. His gaze flicked down, then up. "And the rest of you is pretty amazing, too."

Hannah was close enough to read the truth of his words in the way his pupils reacted and his pulse rate. Though only a small part of her brain noted it. The rest was hoping he was about to keep his promise to kiss her troubles away.

"Usually men aren't that impressed by my brain," she murmured.

"They're fools."

She wanted to ask him questions. Some of them about when he first noticed her, but some about the future, too. She was a woman and a scientist. She liked to know what came next. Only —he was a guy. She knew from listening to her brothers that guys ran from questions about the future. Would "what is this?" scare him? It scared her. It made her vulnerable if she asked it and he ran. The dead couldn't talk, but the living often didn't say the right things anyway. If they even knew what they needed to say.

"Keep your promise," she muttered, spreading her hands across the sides of his face. She didn't tug, except with words. He'd promised to kiss her troubles away, which was kind of funny, because he was the biggest trouble in her life.

His mouth came on hers in a rush that pushed her back against the hard couch edge. She didn't care. The discomfort was nothing. Everything was fusion. Heat. Life. Feeling alive. She hadn't known how numb she'd been for so long…

He broke from her, his chest heaving, face flushed, heated gaze scorching over her on-fire face. "Hannah—"

Whatever he'd intended to say was halted by the knock at her door.

"You expecting someone?"

Hannah shook her head, tried out her voice. It was huskier than usual. "With my family, I don't always get advance notice." She scrambled upright, her knees on the spongy side, but made it to the door's peep hole. "I think it's UPS."

This knock was louder.

"He can see the light," Ferris said. "He knows you're home."

She looked at her watch. "Kinda late."

"You expecting anything?"

She shook her head.

He pulled his weapon and stepped to the side of the door. It was a bit overprotective, but nice. He nodded. She opened the door, stepping to the side closest to Ferris to block him from sight. Over the guy's shoulder, she saw the red glow from that same parked car.

"You're out late," she said.

"Picking up a route for someone. Need you to sign here, ma'am." He held out his machine, and she squiggled something on it with her finger. He handed her a small box.

"Thanks. Good luck with the route pick up."

"Thanks." He made a vague gesture and took off without looking back.

Hannah turned the box over, noting the return address was local but not familiar. Before she closed the door, she looked at the car again. No glow. Was it her imagination that made her see the vague outline of a figure? No reason to think it had anything to do with her, but she still felt uneasy. She locked the door and looked at Ferris before lifting the package and giving it a small shake. It rattled softly.

"Something small." She looked at the address again. It didn't ring any bells—or did it? She handed it to Ferris, and pulled out her phone and entered the address. She stared at the result.

"What?" Ferris asked, giving the box a small shake, too.

She held up the phone. "Happy Endings Retirement Community."

Ferris looked confused for a minute, then his eyes widened. "Charlie?"

"Ironic and romantic." She tapped the box. "And unexpected. I have to meet this guy."

Ferris held up the box. "May I?"

"Please."

He ripped at the tape and pulled the flaps back, then dug through the paper and pulled out...

"Your missing evidence." The ring had been cleaned and it shone in the light from her overhead lamp.

"Is that all?" Hannah took the box and sifted through what was left. At the very bottom she found the note. She held it up, then opened the single fold and read, "If you're determined to meet me, lose the parade."

CHAPTER 9

"WHAT?"

Dunstead heard her shriek through the walls. They might have heard it in Mississippi. He didn't know the old broad had it in her. Alone in the room next to hers, he allowed himself a grim smile. She thought she was playing him like old Miz St. Cyr had played him. She was wrong, but by time she realized it, he'd have what he wanted. And she'd pay for it. She'd pay for it all and give him his walking away money.

He moved closer. The more he knew, the better it was for him. She was hiding something. Her voice was quieter, as if she'd remembered, but stress and panic kept it shrill and penetrating.

"What do you mean—science? Harold didn't care about science! He added and subtracted, he didn't—exactly which organs did he donate to these *grateful* recipients? Problem? Of course not, it's just such a shock. And his funeral—having it without his body makes me uncomfortable, Mr. Jensen. It's a jazz funeral, too."

Like that made a difference. Dunstead almost snorted.

Women. There was a longer pause, but he heard her efforts to calm her breathing, even through the wall.

"I just think that is something you share with your wife. I don't understand—distress me? Well, he was right about that. The thought of—"

Dunstead has a feeling she paused for a shudder for the lawyer?—he figured it must be the lawyer catching it—that he couldn't see.

"—someone doing that to dear Harold, parceling him out like, well, a buffet or something. It's very distressing. And knowing he'll never be decently buried—I can't imagine what he was thinking. Or what he was helped to think."

That last comment held a chill that Dunstead was glad wasn't directed at him. And confirmed his feeling that he shouldn't trust the broad further than he could toss her. He wouldn't be turning his back on her either. Oh no, he wouldn't.

"I want to know who got Harold's parts, Mr. Jensen—what do you mean it's confidential? They know about Harold—oh. That's confidential, too." There was a pause. "I just have this fear I'll be walking down the street and Harold's eyes will look at me from some stranger. I don't think I could bear that."

Dunstead's gaze narrowed. She hadn't seemed that stupid to him. So what was it about the scattering of her husband's parts that really bothered her?

———

"Parade?" Hannah sank onto her couch and looked up at Ferris. "Does that mean—that sounds like he thinks someone is following me?"

"Parade implies more than one someone." Ferris sat down next to her, the ring sitting partway down his index finger. "Good calling card. I wonder if that's why he pinched it?"

"I'm still stuck at wondering how it ended up in the coffin. And what happened back then? And—" she stopped.

"—if your dad knew anything about it?"

She looked at him, knew her eyes were wide, figured they were worried, too. "Yeah."

"You're assuming he'll tell you what happened."

"Charlie? If he's like Zach, he might not." She frowned, absently tapping the note with one finger. "But he sent me the ring. Interesting move." This was back in the realm of living motives. Her "corpse" had abruptly come to life. It was disconcerting. And exciting. Someone with actual answers IF he was willing to cough them up. If.

"Either he wants you to stop looking. Or he—they?—need help," Ferris said, using his thumb to push the ring around and around the first joint of his index finger.

That made sense. She realized something else. "If he thinks I'm being followed, then he must be following me." Did she believe him? It was on the creepy side, thinking of being followed by anyone. "I can't think of one person who'd want to follow me, let alone a parade of them."

"Guido Calvino?"

Hannah's frown deepened. Was this round two? Since round one got called on account of a rain of bullets? The coffins were what had brought her to the attention of St. Cyr and Calvino. Afoniki had probably gotten a report about the meeting. And it was the only thing she'd done recently that was, well, slightly interesting.

"That's not good," she finally concluded. She sure didn't want to lead him to Charlie. Would he know who he was? "Would he care about him or them now? He wasn't even born." Most of them involved now hadn't been born then. "The only one who might still care is Afoniki, the old one." So if Guido was, possibly, having her followed, who else was in the "parade?" She looked at Ferris. "He wouldn't have someone on Ingrid, too, would he?"

In his eyes, she saw him connect the dots.

"I doubt it, but we should probably have her take a good look around." He looked worried. "It's kind of crazy, but what if Afoniki and St. Cyr are having you followed because Guido is? That's the only reason I can think of for all the interest." He rubbed his head like it hurt.

"That is a bit crazy, but I can't think of another reason either," she admitted. "I'm not that interesting."

"Maybe they expected something else to be in those coffins."

"Guido did look a bit relieved," Hannah recalled. "I thought it was weird."

"Or they are all paranoid."

"They probably survive by being paranoid," Hannah said. "And I just happened to have fueled it by doing something sketchy." She covered her face with her hands. "Maybe I panicked for no good reason? If I'd left Charlie's ring there, listed it, it would have been one more weird thing. No second visit from Guido—" And she wouldn't have been there when he got shot at. Thus fueling his curiosity and hers, she had to admit. No case, no—would she and Ferris still be hanging out if she hadn't?

He touched the back of her neck. "No matter where you

left it, it would have gone missing. Charlie apparently knew it was in the coffin. He went there to get it back."

"I suppose." She took the ring from him and studied it. "It's just a class ring."

He covered her hand with his. "What happened to yours?"

She hooked her thumb over his. "I never got one. I didn't graduate with my class."

There was a pause while she waited. She didn't know why she hated telling people she graduated early. He smoothed her hair back from her cheek.

"Lucky you."

She looked at him then, a small smile tugging at the edges of her mouth. "Do you think he took the brick, too?"

"You can ask him when we meet him."

"If Charlie hadn't thrown in the warning, I'd have gone over there tonight." She took a steadying breath, feeling a small pang for the kissing interruption. She thought about that. She could totally believe Charlie was related to Zach. "So how do I lose my parade without looking like I need to lose my parade?"

———

"She should have it by now." Ellie looked up from the book she'd been pretending to read. "You sure you weren't too cryptic?"

It was still a trait that frustrated her in this man of hers. If he'd been a little less cryptic—then Toni would never have been born, she reminded herself. As bad as those years with Bett had been, she could never regret Toni. And now there was Nell.

She ached to see Nell with her own eyes. Her arms had been empty for so long. They'd wanted—but the danger. They couldn't risk it. Hadn't dared risk staying in contact with Toni and Phil. She'd never tried to find them. She wouldn't be here now if Nell hadn't—her hands curled into fists.

His big hands covered hers. "She's smart that one. Don't know how Zach managed it. Must a got her genes from her mama."

Her gaze lifted, met his gaze. The face around the eyes had aged, but the eyes were the same. First time, she knew. Still knew. This was the one for her. She freed one hand so she could put it against his cheek, rough because of the late hour.

"There's risk for her."

"And for us. But it's time, Ellie. We've been hiding long enough."

"I know." She hesitated, but not saying it didn't mean he didn't know what she was thinking. "Do you think I'll get to see her before—"

"We'll make it happen."

"Do you think she'll understand?"

"She's got your face, Ellie. I'm betting she's got your heart, too."

———

"How can you be sure that her death will be blamed... correctly?" she asked, once more in her sweet, old lady mode as she handed him the information he'd asked her for.

Dunstead wasn't fooled. Not that he had been. But now he was sure she weren't no sweet old lady. There was something about her, something that stirred an old memory. Was it her eyes? He wasn't sure. He didn't like thinking on the past.

"I know where to drop the scoop where it will do most good. It's all in who you tell," he added when she looked skeptical.

He didn't mention it wouldn't forward her goals, just his. He also didn't tell her he was using the plan created by old Lady St. Cyr. In that plan, the murder would have implicated her niece, what was her name again? Oh right, Mira... Mirabelle? Stupid name. Old Lady St. Cyr had gone off her own script when it didn't work out the first couple of times, but that didn't make it a bad plan, just bad luck. Timing was everything and this time, the timing felt good. He'd get what he wanted, and she'd pay for it.

"I don't want this traced back to me. I'd be very...upset...if that happened."

Her lashes lifted and Dunstead felt ice in his veins for the first time. His throat dried. And the memory kicked again, then slid away, leaving him with a feeling he was messing in something bigger'n he thought. She planned to kill him when he was done. He'd seen that look before. Well, he'd just have to make sure he got in the first shot. He wasn't going down this time. Sure wasn't gonna die without some people paying for what they'd done.

"It won't, ma'am," he said. He knew how to sound respect-ful. Cowed. He'd had lots of practice. His dad had talked of being loyal, staying strong. They'd fooled him, too. They demanded loyal, but they didn't give it. Not to likes of him, maybe not to anyone. Don't give it, don't get it. That's what he'd tell his dad—memory flashed again. But this wasn't the place for remembering.

He rose, knowing exactly how to look dumb and loyal. "I'll take care of it. You want a war? You're gonna get a war." He touched a finger to his temple. He could tell she liked that.

Her smile was that of a cat in front of a bowl of tuna. "I had a feeling you were the man I needed, Roger."

Even her voice kinda purred.

Dunstead had to turn his back on her to leave. He didn't like it and he didn't plan to do that again. Back in his car, he flipped open the folder she'd given him. The mark looked into the distance, unaware she was being photographed for death. It was too bad. Not a bad looking broad for a morgue doc. She shouldn'ta been born a Baker. And her big brother shouldn'ta messed in his business.

CHAPTER 10

HANNAH STUDIED herself in the cheap full-length mirror, curious why she was reluctant to leave her apartment. On some level, she was aware that she wasn't immune to the usual body image issues. And she might have her own version of those issues when she factored in her brainy girl thing, in particular the blonde brainy girl thing. It was messed up and only Google knew by how much. Not even a Facebook meme could help her, though she lived in hope.

Periodically she applied science to her feelings. She knew that what she saw when she looked in the mirror was not real. Even the camera added five pounds and how much she added depended on that dreaded "time of the month." How much she hated that depended on which day it was in the month. She couldn't say she ever had "thin days," but there were days she felt less fat and her hair always looked better on those days, too, even though she hadn't changed the cut in ten years.

For some reason this made her think about Logan Ferris. What did he see when he looked at her? And why did he persist in showing up at the end of her shift when even an okay hair day had lost the battle with heat and humidity?

Today did not seem to be a "less fat" day or a decent hair day. At least her scrubs' elastic waist accommodated all her days. Having eliminated all other possible variables, she was forced to conclude that her current level of self-consciousness was inextricably related to the parade which may not—but probably was—waiting for her outside her front door. It was positively IQ lowering to contemplate. When one came from a large family, the center of attention position was because something had been traced back to you, resulting in getting grounded or, worse, a Zach lecture.

A girl could acquire a severe case of agoraphobia—if she didn't have a pile of suspicious, overprotective siblings who would notice and start asking questions. So those were her choices. Center stage with the siblings and Zach or center stage with the possibly creepy parade.

The parade seemed the better option. At least they weren't likely to comment. And she needed to go work. And eat. Ferris had advised her not to change her routine now. Besides, they didn't know how long she'd been under surveillance.

Ferris. When would she ever be able to call him Logan?

And yes, she was stalling.

She took a breath and gripped the doorknob. It was a bad time to remember she'd never been picked for any part in any play. Ever. Not that she'd tried out, but still. Not an actress, though she'd seen some—

Still stalling.

She should think about something work related. Or some science. Surely now, when it really mattered, she could lose the plot? It was a pity she didn't have a really puzzling autopsy to mull—would she have picked Happy Endings if Charlie hadn't come clean on his own? She'd like to think she would have. Was it ironic? Or honest? Maybe Ellie picked it? If she had, did that mean Charlie had sucked it up? She sure couldn't see Zach choosing to live in a place called Happy Endings.

Maybe Hannah was the only one who thought it was the ironic choice. Did that mean she wasn't romantic enough? Was it weird to feel like she knew Charlie, even though they'd never met? She was kind of excited to meet him. And Ellie—had they contacted Nell? What if they hadn't? Man, what if they had some weird excuse for not seeing her and then Nell found out Hannah knew and didn't tell her? That would kill whatever sister-in-law thing they might have had if she did marry Alex—

"Can I take your order?"

Hannah returned to the present with a jerk and saw her usual server giving her a patient look. Science had come through for her again. Though she had to resist the urge to look around. Still, if she was going to get a handle on being followed, and figure out how to lose them, she probably needed to, you know, look around. Without looking like she was looking around. Couldn't lose a tail if she didn't know who was tailing her.

And she would. After breakfast.

She gave her order, which she noticed the server had already written down. It was probably not a good idea to be that predictable. Guys watching her could phone it in without having to actually follow her. Maybe she could be so boring she put them to sleep at the wheel. And maybe they wouldn't notice when she went unpredictable.

She sipped some juice. Almost spit it out when someone spoke behind her.

"Don't turn around, Doctor, or may I call you Hannah?"

She didn't have to look and wasn't sure she could turn around. She would have liked to forget that voice, with its faint, sinister infections. It took her a minute and some deep breathing to get her voice calm enough.

"Mr. Afoniki."

Hannah gripped her glass with one hand, the edge of her bench with the other. It was probably a good thing she'd never aspired to be a spy.

"Do I dare hope you remembered my voice?"

For some reason that cleared her brain. "What do you want?"

"It's a very long list." He sounded amused.

"I'll bet world peace isn't on it," she muttered.

He chuckled. "You wound me. Though peace isn't always good for business. It depends on what kind of peace."

She was so not up for a philosophical discussion with a wise guy before breakfast. And possibly not after. She really tried to avoid philosophy until after lunch when she could nap through it.

"That attitude wouldn't win you a Mr. America contest." Hannah was a little surprised at herself, but it was easier to spar when she didn't have to look at him.

"I wish I could sit with you, see you," he murmured, "but you are attracting so much attention. It seemed wiser this way."

"To do what?"

"Why, just to offer you my help. If you should need it. I will admit I'm a bit surprised at Guido—but Claude." He sighed.

"Claude has so much to prove, doesn't he? No, I'm never truly surprised by what Claude does."

Her food appeared in front of her. It took all her resolution to pick up her fork. With some deliberation, she cut off a bite and propelled it to her mouth. She chewed, swallowed, and prayed it stayed down. She didn't have to be a child of Zach's to know that this much attention was not a good thing.

"If I needed help, I'm sure one—or all—of my brothers would line up." She wouldn't even have to ask. Or need help.

He chuckled. "But do they know? Other than a brief glimpse of Alex, they seem to be amazingly absent."

"I'm quite capable of eating my breakfast without assistance." To prove it, she took another bite.

"I have a feeling they are out of the, um, loop."

"If I had a loop for them to be out of, it would only take a text to bring them in. If I had a loop, which I don't. I'm loopless." And need to quit talking. She clamped her lips tight.

"But you won't." He sounded quite certain.

And he was right, but not for the reason he thought. Unless he did know and thought it hilarious she was seeing her brother's younger partner. *I'm not a cougar.* For one horrible moment, she thought she'd said it out loud.

Something buzzed from his direction. He stirred, said reluctantly, "I must go."

She'd have been flattered by the reluctance, except for who he was. So she wasn't.

"If you need my help…"

There was the soft sound of someone sliding off a bench. A soft, nice smelling puff of air as he walked past. She didn't realize he'd left something on her table until he'd gone outside. A business card. She sighed.

"Lovely."

"Ma'am?"

Hannah looked at her server and managed a smile. At least she thought she did. "Could I get my check? I'm running late…" Which was also predictable.

"I'll wrap that up for you, ma'am."

Hannah sighed again. She definitely needed to switch things up, do the unexpected. In unpredictable ways. And no, she did not know why that made her rub her lower lip with her pinky. She could text Ferris, but he was probably picking up Alex right now. How had her life gotten so complicated? Oh right. An exhumation of a couple of coffins. She should get herself a tee shirt inscribed with "be careful what you dig for" on it. And on the back, "don't do favors for your brother."

———

A bullet was Dunstead's preferred way to kill. It was quick, clean. The cops knew that, though. If he did the hit like he usually did, he'd be back in before he got used to being out. No, he needed to be creative. And he didn't have to think that hard. He'd do it the way the old lady had planned, but with a twist. An idea had been simmering in the back of his brain all while he was in. What he'd do if he got the chance.

There was a bit of…balancing to be done, accounts to be settled. Both now and for his pa.

The target was not his first choice, but there was a certain finesse to the idea, something the cops also wouldn't expect from him. Probably thought he didn't know what that word meant. Well, let them think it. He didn't want the credit for this one.

All it took was a few minutes on a computer at a local library—it was ridiculously easy to learn how to blow up a car —and a chat with the right gal to get the stuff he needed, and he was halfway to a hit with finesse.

He had a guy watching the doc. According to him, he wasn't the only one following the doc around. A bit of a surprise, but not a deal breaker. They would widen the suspect pool for him, though they also upped the difficulty level in planting the bomb on her car.

He tossed the cigarette butt away and straightened. He looked both ways down the dispirited back alley and then headed back to his wheels.

Maybe he'd learned a little something from his time with old Lady St. Cyr, so it wasn't all bad. And the best part? If the cops didn't blame one of the guys following her, they might pin it old Lady St. Cyr. Everyone knew Dunstead preferred a bullet.

————

By the time the server had returned with her change and her wrapped-up food, Hannah had found her backbone right where she'd left it. Afoniki wasn't her big brother. He didn't get to yank her chain. The parade, too. She was over it. So over it. Wasn't it hard enough to be a gal working in the city without a bunch of idiots deciding to examine her lame life? Really? And for what?

She'd bet money not a one of them knew why they were doing it—not the guys doing the following or the guys doing the hiring.

She'd wager it was like Ferris figured, that one of them

started it and the others just followed along because. Jerks. She could almost hear them all **not** thinking.

She halted in the doorway and did a sweep of the parking lot. Identified three possibles.

They were all driving cars that were a variation on a cliché theme. A bit old, a bit inconspicuous, with a dude in the front seat of each. *Smoking*. Cliché guys in their cliché cars. And that one car, it had been on her street. She remembered the plate number.

She went for him.

When he tried to pretend he was invisible, Hannah rapped sharply on the window. He rolled it down and tried to look stupid. He kind of managed it, but she wasn't gonna be deterred by what she already knew to be true. She had some steam up and needed a direction to blow it.

"Get out. Now." She'd practiced this tone on her sisters, so she wasn't surprised when he complied. Or that he stood there looking sheepish and trapped, with a bit of wild-eyed.

"Who?"

"Ma'am?" He blinked.

"You know what I'm asking. Who?"

He swallowed, looked around for help and didn't get any. "Mr.," he swallowed and lowered his voice, "Mr. St. Cyr, but please…"

"You tell him from me that I'll be sending my brothers around to ask why he feels the need to monitor my movements unless he wants to reconsider his decision-making process."

"Yes, ma'am."

"Get out of here."

He complied so fast, he tripped over his feet and the edge

of the car. He managed to leave without hitting anyone or anything, though it was touch and go.

She looked at number two.

He tried to leave, taking it casual, but she wasn't fooled. Number three must have left when she was chewing on number one. It was probably not the way Ferris would have recommended her to lose a tail, but it appeared to have worked.

She studied the various cars in the lot. No obvious signs of anyone else interested in her. She couldn't think of a fourth person who would put a tail on her, but she didn't assume things inside the NOCC. Maybe she should take that policy into the outside, too.

Charlie had called it a parade, not the three dudes following you.

There were people around, but none of them looked particularly shady, clichéd, or interested in her. That didn't mean someone wasn't.

She bit her lip. If she were clear of tails, how long would that last? She didn't know why they'd been put on her in the first place. It could be about the coffins, but she'd just vowed not to assume, unless she should assume. And then she would. But no assuming right now.

Okay, that thought train had been painfully complicated. Maybe she should just move on—she saw the streetcar approaching.

She might not be a detective, but she didn't need to be one to *carpe diem.*

———

Dunstead's drop phone shrilled. "Yeah?"

He listened, and was a bit impressed. Doc had managed to shed herself of all three tails. Good for him, not so good for her. The jump onto the streetcar gave him pause.

Did he want him to follow her? She'd be on the alert for a while and might spot his guy. And he didn't care where she went, now that he considered it. Soon enough, she'd have to come back and pick up her car. And then it wouldn't matter. She'd leave the world in a blaze of glory.

"Stay with the car. I'll be there in ten."

It would be tricky in daylight, but it felt kinda like a sign. A public place was very different from official parking behind the morgue.

"Check around for cameras," he ordered, before ending the call. Almost he smiled. How appropriate they called it "Baking" a scene.

————

Hannah had brought with her the wrapping from the package and Charlie's ring. She smoothed the paper now and studied the return address. She held it closer, turning it so the light could find it.

Was that a number lightly penciled in after the street address? She tucked it back in her purse and studied Happy Endings.

She'd seen worse, she decided, but was starting to feel more certain it was an ironic choice. There was some flash, the kind of exterior that reassured both relatives and potential inmates, er, residents, that happiness could be found within. Why, she wondered, did so many retirement homes stick palm trees all over? Was it about upkeep or a subliminal Florida-ish message? Well-maintained exterior. Smooth walks and enough flowers to appear cheerful.

She skirted the activity center and dodged some gray hairs, as she studied the numbering system. She paused by a bulletin board, using the time to make sure she was still without a tail. If she'd been tailing herself, she'd have stayed out on the street, but she was pretty sure she was clear. She'd walked completely around the block before approaching.

She moved on, trying to imagine Zach in a place like this. She couldn't, of course, but then it was hard to imagine Zach anywhere but at home.

She supposed all kids, even grown ones, had blinders on about their parents. Every now and again, the blinders would shift, giving her a glimpse of the man instead of the dad. These glimpses did not provide clarity or even understanding. True understanding, she'd heard, wouldn't happen until she became a parent herself, but she did feel…compassion for the man who'd lost two women he loved and been left to raise a lot of children on his own.

While she could be thankful he had not married a third time and added to his Baker's dozen, she also felt sad that he had been so alone for so long. Of course, those feelings didn't stop her from feeling conflicted about him dating again. But she felt they indicated some maturity or perhaps personal growth.

She almost thought she heard Zach snort at that last thought. Okay, it was a bit pompous but that didn't make it any less true. Which made it kind of odd that she was relieved to spot the number she'd been looking for. It's not like Zach could hear her thinking about him. Good thing since her thoughts had gone off track again. But thankfully, he was miles away.

With one last look around, and a rapidly beating heart, she approached the door. She lifted her fist and hesitated, but the can of worms had already been opened. She closed her other hand around the ring she'd brought with her and knocked.

She was prepared for Charlie to look like Zach. But...

She blinked. "Zach?"

"Took you long enough. Get in here."

CHAPTER 11

"HERE SIT DOWN, HONEY," a soft voice spoke from out of an old Nell's face. "She looks like she's going to faint. Charlie, help her."

"My kids don't faint," Zach snapped, and then grabbed her other elbow and steered her to a bland couch. It went, she noted vaguely, with the bland room, if not the inhabitants. Okay, she didn't know they hadn't picked it, but it didn't seem to go with the hiding/not hiding deal. Maybe they'd gone with boring because their lives had been too exciting.

A hand shifted to her neck, and he pushed her head down between her knees. Hannah stared at the tan carpet inches from her nose. Zach avoided tan like the plague. Had almost a love affair with plaid, the bigger the stripes the better. Surely her dad's brother—

Her thoughts fractured then, and she pushed against Zach's hold. He let her sit up again.

"You okay?" his tone was gruff, his gaze worried.

She nodded and managed a shy smile for Ellie, then looked

at the other man in the room. He was a bit taller than Zach, and of course, older. He looked like him, but didn't.

It was the eyes she decided. They had the look of someone who'd taken the long, hard road and still hadn't found real peace. Maybe he never would.

"Hi," she managed, blinking a bit.

Charlie grinned. "Hey."

Hannah looked at Ellie again. "Wow. No wonder—" she stopped, not sure how Ellie felt about not being unique.

Ellie sighed ruefully. "Yes. It was rather a shock when we realized Nell had come here to live."

"Did you know where—" she stopped again, so many questions crowding her throat.

"No." The shadows in her eyes deepened. "We cut off all contact. We—it was the only way. Or so it seemed then."

The sound of the words was less certain than the words themselves. For an instant Hannah thought she saw Ellie's personal hell in her eyes.

"No," Hannah agreed, comfort the goal, though she didn't actually know how to give it. "Though maybe someone should have told Nell…"

"Bit of a shock when we saw her picture in an online magazine article," Charlie agreed.

"She's very good." Wow, that was lame and earned her a look from Zach that confirmed lame.

"Of course she is," Charlie said, almost protectively.

"Does she…"

"Not yet," Ellie said. Her lips twisted. "We got here the week the shooting started."

"I think she'd be relieved—" Hannah stopped again. Sarah

thought she'd be glad to have a law-abiding grandma, except —could they tick off the law-abiding box when they'd faked deaths and identities? Hidden for years and years? Of course, they had better reasons than Nell's other relatives for their law skirting activities. "There was a lot…going on."

Zach rolled his eyes, and Charlie and Ellie seemed amused. It helped focus her thoughts some. "Why am I here?"

"That's a good question," Zach growled, shooting his brother one of his looks.

Interesting that it bounced off. Hannah would take that class if Charlie offered it.

Charlie didn't speak. He looked at Hannah, not Zach, one brow arching.

"You need my help." She held up a hand when it looked like Zach was going to protest. "I'm actually pretty good at what I do, Zach. But this—" she gestured with her hands, "isn't usually what I do."

"And yet here you are, not doing what you usually do," Charlie said. He waited until Ellie sank into a chair, then sat in the chair opposite Hannah. "Sit down, Zach."

To Hannah's surprise, he did. This was a new side of her dad, the sibling side, she realized. She'd heard just that tone in Alex's voice a time or three million.

Charlie, as if he felt the questions trying to scramble out her mouth, held up a hand. "I know it's not fair, but we need to know what you know."

Not fair, but life seldom was. "Did you become a cop, too?" she asked, before she thought about it.

Charlie looked amused, but just shook his head. "Later. If there's time."

It felt like a cloud moved across the high, hot sun.

"I don't *know* that much," she said.

"You know more than you think you do, or they wouldn't be having you followed," Charlie pointed out.

"What—"

"I'm fine, Zach." She covered his clenched fists with her hand and squeezed. "Later I'll tell you how I lost them." She grinned and saw the reluctant twitch at the edges of his mouth. "I'm not sure the tails are related to you two."

"But you're not sure they aren't," Ellie said.

"I'm not sure of anything," Hannah admitted. Charlie arched his brows skeptically. "Feelings aren't facts."

Charlie grinned, slanting his little brother an ironic look. "Well, give us the facts you *feel* are important."

Hannah considered this. "Well, it started with the coffins. You know you're going to have to explain that, don't you?"

Ellie laughed. "That was Toni's idea. None of us thought they'd bury the coffins without looking inside. It was so…convenient."

"Maybe they wanted to believe it?" Hannah said. "So the ring, if they noticed it, was meant to be a slap in the face to—" she stopped as the shadow came back to Ellie's eyes but her jaw firmed.

"He ran Charlie off. I wanted him to know we found each other, that his daughter didn't want him either. I wanted to hurt him." She looked sad. "Now it doesn't seem to matter that he never got the message. Age tends to reorganize your priorities."

Hannah felt the question hovering but couldn't get it out.

As if she'd asked, Charlie shook his head. "I, we, didn't kill him."

Zach gave him a very cop look, which made Charlie's gaze turn stern.

"If I'd been gonna do it, I'd have done it then. But we didn't," he repeated. "He wasn't worth it then. Not worth it now." He met Zach's gaze. "I told you that back then."

Hannah felt a sort of sigh go through her at the look on Zach's face. "So you did help them."

That made the cop look leave. Charlie bit back a grin.

"Did you know they'd come back?" she asked Zach, who shifted uncomfortably.

"He didn't," Ellie said firmly.

"But you guessed?"

"I wondered. All the publicity—I figured they'd show up at some point."

Ellie looked sad. "Maybe we shouldn't have, but to *see*—we didn't know about Toni, not until—"

Charlie took her hand and lifted it to his mouth. The look they exchanged shouldn't have had an audience.

"Girl needed to know—well, she needed to know," Charlie said heavily.

"We've been hoping things would calm down. We don't want to make it harder for her." She looked down for a few seconds, then back up at Hannah. "And, well, we weren't sure she'd want to see us. We—all of us—let her down. Put her in danger. And there was…Bett."

Charlie's hand tightened on her. "In hindsight, the message we left was a very bad idea."

"I told you that at the time," Zach growled.

"What were you afraid he'd do?" Hannah asked. It was such old news. Then she got it. "Nell? His own granddaughter?"

"If he thought he could punish me? He didn't know her."
The shadows in her eyes deepened. "His love for Toni wasn't
healthy. She belonged to him. I belonged to him. And we both
betrayed him. He was just waiting. Biding his time."

"Is that why you took the ring?" Hannah asked.

Charlie nodded. "Why didn't you log it in?"

"She was afraid it would create trouble for Zach, of
course," Ellie said impatiently.

"Would it have?"

Charlie hesitated. "Maybe. If he thought Zach helped Ellie?
Then yeah, it would have."

"What I don't get, why the brick?"

Charlie and Ellie exchanged puzzled looks. He said,
"Brick?"

"Someone stole a brick from one of the coffins."

Charlie looked interested in that. "They must think that's
where—" he glanced at Ellie, who hesitated, then nodded. "—
we hid the proof."

"The sheets of code?" Hannah asked. Ellie nodded.

"I stole them for Toni, as protection for when—I thought
he'd guess, but the papers would keep him in check." Ellie
looked puzzled. "Why take a brick from a coffin?"

Zach and Charlie both frowned, obviously thinking. Finally
Zach said, "Maybe one of them wanted the other to think they
had found it?"

"Assuming any of them still cared," Charlie said.

"They were still interested enough to insist on representa-
tives when the coffins were opened," Hannah said. "What are
they?"

"It's some kind of agreement to kill Zafiro, or proof of it, I
think. I just heard bits and pieces. I wasn't supposed to know,

of course. The papers were in some kind of code to protect each of them from each other. And the rings each had a piece of the solution to the code, part of the key, he said, engraved on them. I took them because I could tell he was afraid of losing it."

"There's no statute of limitations on murder," Hannah said.

"Everyone knew they'd killed Zafiro," Zach said, "but there was never any proof. We all wondered why they were so eager to get along."

"That would explain why they were stolen," Hannah said, thinking out loud and forgetting they didn't know. "But not by who…"

Ellie's shoulders dropped a little. "So they are gone."

"Frank made copies." Hannah watched them and saw them exchange looks.

"But without the rings?" Charlie looked grim.

"Frank probably had photographs taken of at least one of them…" She hoped. "These days, with computers, even a portion of the key might be enough. We'd need someone with real expertise to look at it. I'll email Frank and see if he found someone. He was looking."

"I'm surprised they trusted each other with anything," Zach growled. "Only one it could affect now is Aleksi Afoniki."

"I'm not so sure. There was some kind of trigger—that's what Bett called it—if one of them died," Ellie said. "They rose and fell together. Until the end."

"So it might still bring the heirs down?" Hannah's eyes widened. That was a reason for all of them to have her followed. They'd be afraid of what she'd found. And what she might do with it. Except—someone did know she didn't have it. Because they had it. And at least one of the mob rings.

"I wonder if Helenne found out about it and that's why she had Phineas killed?" Zach looked thoughtful. "And possibly why she went after Nell. She wouldn't want anyone stealing her thunder.'

Hannah wished Ferris was there, while being glad he wasn't. It was hard not to shudder at the thought of Zach opening the door to them both.

"Aleksi Afoniki is the last one standing and he's got a couple of feet in the grave. I guess Helenne could have—but I don't understand why he, Bettino," Hannah said awkwardly, "would make the same mistake as Phineas St. Cyr? He told his bodyguards to wait by the car. If you believe them."

"Bett wouldn't have crossed the street to meet Helenne," Ellie said with conviction.

Hannah hesitated, then said, "Would he have come to meet you?"

She didn't answer right away. Hannah was impressed. She sensed Charlie wanted to jump in, but Ellie shook her head. "Yes. He would. He wouldn't be afraid of me either." She looked up, met Hannah's steady gaze. "And I can't prove I wasn't there."

"As she said, Aleksi is the only one left with skin in the game," Charlie said, his tone suggested they'd been arguing about this.

"He wouldn't know how to lure Bett out into the open. I think it was a woman," Ellie said. "Bett would never have feared a woman."

"Was there another woman from back then?"

Three heads turned toward her.

"It's really the only thing that makes sense. Or at least a viable possibility. All of this is, has been about the past. We—I wondered about a new old player. Or an old, unknown player. When I wasn't sure you were, you know, alive to be the ones."

Charlie looked at Ellie, then at Zach. "I wasn't in position to know who Bett might have dated."

"He wasn't faithful, if that's what you're wondering, I never knew—didn't care enough to find out. It was a relief when he looked elsewhere."

"Zach?" Hannah looked at her dad.

Zach frowned. "The only one who might have known is Curly—William Gastonieau." Charlie looked a question. "He was my partner. He'd be in jail, but he's in a coma. Had a stroke."

"He tried to kill Nell," Hannah explained. She didn't make the mistake of patting Zach's hand this time. That wound ran deep. Sadly, crooked cops were not that rare back then.

"I can see what I can find out," Zach said in a particularly expressionless voice, "he might have had someone, but why she would—"

Hannah felt Charlie's gaze on her and looked up.

"What do you *feel*, Hannah?"

The question wasn't sarcastic, but there was a hint of humor in it. She didn't speak for almost a minute, but only Zach shifted as if impatient.

"Old...cold..." she finally said. "It's an old, cold case that doesn't feel old or cold. It feels...like it's about to explode."

———

Dunstead dialed the broad's number. When she answered, when he was sure it was her, he said, "You'll want to keep track of the news today."

He hung up without waiting for an answer. He turned to his guy. Smiled. "Let's get something to eat," he said. "Some place quiet, where they have a TV."

His guy grinned, exposing the gap in his teeth. It was a pity this would be his last meal. Good help was hard to find. He wouldn't make the same mistake as last time. No one could say he didn't learn. He thought about the broad. He wouldn't feel sorry when he shut her mouth. It hadn't taken him long to realize that she had a whole lot of crazy under that smile. A whole lot—

He frowned as something in his head twitched again. Like an itch that wouldn't be scratched….

———

Hannah's pace might have lagged a bit as she followed Zach to his car. Questions simmered in the air between them. Actually, they were almost at a boiling point. His problem? She had questions, too, lots of them. They hadn't gotten through even half of the information that needed to be exchanged when she'd got called from work. Apparently her "I'll be a little late" had gone on a little too long.

She needed time to process. It was how she handled, well, everything. Take information in. Ponder it. Process it. Arrange it in a manageable order. Only she wasn't going to get that time. She hadn't gotten processing time for days, or so it felt.

She peeked at her dad. He looked grim and a bit shell shocked. She saw her face in the rear view. She'd never looked so much like him. She opened her mouth. Closed it. Opened it again when he turned toward the NOCC.

"I...need to pick up my car." She'd felt so clever when she left it for the streetcar. Pride really did go before the fall. Or opened one up to parental grilling.

"And where is your car?"

She gave him the address. How did he manage to make her feel about seven years old? Had she felt seven when she *was* seven? Dimly she recalled hearing Zach tell someone that, "Hannah is seven-going-on-thirty."

Did that mean she was thirty-three-going-on-fifty now? Oh crap, maybe she was a cougar where Ferris was concerned. Unless she was thirty-three going on seven, which she didn't want to think about.

"You're being followed?"

"It's not my fault," she said and then clamped a hand over her mouth.

"I suppose it's Alex's fault," Zach growled.

She choked. "Actually..."

A red light gave him a chance to give her the dad "look."

"They were his girlfriend's relatives' coffins," Hannah felt compelled to point out.

He choked this time. His mouth twisted. Luckily the light change saved him.

"If you turn here—"

"I was finding my way around this city before you were born."

"Yes, sir," she said meekly and had the satisfaction of seeing him bite his cheek. And here she'd thought she got her sense of humor from her mama.

Logan Ferris found it hard to relax, knowing that Hannah was out there being followed for unknown reasons by an unknown number of bad guys.

Lose the parade.

She was a doctor, not a cop. How was she supposed to spot, let alone lose the parade? He itched to call her, but it was tough to do with her big brother at the wheel next to him. He had no desire to yank Alex's attention his direction either, not with that level of scowl on his face. He opened his mouth to ask about Nell. Closed it. No point asking about Dunstead. Nothing to know until they got to their desks and could look at reports.

Who would have bailed him out? Ferris would have said the guy had no friends left. It sucked to be wrong.

Their radio chose that moment to come on. Vehicle explosion. Fire department at scene. One fatality. Suspicious circumstances. That was the part that triggered their involvement. Ferris flicked on their lights as Alex applied some pressure to the pedal.

They weren't far from the scene, but the traffic got worse the closer they got. Even their lights didn't shift it out of their way, not when cars had nowhere to shift to. In a rare, missed opportunity, no Lucky Dog truck had shown up yet.

Finally Alex was able to nose their car through the tangle and into a spot enough out of the way to count. They still had a bit of a walk. They headed for the mob of people and the thinning smoke billow rising into the washed out, mid-day sky.

"Car bombs are kind of rare," Ferris said, more thinking

aloud than trying to get conversation going. He wasn't surprised when Alex only grunted.

When they finally broke through the crowd, a uniform waved them through the police line. They paced around a fire truck and got their first look. The fire was out and the body had already been bagged and tagged. Ferris couldn't be sorry about that.

Through the babel of talk, he heard one of the crime scene techs—not a Baker—say something about the explosion probably killed the driver before the fire....

He gave a bit of a shudder.

The front end looked like something from an Iraq news story. Gutted and twisted, the damage extended almost to the back seat. The interior was completely burned but firemen must have got it out fast. Burn marks streaked along the rear, with some of the color showing through the carbon—

His thoughts slowed, as color and model registered. Like he had the night before, he went around the side of the car and looked down. He remembered opening a door just like this one, down to the scratches around the lock.

His mind registered the plate as if from a great distance. Then he looked up, saw the grim face of the uniform talking to Alex. He watched color bleed from his face leaving it gray and ashen. He swayed once, but he shook off helping hands. His big hands curled into fists, but there was no one to hit—

He should go to him. He couldn't help, but Alex was his partner, his friend. No one noticed Ferris stagger back two steps, hit the side of the fire engine and sink down on the running board.

It was a crap time to realize that he'd just lost the woman he...he...

He couldn't think it because if he did—he dropped his face in his hands and groaned. He could. No one heard him. No one looked at him. All eyes were on Alex. He just needed a little time...a little more time...to...to...

...wish he was dead, too.

CHAPTER 12

ZACH'S PHONE SHRILLED. He was driving so he ignored it. It stopped and started again. If a phone could sound insistent, even urgent, then his did.

"Sometimes these dang things…" he pounded a finger on answer and snapped, "What? I'm driving—of course I'm sitting down. Would I drive standing up?—What about Hannah?" His eyes widened. Widened some more. "Listen to me very carefully, Alex. Hannah is sitting right here with me in my car—do you think I don't know my own daughter?" Another longer pause. "Just because I mix up their names— We'll be right there—okay. Fair point. Hannah needs to report to work. Meet us there." He ended the call and looked at her.

Hannah resisted the urge to repeat the "not my fault," possibly because the look is his eyes was so grim. "What?"

"Someone blew up your car. Alex thought you were in it."

"Someone blew up my car!" She got the "look" again. Man, he was dishing them out today. "Sorry," she muttered, even though it really wasn't her fault. "Is Alex okay?" Though why he wouldn't be…wasn't his car—Ferris. He'd have been with Alex. "So, they—he's meeting us at the NOCC?"

Zach had started to turn back to driving, but he stopped and looked at her again. "That's the second time you've done that."

"Done what?" She'd learned early to never admit anything. Ever.

"Changed plural to singular."

She swallowed, hoping he hadn't noticed and wondered if she'd ever heard her dad use a sentence with—

"Well, in our family, it's not easy to get over using plurals…" Hannah pointed out. Not her best, and sadly, not her worst attempt at deflecting Zach.

"Right. How about we talk about those plurals while I drive you to work. And then you can tell me what else you aren't telling me."

———

Leblanc knew better than to show surprise when she came back. He'd heard about Calvino, of course, but Afoniki, well, it had not hit the news yet, he supposed. Her husband had died since they last met, so he murmured condolences as he got her settled and then took his seat behind his desk. He very much hoped she didn't invite him to the funeral. It was a conflict of interest that she might not understand. She'd draped herself in tasteful black and wore a gentle air of sorrow, but her eyes showed her to be embracing her heritage with an almost unbecoming eagerness. To head off an invite, to give the visit a business-like theme, he spoke first.

"You have the, er, items, Ms. White?"

She opened her purse and pulled something out. "I have two of them." She opened her hand.

Leblanc considered the two rings with no outward sign of emotion. He'd never seen the rings, except in photos taken by his grandfather. "May I?"

After a short hesitation, she handed him one. Leblanc did not smile at her obvious distrust. And it was…mutual. He pulled out a loupe and studied the stone. It was a fine stone, almost unblemished so that the numbers etched in the setting could be seen. But the outer band was not as pictured. Had Zafiro added something after delivery? It was, he supposed, possible, but out of character. If he had trusted a Leblanc with the secret, why not with all the secret? He studied the engravings through the loupe. The series of numbers and letters meant nothing, could have referred to anything.

Without speaking, he handed this ring back, accepted the second from her. He had no reason to doubt its authenticity. Though, he noted, the numbers and letters were different from the other ring. He handed it back.

"And the third ring?"

"That stupid old man won't leave his house," she snapped.

Leblanc waited without speaking.

"Well, I thought maybe there'd be something for two out of three."

"No," he said, managing to infuse spurious regret into the single word. The world, not just his world, but the world, would be a better place if she failed at the task set before her. He'd wondered when he read of her husband's death. He didn't wonder now, though he was curious how she'd managed it. Impressed she'd managed to take out Bettino Calvino, though with him, she would have surprise on her side. Aleksi would definitely be the hardest nut to crack.

The flash in her eyes almost—but she needed him. That knowledge held her in check. For now.

Her mouth opened and almost he guessed what she wanted to say. What did it matter now if he told her what he knew without that last ring? Her lips curved, like a tiger, waiting to pounce.

"How loyal you are," she murmured. She tucked the rings back inside her matching black purse and closed it with a loud snap. "I feel so...comforted by that."

Leblanc waited until she was gone before tugging at his tie. It was too late to undo what he'd done, and it went against his deepest grain. Of course, he was unlikely to live long enough for an ethics probe, assuming someone complained about him. He extracted his cell and dialed. Had he always had this number on speed dial? Interesting that he'd only just realized—

"It's Leblanc. I was wondering if we might meet today?" He paused and looked at his full calendar. "I'll be free all after-noon." Then he buzzed his assistant. "I'll need you to clear the rest of my calendar for today."

It was unusual and he wondered if the man would remember later and if he did, if it would help the police.

———

Hannah could only be grateful when the way-too-long ride with Zach ended at the NOCC. He followed her inside, but even he wouldn't grill her at her workplace. Or in front of other people. She hoped. She was on track for the lab when she saw Miz Cookie looking sweetly tragic in the hallway. Hannah halted so abruptly Zach almost bumped into her. She stepped into the scarce shadow of an office door, acting on instinct. Not sure why she expected Zach to say something, but other than glancing down the hall, then at her, he stepped out of the direct light as well.

Well, he was a cop, even if he was retired.

"Scary," he muttered.

And she'd needed Sarah to give her a heads up on Miz Cookie. Hannah made a mental memo to sigh once Zach was gone. Would he leave after she'd almost been blown up? Her world tilted a bit, but before she could fully process this, the receptionist looked around for help and spotted her. The least she could do was spare Zach, so she stepped out.

"Something I can help with?"

Miz Cookie turned, her careful smile faltering as she spotted Hannah. A puzzled look of 'should I know you,' then the color drained from her face, and she swayed, her eyes almost rolling back in her head. Hannah grabbed one arm, knew she couldn't keep her off the ground by herself—

"Help me," Hannah snapped. The girl jumped in and so did Zach, though he retreated as soon as Miz Cookie was in the chair. Lucky man that he could. Hannah eased her head down until she stirred and pushed against her. After a minute Miz Cookie sat up, but kept a hand over her face, a small moan escaping her lips.

"This place," she faltered, "is so distressing."

It hadn't been that distressing until Hannah joined the

discussion. Had she recognized the prime rib cutter from her party? But why would that make her almost faint? Hannah arched a brow at the girl.

"Mrs. White wanted to claim her husband's body, but he donated it to science," she explained.

"Science can have him. I just want him until after the wake. I need closure, I need to say goodbye to my own dear Harold."

Hannah looked a question at the girl, who shook her head.

"It looks like science already claimed him, ma'am," Hannah said. "Is there someone we could call for you?" If she had science's number, she'd have called them.

Miz Cookie said in faltering tones that now sounded fake, "My driver...he should be right out front...."

Hannah felt a bit mean thinking she was faking it. The lady was still very pale. Whatever had shocked her, that had been real. Left alone with her, the silence felt awkward, though Hannah had no idea why. "Can I get you some water or something?"

The hand lowered. Yeah, she was pale, but the sugary smile was back. It looked a bit odd with her expression. Once again, Hannah wished she had better people reading skills.

"You're wondering..." Miz Cookie gave an exaggerated shudder, and indicated Hannah's ID. "Your name."

"My...name?" Hannah touched the ID.

"I heard it on the news on the way here. That you'd been killed in an explosion or something. This place, my recent loss...then, well, a dead woman walking toward me—I'm afraid I felt faint."

Hannah blinked. She wasn't sure she'd make that connection from a radio news story, but okay...

"I'm sure it's no surprise, ma'am—" The approach of the driver was salvation in a uniform. With perhaps too much alacrity, Hannah rose and let the driver have her spot. She managed to escape with a mumbled something or other. She was glad to sink down at her own desk, even if Zach was waiting for her.

"What was that about?"

"Science got her husband's body before she did," Hannah murmured, wondering what kind of person heard a random name on the radio and remembered it enough to faint when that person turned out to not be dead?

"What's wrong, baby girl?"

Zach hadn't called her that, well since a new baby girl had replaced her. Which would make it a very long time. She felt actual tears sting the corners of her eyes.

"I'm not sure, daddy," she said and sniffed, then gave a laugh that was more wry than amused. They'd be drowning in sentimentality if this went on any longer.

His answering smile was also wry. "Well, much as I hate to admit it, if anyone can figure it out, it's probably you. You got your mama's brains."

"You sure about that? My dad's a pretty smart guy."

"Is he?"

He was worried, she realized, puzzled for a moment. Then it hit her. "That was a pretty clever dodge you pulled off back then."

He grimaced. "Not my finest hour."

"So we don't serve and protect family? I can't see what else you could have done." If he'd tried to do it legal with Curly there in the wings, and on Zafiro's payroll… "I can't imagine how hard it must have been." Trying to protect Charlie. Not sure who he could trust, so trusting no one. Knowing him, he wouldn't have shared that dangerous burden with anyone.

"I've seen the way you kids have looked at me since…" he stopped, scowling.

"If we have, it's only from the shock of realizing you're a real person and not just our dad." It wasn't the whole truth, of course.

They had been looking at him with questions in their eyes because who they thought he was had gone out of focus. But at the back of it was a certainty that he'd done his best. And perhaps a belated realization he wasn't perfect.

"I know this will come as a shock, but we never really thought you were, you know, perfect."

That startled a laugh out of him. "When did you grow up?"

"While you were working," she shot back and grinned. "You might mention it to Alex when he gets here—"

The door slammed back and Alex filled the opening, his gaze both angry and worried.

"Mom's here," she muttered, for Zach's ears only.

He coughed and she stood up, totally not as a defensive move, but because she felt like it.

"Not even slightly singed."

She fought the urge to edge behind Zach for protection.

The other door swung open, and there was Ferris, filling the other half of the opening. The worry and something else in his face, well, it made her catch her breath.

Aware of Zach watching, she tried for light, but before she could do more than give him a wavering smile, he surged past Alex and grabbed her, pulling her tightly against his chest. Okay, she hadn't expected that move. It was very nice, but hard to completely enjoy it with her dad and her brother watching.

"Alex said you were all right, but I couldn't—didn't believe him," he growled in her ear.

At loss for a witty comeback or a clever deflection, Hannah opted to bury her head in his shoulder and take comfort from the frantic thumping of his heart. His hands touched her hair, her shoulders, then clutched her again and it finally, fully hit her that if someone hadn't—what?—tried to steal her car maybe? She'd have been the one—

It was a good thing he had a tight grip on her, because her knees went weak.

———

It had been easy to get his arms around Hannah. Under the laser regard of her dad and her brother, it should have been easy to open a distance. Only it wasn't. It felt like...retreat. And she had her head buried in his shoulder. He'd believed her gone. Holding her was the only way to prove she wasn't. To know that she was very much alive.

Would he have preferred this proof to occur in private? Oh yes. So much did he wish that, well, yeah, it was a very deep wishing. Wild ideas of escape passed through his brain. All of which, he suspected, would be ruthlessly squelched by Alex, who had shifted so that he blocked the whole of the exit. Zach, he looked on the enigmatic side there, possibly a bit thoughtful. Who'd have thought the dad would appear more reasonable than the big brother? Appear being the operative word.

"This is kind of awkward," Hannah whispered.

"Yeah." The agreement was a breath of sound that he hoped didn't reach other ears. "Any idea how—"

"—we get out of it? Um, count of three we both step back?"

To his surprise, his hands tightened. "I'll try."

The feel of her silent chuckle helped. Her head lifted, her hair brushing against his face as her mouth—not the time for that, Ferris reminded himself—then her eyes came into view. His arms slowly dropped. He saw her lips move in a silent count and at three, he took one step back.

"I'm," he had to clear the huskiness from his throat to continue, "glad you're all right." The formal tone was way too late.

"Thank you." Her formal response was also too little, too late. Probably be funny later. If he survived to later.

"What the—" Alex began ominously.

Hannah swung around and silenced him with a look that impressed Ferris so much he almost grabbed her again.

"It's pretty obvious what is going on, Alex, and if you weren't so primitive about everything, we'd have told you," Hannah said, with admirable calm. Then spoiled it by flicking a look at her dad.

To Ferris's surprise, when he spoke it wasn't about him, them.

"What happened with Hannah's car?"

"A guy shouldn't date—"

He had to give Alex credit for persistence. Zach apparently didn't agree.

"Last time I checked, both of them were of age and living in a free country," Zach's tone was so mild Hannah's eyes widened, then she hurriedly changed it to a "so there" one for Alex. The edges of Zach's mouth twitched, but he held it together. "And I'm more worried about what happened to her car than who she's dating."

There was a bit of "for now" to that, so Ferris didn't kid himself he was home free—wherever and whatever that meant. He was in deeper than he'd realized and so far it didn't feel that bad.

"Fine." Alex gritted out the word. "While I'm still on this case, I'll need your statement."

Hannah exchanged what even a guy would call a significant look with Zach. Where had they been when her car was being blown up?

Zach's face turned grim again. "What caused the explosion?"

"They found the remains of a cheap cell phone," Ferris said, because for now they were still partners. "Various pieces tested positive for explosive residue at the scene."

Hannah sat on the edge of her desk. "Someone seriously tried to blow me up?"

"Or it could be a case of someone wiring the wrong car." Alex took two steps away and then turned back. "Can you think of anyone—" he stopped. "Any cases that might have upset the wrong people?"

"Nothing you don't know about." She hesitated, then added with obvious reluctance, "Claude St. Cyr had someone following me this morning."

Alex stared at her. "And you know this how?"

Hannah licked her lips. "I may have…asked him who hired him."

"And he just told you?" Alex scoffed.

"Well, I may have mentioned my, um, brothers." She

shrugged. "It used to work in high school. He took off like a scared rabbit. Didn't even have to threaten the other two—"

"Other two?" Alex didn't yell, but that didn't make his tone less ominous.

"Dimitri Afoniki didn't admit one was his—"

"What?" Alex's tone got louder.

"...but I'm pretty sure he was in on it, and he said Guido had sent the other guy. I know it's hearsay, but I believed him. That's what ticked me off—" she stopped, looked at each of them in turn and then shrugged again. "Well, it did tick me off. So I chewed the one out and the others went away."

"If one of them—" Alex ground his teeth together.

"I don't think it was one of them. I mean, why follow me if you're just going to blow me up?"

Ferris straightened. "You think...X?" They'd both felt like some unknown someone was involved somehow.

Zach looked thoughtful. "Doesn't explain why."

"Who the—" Alex paused to edit out the string of swear words he obviously needed to set loose, but couldn't in front of his dad, "is X?"

"Well, that is the question, isn't it?" Hannah's gaze lost focus.

Dang the girl was cute when she slipped into what he called her geek zone—as if he heard that, Alex's gaze shot toward Ferris. Mentally whistling, Ferris looked away. Dating. Zach said they were dating. Hannah hadn't admitted it yet, but her dad had. Was that good?

"Or would that be the equation?" Hannah murmured.

"What—" This time Alex forced it out between gritted teeth. "—are you talking about?"

"X is always the unknown in an equation, isn't it? At least it always was in my math classes."

Alex opened his mouth. Caught a glare from Zach. Then closed it again.

———

The text came while she was still in the car, still shaken. Had she almost fainted? And what had she given away? Gladys White looked down, her hands clenching at the sight of the text.

Did you see it?

It was true the news was still reporting the doctor as the victim. But she knew the truth, didn't she?

Appearances can be deceiving. Did I mention how much I dislike failure?

The response took a long time to come. She was sure he did some checking or some thinking. Hopefully both.

I'll take care of it.

She didn't bother to respond. She really did dislike failure. First the lawyer, then they wouldn't give her Harold's body, now this. She needed something positive. This was a day seriously in need of at least one positive. One couldn't live forever on the glow of not just fooling Bettino Calvino but removing him from the picture. He'd been so surprised. And then he'd died. She had no idea how lovely it could be to take a life.

Today was supposed to have been, well, not that perfect since she had to farm out the second death. And just because someone had died in the car, well what did she care about that? It was just someone who got in her way.

And Dr. Hannah Baker was someone who hadn't died

when they were supposed to. She hadn't mattered either. She tried to remember why Dunstead thought she was the perfect choice.

She shouldn't have to deal with details. She was supposed to be the Red Queen. She had minions for the details. She liked that. Minions sounded better than pawns.

Dunstead was supposed to be the minion who got her mob war started by killing Hannah Baker. She frowned, wondering why it had seemed so logical then but was less so now? Something about the Bakers thinking the mob did it? That was it, like that show she saw…she huffed out a sigh. For just a tiny minute, she thought Dunstead had tried to fool her, that wasn't possible. He wasn't clever enough for that.

Now Hannah Baker, well, she looked clever, but was she? What if she began to suspect Harold's death wasn't quite natural? Or worse, that Gladys knew something about the bombing of her car? She'd practically given her a memo, but it had startled her so. Her face, her face had been familiar before —where had she seen her before? She frowned, but she was too upset, too angry. So angry she wanted to kill Dunstead, Leblanc and yes, Hannah Baker.

Surely she could still make something good from the day? Turn the negative into a positive?

She still needed Dunstead and he'd promised to take care of the doctor. That left Leblanc. Did she need the lawyer? Surely lawyers arranged for their affairs to be taken care of after they died? They were lawyers. That's what they did. Arrange things. And perhaps the next person would—get the memo—that it wasn't wise to cross her? Yes, someone new might be more reasonable about that silly third ring.

Now see, already she felt better. She just needed to decide

how. Nothing too complicated. In the books, complicated always went wrong. Hadn't there been something in that one book? Or maybe it was a television show. She forgot which... as she pondered this, she had another happy thought.

If not tomorrow, then surely the day after, the war would erupt into a lovely bloodbath. If Dunstead did his part. Which he'd better. Not that she could let him live. Already she could see it, the city erupting with a great big bloodbath, started by her.

Can you see me now, Great Grandfather? Can you see how like you I am?

CHAPTER 13

LEBLANC HAD NOT SEEN Cinzia Calvino for some time, though he followed her career as he did with all three families, using tracking software. He needed it. Family members arrived and disappeared with no obvious rhyme or reason. Cinzia was a particularly beautiful woman, lush and tempting to those so inclined.

He had never been tempted to stray, though some of the firm's female clients had tried to tempt him at various times over the years. Not, he knew, because of his personal appearance. Always they were drawn to what he knew, what he could have told them. Knowing was a strange and dangerous power. He'd always believed his wife didn't know, but he might be wrong about that, he supposed. He'd been drawn to her because of her stillness, because she wasn't like any of *them.* Here, at the end, with sharpened clarity, even she seemed changed to him when he called to tell her he would be late. Did she sense he would not be coming home tonight or ever? Would she miss him? Would anyone?

The firm's affairs would transition almost seamlessly, as they always had. Death, even by misadventure, was a minor annoyance. It was possible that no one within the firm would know what he'd done. On the other side—if there was another side—he might have some explaining to do to that original client, Zafiro. Almost that thought made him smile. He would like *her* to know, but that might have to wait for the other side as well.

His thoughts circled the question he did not wish to dwell on. How did he feel about dying? The shadow of it was always there, particularly with his clientele. The law covered everything about death, even in some cases, how to do it. It gave no guidance on how to feel. He'd always liked that about the law. Until…

It was a relief when she arrived, and he could focus on business. It was, had always been, his anchor, in the constantly shifting seas as a lawyer to the mob.

She had not changed so very much from their last meeting, at a holiday party, if his memory served. There was no question she was a Calvino, not with that dark hair. Her physical attributes were considerable and, he knew, somewhat deceptive. She played the bimbo on occasion, but even Bett had underestimated her. It was not the first time Bett underestimated a woman, of course. Eleanor Calvino had even surprised Leblanc.

"How can I help you?" Cinzia said, pausing for just the right amount of time before adding, "That is why you called me, is it not?"

"Yes," he agreed. There was still time to pull back, but he found that revenge was sweeter than loyalty here at the end of his life. His hand on the envelope he'd prepared, he did give her a chance. "You should tell me no. This is no gift."

"In our world, few things are." Cinzia leaned back in the deep chair, crossing her legs, her hands resting lightly on the arms. "And curiosity was ever my curse."

Leblanc pushed the envelope toward her. "Don't read it here. And if you change your mind, burn it."

Her sculpted brows arched. "Anything else?"

"I would appreciate your...protection for my family. My wife and my son."

The lovely head tilted to the side. "I give you my word I'll do my best."

Her best was all he could hope for. It might even be enough. "Then I am content."

"I could offer you the same..."

He shook his head. "Certain...triggers will go into effect when I am...gone. Otherwise—it is better for the firm, for all of you, if I don't disappear. But this meeting—" he indicated the envelope she held, "that is for me—if you decide to act on it."

"Then I will do my best for you," she said, her tone almost regretful.

"Be careful when you leave," he warned. "Bett was not careful enough." It was all he could do for her after handing her a live bomb. Still he walked the line, even though it blurred at the approach of death.

Her lashes flickered at this, and she nodded, looking thoughtful. She rose in one, fluid motion and picked up her purse from the small table next to the chair. She tucked the envelope inside it, then looked over her shoulder at him. Her lips parted, but she just nodded again and left.

Leblanc watched her go, content he'd picked better than he'd expected. She was smart enough to know that neither goodbye or God speed were appropriate. The devil take you? That was, he supposed, already the plan.

———

It wasn't snowy, no woods in sight, but Hannah definitely had miles to go before she could sleep—at least miles of siblings—which had apparently not been Robert Frost's problem. The lucky man. Amazing how tired one could be when all one had managed to do all day was to **not** get blown up. And listened to a lot of people marvel at her not getting blown up.

She wanted to go back to her place, but she wasn't stupid. If someone did want to kill her then going back there was like saying, "Here I am. Kill me dead this time." Though that option didn't seem half bad after getting hugged and exclaimed over by twelve siblings, all of whom paused to cast speculative looks at Logan Ferris. She probably needed to Google some quotes on bravery. He deserved them all for standing—well, sitting fast in the face of Zach's Baker's dozen. And Zach.

"So, as long as you know your alphabet—" Ferris murmured in her ear during a break in the…wake seemed sort of apropos.

Hannah nodded. For their sins, they were Alex, Benjamin, Calvin, Daniel, Edward, Frank, Gideon, Hannah, Ingrid, Jillian, Katherine, Laura, and Madeline. Not that this naming scheme had stopped Zach from messing up who was who on a regular basis.

Mostly he called the boys "bubba" and the girls, well, his

dealings with his daughters had always been complicated. They'd all had a short stint as "baby girl," but it was Maddy who got stuck with it. Except, apparently, in times of dire stress when it spread to other, older daughters. She made a mental note to remember this rare sign of Zach under stress.

Eventually the sibling storm cleared, leaving Alex who still lived at home—though reluctantly—along with Ben and Frank, who both dealt with organized crime at the NOPD and FBI respectively. Reducing the big brother presence by three did not help as much as she'd hoped.

She looked at Alex. "Don't you have a date or something?"

This hint that he was surplus to requirements either went over his head or was ignored. Maybe he was still hoping to tear a strip off Ferris. On the positive side, Alex was the only one who had pretended to take her statement. Apparently both Ben and Frank were too big with news to remember that key step. Not that she was sorry, though oddly enough it kind of annoyed her, too. It was possible that—as Zach used to say—she wouldn't be happy if she were hung with a new rope.

"Rumors are flying about who ordered the hit. Who you blame—St. Cyr, Calvino or one of the Afonikis—depends on who you talk to," Frank was saying in his grim, FBI voice. "Only thing anyone seems to agree on, Mirabelle St. Cyr was hired for the job."

Ben frowned. "Car bomb isn't her usual MO."

"Well, she wouldn't want her fingerprints on the hit. They have to know we'll all hunt them to their grave if they hurt one of ours," Alex asserted.

"Word is they plan to deal with it…internally," Frank said, "which could mean war."

"My money is on Claude going down. No one thinks he has the—"

Zach coughed.

"—the guts for it," Ben amended hastily.

"I think they underestimate Claude," Hannah said to Ferris. She angled so she could see him without moving too far away. Alex's eye had finally quit twitching at the sight of him, which either meant progress or he was as tired as she was. She settled against the couch arm and rested her elbow on a raised knee and her chin in the palm of her hand. "He's hungry for it."

"You think he's behind the bomb?" Ferris asked, moving a strand of hair back off her face. His gaze was warm, maybe more than warm.

She didn't want to talk about any of the bad guys, but she wasn't sure she wanted to talk about *them* either, even if all her brothers and her dad weren't in the room. But she liked the feel of his fingertips brushing against her skin. So, instead of shaking her head, which would break contact, she said, "No, I don't. I don't think any of them are behind it."

His brows arched, so she added, "It doesn't make any sense for any of them to pi—tick off a bunch of Bakers." Her tired brain twitched, as if it wanted to connect that thought with something else. She really needed some thinking time. And some sleep.

"X?" he said. "I've been digging, but still haven't uncovered anyone from that time who could have an ax to grind now."

"One thing that puzzles me," Hannah said, a bit dreamily, "is why Zafiro didn't have an heir instead of the three wise geezers. Seems like picking three gung-ho bad guys was a bad idea from the get-go. Was bound to go bad for someone." Her gaze narrowed. "I'll bet it was Afoniki who came up with the idea. He's still the chill one." And the lone survivor. "And while none of them managed to have a direct heir, they each found a relative to take over." And that's one of the questions she forgot to ask Charlie. Did the fake Ken mean anything? Or was that what he meant? That none of them were real heirs to anything they had?

"Maybe he didn't have a male heir," Ferris said, his voice a bit on the sleepy side, too. "It happens. Ask Henry the Eighth."

"Ask him what?" Zach unexpectedly joined the conversation.

"I was wondering why Zafiro didn't have an heir?" Hannah explained. "Was he ever married?"

"His wife died. In childbirth, I think." Zach's face shadowed. "I sort of remember something about some miscarriages."

"And he never remarried?" Ferris asked.

Calvino had never remarried, but the reason seemed a bit obvious now. He wasn't sure he could legally remarry, though that was kind of funny to think about. A wise guy worried about legalities. But she bet he did. He'd want kids legal. No questions. Afoniki had never married, and St. Cyr had been—what—too afraid to kill his wife?

Zach shook his head. "No. There were women..." He stopped and looked at his daughter.

Hannah tried to look innocent. Probably failed. Then her thoughts drifted on. Would Zafiro have done the same thing? Run off a wife? Or even banished one—and a daughter? In that time, to him, it would have mattered. In places in the world it still did. Henry the Eighth hadn't started out lopping off heads. He'd just wanted a son. And eventually had gotten enough absolute power to keep trying.

Zafiro had power in spades, enough to divide three ways, but not enough to get him that son…

She spoke her last thought, "Even now it's the boys that get all the goodies." Did it bother Cinzia Calvino and Mirabelle St. Cyr? "Surely they both left the girls something?"

"They had things set up so there was no probate," Ferris said. "Guess neither of them liked prying eyes on their stuff even after death."

Hannah had to ask, "Is Mirabelle really a hit woman?"

Ferris shrugged. "That's what they say."

"And the other one, Cinzia, isn't it?"

"No one is quite sure what her deal is," Ferris said, "at least not anyone willing to tell me anything."

Hannah smiled a bit absently. She wished she weren't under house arrest. She had an itch for some girl talk. She even knew it was kind of whacked to think about it. Particularly with her people skills. But a couple of mafia princesses weren't like real people anyway. Did they hang out together or compete? Was there a school for mafia princesses? She couldn't do it, of course. It was crazy, but it would be kind of interesting, especially now that she'd met the boys.

The silence finally penetrated Hannah's thoughts. She looked up and found all three brothers looking down at her, their brows all raised interrogatively. She looked at Zach. "Those are some powerful genes you passed on."

That popped his brows up, boosting the likeness through the stratosphere.

"What?" she asked.

Next to her, Ferris choked.

"We want to talk about how to keep you safe," Alex said.

Not highest ranking, but oldest, so he got to talk first. He was already on the defensive, expecting her to be difficult, she noted. Flattering.

"If I hide out, the killer will just go to ground until we all get tired of me hiding out," Hannah pointed out. She'd been mulling this problem, too, in between mafia princesses and unchecked power. While she didn't mind Ferris guarding her, more than a few hours with her brothers and she'd be begging to get blown up.

"And what was the result of this thinking?" Frank cut in before Alex could.

Was there a bit of sneer in there?

"I could ride along with Alex and—" she had to gulp to get it out. It was the second time she attempted his name, first time in public, but if she didn't do it, she'd undo everything she may have accomplished with Zach's help, "Logan on their shift tomorrow. Might be interesting to see the other side of my corpses, so to speak." And Ferris and Alex wouldn't be alone together until Alex had time to cool off. Assuming he could.

Alex, Ben and Frank exchanged "Is she crazy?" looks. But before they could say it, Zach spoke.

"I think it's a good idea."

Hannah gave him a look. Of course he liked it. It kept him from being tied down at home with her. The crafty old devil. Left him free to sneak off for more Charlie time.

After some grumbling, the brothers agreed to give it a try, if she stayed out of sight during calls. Naturally she hadn't thought of this herself. And yes, she'd wear a vest. Huge sigh.

"Oh, and Frank?" He turned with justifiable wariness.

"Any chance you could get me a look at what you guys have on Zafiro? I mean, he's old news, right?"

"Why?"

"Curiosity." Mostly. "It's an idea I have about those sheets of code," she added. She knew which of his buttons to push.

He didn't look happy, but he nodded. "I'll see what I can do."

"Tomorrow? So I'll have something to read while I'm riding around?"

"I'll see what I can do," he repeated.

"I better get moving," Ferris said, giving her an apologetic look, "or I'll be too tired to ride around."

"I'll walk you out," Hannah said, getting up with him. Alex's mouth opened and she held up a hand, "Don't say it, or I'll dog you and Nell for the next year. And you know I know how."

His mouth snapped shut.

"I won't let her go outside," Ferris said.

Not that it helped, but it was a good try. "He'll cool off eventually," Hannah said, leaning against the wall by the back door. She was too tired to parse anything, so hoped he wouldn't go all "we need to talk" on her.

He didn't.

"I'll see you tomorrow," he said. The kiss was brief, but very nice. She waited until she heard his engine fire and then headed through the kitchen and living room without stopping, except to kiss Zach on the cheek. They were her brothers, not her keepers. It might have depressed her to be back in the room she'd shared with her sisters, but she'd lost the ability to feel anything halfway through the living room. It had been a long day.

———

Though she'd rather expected it, Cinzia was still surprised when Aleksi Afoniki let her in. And not just in the house. She was ushered into his bedroom. Granted, he held a weapon and pointed it at her, but that was just common sense, even though she'd been patted down by his staff. Twice.

She held her hands up. "I can keep them up if that would make you feel better."

Something that might have been a grin twisted his ravaged face. It wouldn't be long. She guessed that he held on by sheer will. He gestured to a chair pulled close—but not too close—to his massive four-poster bed. She sank into it, with just a hint of sexual provocation. He couldn't and she wouldn't, but it was a sign of respect. And a gleam in his eyes told her he got it. Slowly, carefully, she lowered her arms to the chair sides, keeping them in clear sight. She hadn't come to kill him, but he wouldn't know that.

"Well?"

She found she couldn't start, not with her hands gripping the chair arms. "It's oddly hard for me to talk without my hands. I am Italian. If I keep them in sight, may I?"

His chuckle set off a paroxysm of coughing.

"Shall I get you help?"

He gestured toward the glass of water, and she jumped up, held it to his lips until the coughing eased. She made no effort to take the gun, though she could have. Besides, it was not the gun she wanted. When he was calm again, she retreated to her chair.

"Well?" he asked again.

She didn't need her hands after all. Her lips curved into a smile she knew was sexy, provocative and confiding.

"I've come to ask you for your ring, Aleksi."

"Ask?" he said with a scoffing sound that almost made him start coughing again.

"Yes, ask." She paused to let him see the deep sincerity in her eyes. She knew, it was a new look for them both. "Whoever killed Bett and Phin was after their rings. You know what that means. If you give it to me…"

She shrugged, well aware it made her breasts move interestingly. Though not enough to kill him. She wanted him alive when she left. Besides, he was smart enough to read the writing on the wall.

"And what does it mean?" he asked, as if stalling for time to think.

"Why, not just check, but checkmate. And so much frustration for someone."

"How do I know you don't already have the other two? That it was not you who killed Bett?"

"Well, you don't, I suppose. Except, if I had, you'd already be dead. I'm asking, not taking."

"Who told you?"

"A…reliable source who also desires a checkmate. And no I didn't kill him either."

"He is dead?" The heavy brows creased.

"I fear if not already, then soon. This enemy—no, he didn't tell me who—is quite determined." She smiled again. "But I think they might, just possibly forget to watch a…pawn?"

That pleased him, though she felt the sting of the self label.

"Bett underestimated you." And then, "Dimitri could do worse."

"And I could do...better." He'd had his chance. She couldn't become another Helenne pining for a man who didn't want her. "I'm not Helenne," she said, just in case he didn't get the point.

His smile almost...almost...made him look human. He tugged at the ring, then thrust his hand toward her. "Take it."

CHAPTER 14

DUNSTEAD SHUT off his phone and tossed it on the bed beside him. HelLooked glumly around the shabby room of the crappy hotel, cut lose a string of curses.

He was tired of living like this, tired of doing the dirty work for folks who lived better'n him. Take that old broad, living in that fancy house, giving him orders like she knew what to do. He'd bet money she was using television to plan her moves. She was as whacked as her ideas.

He couldn't believe she bought his line about how killin' a Baker would launch this mafia war she wanted so bad. She'd made his payback so easy. He frowned. Why? That was the question bugging him.

Why would she want it, need it so bad? Lady like that? She had nothing to do with any of 'em, had plenty of money or she couldn't afford him. Nice house. Fancy car with someone to drive her around. What was her beef? Had one of 'em killed her old man?

If he was a betting man, which he was, he'd bet she wasn't that sad her old man was gone. She seemed to like mourning, draping herself with black like that and dabbing at tears she weren't shedding.

The funeral was tomorrow. Maybe he'd pay his respects. She'd hate that, but weren't nothing she could do 'bout it. And, meantime, maybe he'd snoop around some. He'd always liked secrets, knowing 'em and—if the price wasn't right—sharing 'em. And he knew who would be very interested in knowing who was trying to gin up a war.

It was just a matter of deciding who'd be most interested. Almost, almost he was willing to give it to them all.

The old broad was smug, so sure she was in charge. It would be interesting to see how she handled them coming after her. Maybe his old man was kinda right, about loyalty—at least sometimes, for the right price—

He frowned. Now why did thinking about his old man give him the itch? He didn't like thinking about him but made himself do it. This once.

"They're lucky, boy, real lucky that Zafiro don't got no one to avenge him. Now there was a man who knew how to reward those with him and get those not."

Dunstead shook his head angrily. Zafiro was long dead and so was his old man, but it was uncommon, weird to be thinking 'bout him now. Almost made him feel bad, thinking about going to the wise boys, but his old man also used to tell him you worked with what ya got.

Well, what he had was the right to change the deal to one better for himself. The doc would be on guard and so would a passel of Bakers. Only what if they was looking the wrong way? Protecting the wrong person?

———

Hannah wasn't sure whether she felt relieved or disappointed that her ride-along wouldn't be in a squad car. Zach had been out of a squad by the time she was born, so she'd never actually ridden in one.

She had sat in one the other day, but that wasn't exactly the same thing as racing through the streets with the siren blaring and the lights flashing. She'd always wanted to ride in a fire engine, too. And a real train. And a helicopter—

"Are you getting in or not?" Alex's voice broke in.

Distracted from what was shaping up to be a sort of bucket list, Hannah studied him for a moment before answering. There were signs he'd gotten some sleep, too. His frustration level was down to mildly annoyed, and he'd only grunted at Ferris when he showed up with their wheels.

"I'm getting in," she said, suiting action to words. She snapped her seatbelt and then allowed her gaze to connect with Ferris' in the rearview mirror. He looked slightly less rested than Alex and broke eye contact as Alex slid behind the wheel. It was possible he had buyer's remorse. Getting out of a relationship with a Baker might be as hard, or harder, than getting into one.

She'd observed, on more than one occasion, that her brothers lost almost all reason and accountability where their sisters were concerned. It was sweet but death to her social life. Of course, so was working in the morgue, without the sweet part. On the other hand, the morgue paid her bills, something her brothers did not.

"Frank left you a file," Ferris said. "It's there on the seat." He flashed her a quick smile, then faced forward again.

"Thanks." It couldn't be the complete file. Frank must have taken out, or not copied, the gruesome stuff. That was also sweet, and she didn't really mind. If she still had a job at the end of her sudden leave, then there'd be plenty of gruesome waiting for her. She was more interested in the photos and personal details anyway. Not that she could have explained to anyone what it was she hoped to find.

It was a feeling that didn't even deserve to be called a gut instinct yet and maybe never would. There were notes about the wife and miscarriages. The most interesting part, though, was that she'd disappeared, not died in childbirth, after the baby died. How had the rumor got started? She turned back to the photos. They were old, but still better than the ones Ferris had gotten for her. His frontal and mandible were very Slavic, more so as he aged, she noted.

She felt that twitch. It was frustrating she couldn't seem to connect any dots. An autopsy could be frustrating, but it was still—mostly—about a single body. This was like having a jumble of bodies and trying to match legs and heads to the right torsos.

She leaned back and tried to mentally mind map, letting the ideas float around and possibly connect on their own, but Alex's voice cut into her drifting thoughts.

"Any sign of unusual interest in us?"

Hannah looked at Alex, then at Ferris. She realized that Ferris was scanning, discreetly, but definitely scanning for interest ahead, to the sides, and behind.

"Nothing yet."

She hated this. It didn't even make crazy sense. Was that her problem? Too logical? She sorted the crazy stuff out of the more logical actions and studied them. Inside her own head she could look her own crazy ideas in the eye without flinching. No one could see them but her. So in addition to the very weird attempt to blow her up, she had…

The bizarre attempt to **not** kill Guido Calvino.

The execution of the four boys who had failed to **not** kill Guido Calvino.

Two missing wives, one of whom was definitely not dead. The other who probably was but might have left behind a child?

The problem was, she could postulate a living heir for Zafiro and even make the case for this heir seeking revenge against the three wise geezers, but she couldn't figure out how that person learned they **were** the heir. No one in this file or in her world seemed to believe there was one.

Okay, it was possible that Zafiro also knew his wife wasn't dead, so why not seek out his heir—the baby was a girl? That girl could have had had a son, but by then Zafiro was probably dead. And everyone—even the cops—agreed he'd planned for one of the wise geezers to take over his empire. So he'd…given up on a male heir?

The rings? Supposing there was a lost heir, the "X" she and Ferris had been postulating. Why the rings? Zafiro made them first. Was there another message associated with the three rings? But again, how would an heir find out? And why now?

Okay, she had a sort of idea about that. Zafiro had expected one of the wise boys to take over. What if there was some sort of trigger in place for when that person died? But that brought her back to how had X found out?

The radio came to life, changing their direction, from squad headquarters to crime scene. When Alex heard the name, he exchanged a look with Ferris and then said, "Repeat the vic's name please?" It didn't change, so he shook his head.

"Who is Raymond Leblanc?" Hannah asked.

"If it's who I think it is," Alex amended, "he's only *the* lawyer to the mob."

Hannah opened her mouth. Closed it. Pulled out her phone and Googled him. He wasn't just the lawyer to the mob, he was the main guy in the firm, the oldest living. Until now. And, according to their website, the firm went back. Way back. Way, way back. She grabbed the file, and there it was.

Leblanc and Fontenot.

Less partners back then, but fewer bad guys to manage. And a possible path to knowledge for an X. It was an interesting thesis. It felt right, but it had one big problem. Not an inch of proof or an inkling of who.

Okay, that was two problems, but who was counting?

———

She was not, Cinzia believed, easy to shock. But old Leblanc's envelope had been, yeah, shocking was the only word for it. And, she was rather surprised she'd got out of Afoniki's place alive.

If Dimitri had known, she wouldn't have. But she'd made sure he was out before she paid her call. Of course, he'd learn she visited, but the why? Well, that was up to the old man whether he told Dimitri or not. She had a feeling he'd keep his ring hand hidden until he couldn't.

And if he died in his bed, would Dimitri remember and put it together? It depended on how long it took. She shrugged. What would be, would be. Always had. Always would. Until it wasn't anymore.

Securing the ring was all Leblanc had asked her to do,

though he must have known he'd told her enough to make her hungry for more. She was a Calvino, after all, even if she was a girl. A Calvino with a measure of honor. She'd put a guard on Leblanc's family. He hadn't gone home last night, but his death—if he was dead—hadn't been reported yet. She felt a little sad for him, a little amazed for her—and yes, a little annoyed at what he'd unleashed on them all. It was, perhaps, a good thing he was dead. Because if she'd known what was in that envelope?

She would not have left the lawyer's office without a name.

No name. No description. She didn't know if it was a man or woman.

And yet, maybe Cinzia did know it was a woman. Bett would not have feared a woman. He'd been a chauvinist to the end. Yes, it had to be a woman. That was the only thing that explained Bett's far-too-easy execution.

Both Leblanc and Afoniki had been certain they were going to die. But without the last ring, the woman would not get anything else. According to the information from Leblanc, this Zafiro heir needed all three rings to unlock the whatever it was that would deliver the empire back to the heir. As Leblanc had written, it was a checkmate as long as she never learned who did have the third ring. It was possible that Aleksi would spill it, but she'd told him just enough to make him dig in his heels. No, he wouldn't tell. And in time, this enemy would have to appear and act. Or give up.

Cinzia could have gotten the other rings—with the name—which is why Leblanc had withheld it. He wanted the status quo to return. For his firm. For his family. Of course, she couldn't appear in the office to claim the prize without some explaining, so perhaps Leblanc had been wiser than she first thought.

She frowned, staring into space without seeing the opulent bedroom that was not truly hers in this house that was now Guido's. Perhaps she could achieve much the same result without the other rings? Was that why Leblanc had mentioned that Afoniki, her uncle Bett and St. Cyr had added to the rings' engravings?

It might just be a "little something" for her trouble. Or it could be more. It did make a girl think. Nor did she plan to stop looking for the other rings. Because everything had a solution, if one thought long enough.

It wasn't that she disliked her cousin. Guido wasn't bad for what he was. But she was rather tired of being seen as someone who only brought her ability to marry someone powerful—even someone as yummy as Dimitri—to the family equation. And no, she wouldn't touch Claude with a barge pole, thank you very much.

One couldn't lobby for female equality with a bunch of, well, murderers and thieves.

But if one's timing were right, one might, just might be able to teach them about girl power by other means.

———

Dimitri felt it oddly appropriate that they'd chosen to meet by one of the recently exhumed crypts. The Calvino one, of course, since he was meeting Guido—and since they were likely plotting against Claude, it wouldn't be wise to meet by the St. Cyr crypt.

There was enough of a risk just asking for the meeting, but

the one thing Dimitri was good at, it was feeling the cold wind of trouble approaching. He did not know if Claude had that skill, did not care, but Guido, well, in an odd way they'd grown up—not next to each other—but parallel. Like shooting stars moving at the same pace and on the same trajectory.

Perhaps it was the strange, and life-long, balancing act of Bett and Aleksi that had formed their almost friendly rivalry. Neither knew exactly what they—or the other—would do when the final curtain went down, but for now, a living Aleksi held them both in check. This might be the last time such a meeting could take place if the surprisingly effective assassin of Bett struck one last time.

Dimitri noted that Guido brought more bodyguards than usual this time but, like him, had to take the last steps without them. What was said here was for their ears only. And the bodyguards were more for what might be out there. Neither was fool enough to start shooting within sight of their guys.

It was quiet, hot and as musty as he remembered, though minus the smell of gun powder. Guido stopped a few feet away. There was trust and there was *trust*. Neither of them ever had *trust*. He knew Guido well enough to know he wouldn't start the conversation. Someone, probably Bett, had told him there was power in silence.

"Do you think it's Claude?" he asked.

Guido didn't complain about the lack of greeting. He shook his head. "Doesn't feel like him."

Dimitri nodded at this. "Someone new?"

He half nodded, but with a grimace. "Feels off though."

"Random. Disconnected. With the occasional flash of competence." That sounded better than successful, since the "bright" moment seemed to be Bett's killing.

"How is Aleksi?" Guido's expression didn't change.

"Watching his flank." And every other approach angle. He hadn't seen him for days. No fear from the old man, but definitely a sense of waiting.

"How can someone be so good and so bad?"

Dimitri shrugged. One of his men signaled. After a nod from Guido, he let the man approach. What he whispered sent his brows shooting up. He sent the man back to his place before saying, "Raymond Leblanc's been murdered."

Guido stilled, like an animal scenting danger. Like Dimitri, he knew there was only one reason they could think of for silencing the old man.

So he couldn't tell what he knew.

———

Aleksi Afoniki had chosen an interesting place for their first—and last—meeting. Gladys couldn't think why he'd finally decided to meet her. He had to know—but perhaps he didn't. He was old, possibly senile. That would make it less satisfying. And possibly make her a bit more careful.

She watched him for a while, knowing he would never expect it to be her. He would have noticed her twenty, possibly even ten years ago. She'd had that something until she fell into the middle age of invisibility. After that it didn't matter if you knew how to dress and do your hair. You were just gone.

Aleksi had probably always liked his women real young. A dirty old man who had one thing she wanted, needed and then no one could stop her. No. One.

She turned from the river drifting past. It was hot and she felt the sheen on her face. Why did these meetings have to happen on hot days? Couldn't Leblanc have dropped his bomb on her when it was cooler? Now she studied the people drifting about below the Moon Walk. None of them had that look she'd come to recognize so well.

He really had come alone, well, he'd needed someone to push his chair and help him to the bench. The same bench where Phineas had drawn his last. She hadn't killed him, more's the pity. His wife had done that, if the papers were right for once. It felt right to bloody the bench for herself. Seal the end of the wise geezers' rule and the beginning of hers.

She strolled closer, still watching for signs of interest. She didn't expect any bodyguards to be in black, but there was a walk, a certain watchfulness that would give them away. But all she saw were tourists, some towing fretful kids.

The calliope was wailing from the river, calling people to board the *Natchez*. She used the sound to cover her approach, but she didn't need it. He didn't even look at her until she sat down. Despite the heavy heat, he wore a coat and had both hands thrust in the pockets, denying her a peek at the prize she'd come to claim.

She didn't look at him, not until the song ended. Then she shifted, turning so he could see her, if he had the wits to *see*.

Aleksi scowled, as if to drive her away, but the scowl faded. And then he laughed.

"That old devil."

She eased her purse down just enough to give him a glimpse of the silenced gun she held.

"Am I supposed to raise my hands? Be a bit conspicuous, don't you think?"

His open mockery made her grit her teeth.

"So, you are what is left of Zafiro. I think he would be as disappointed as he was with your...mother?"

The gun coughed without conscious thought. His body jerked, but his eyes showed life when she shoved the gun back in her purse and moved in. She pulled one hand out. No ring. The other—her chin jerked up hard enough to jiggle her jowls.

"Where is it?"

He laughed once, then coughed. "Checkmate."

CHAPTER 15

NO ONE KNEW, no one but she and Leblanc.

And yet, he'd *known*.

And then he'd laughed at her. Gladys' hands curled into fists in her lap, swaying slightly as her car took a corner a little fast.

And then he'd laughed at her grandfather. The man he'd murdered.

Checkmate.

He'd actually said it to her, like he'd known—the Queens had so much power on the board, but it was Kings who had to be checkmated to win. She tried to breathe. She hated chess. It was a stupid game.

Leblanc. She hadn't talked, so it must have been him.

But he hadn't told them everything, or she'd never have gotten close to the old man.

Had he warned the old man? Just because he wasn't wearing the ring, didn't mean he'd given it away.

But she knew he had. She'd seen it in his disgusting old gaze.

Checkmate.

There were other ways to take back what was hers, but they'd take too long. If that old man had meant to cheat her then why tell her? She frowned.

Unless…Dunstead? He'd given her some odd looks the last time they met. Like he found her familiar in some way.

She looked in the mirror of her compact and adjusted a few strands of hair. She looked like him. She had pictures. Not good ones. She'd had to find them online. The only reason no one noticed was because they weren't expecting it, weren't looking for it. That's one reason she'd wanted them at her house, at her party. To see if they'd see. But they hadn't.

Had Dunstead gone through her things? She had the secret board with the photos of her grandparents, of what she found in public files about that side of her family. And she had the rings and those papers, the brick from the coffin. That had been taken on impulse, because there'd been nothing there to find. At least they'd all wonder if they'd missed out. She'd read something similar in a book. There was that old man who'd looked at her in the morgue. Janitor or something. Couldn't have been him.

Dunstead or the lawyer?

The drawer of her desk was locked, but he was a criminal. He probably knew how to unlock things and get past her security.

There'd been something about her desk that had bothered her when she went to get her gun. She'd pushed it aside, so eager for the meeting with Aleksi.

If Dunstead had been in her house…

He'd been ignoring her calls. Avoiding her since promising to kill Hannah Baker.

What if he'd been lying about that? She'd never read any book where a mob war was launched by killing a cop's sister. She'd checked because, well, because. Not that she was wrong or could be fooled. She'd been distracted with so many things. That's all.

That cop, the doctor's brother, he'd been the one who took Dunstead down.

She gritted her teeth. He'd needed her, because she was the Red Queen.

He needed money so he couldn't run that far. But if he'd been the one to rat her out to Aleksi then he probably had money. What he didn't have was payback. Helenne was out on bail. And Alex Baker? Back on the job, dating Bett's granddaughter, she'd heard, which was rather amusing. He must like that in whatever part of hell she'd sent him to.

She'd done that. Killed two of the most notorious organized crime heads in the city.

She had done what no one else could.

So what if Dunstead had slipped his leash. She didn't need him. She didn't need the ring. She would get what she wanted. She'd earn the name and then she'd take it.

Gladys Zafiro.

She'd show him, she'd show them all she was her grandfather's true heir. That she had his will and guts and his ruthlessness. In fact, she'd show them she was better. And stronger. And smarter.

And she'd start with today's other disappointment.

If Dunstead was trying to hit at Alex Baker, that's where she'd find him. He might even try to pretend he was doing it for her. But she couldn't wait for him to come to her. She'd find him by finding Alex Baker.

Gladys might not have the ring, or what went with it, but she did have one thing that Leblanc hadn't taken from her, that all the good wise guys—even the female ones—in the best books had.

She had his snitch.

————

Ferris couldn't believe it when the call came. They'd barely finished at the Leblanc scene. They hadn't even had time for lunch. He had a bad feeling about the location—a bench on the Moon Walk in the Quarter—even before they got a name to go with their victim.

Aleksi Afoniki, the last wise geezer. It was kind of historic.

They couldn't get the car close to their scene, so Alex told Hannah she'd have to come with them.

"You can sit in the CSU van while we process the scene," he said, scanning their surroundings before nodding for her to get out.

Ferris hadn't known Hannah long enough to know if her abstracted compliance was typical or not. Alex wasn't looking at her. He looked for threats and was probably already thinking about the crime scene.

It was a weekday in the Quarter, so the crowds were light. Still too many people about. She was too exposed for his liking. He couldn't even enjoy the way the sun ignited the gold in her hair or watch her walk, because he had to look around, assess for possible threats.

It had been an unusually silent ride, with only necessary exchanges of information among the three of them. He could feel Hannah's wheels turning and see that thinking look in her eyes when he'd looked back. He'd seen it, as if she'd said it out loud, that she thought he regretted hugging her. He didn't. He was too worried about what might happen next to regret anything except that he wished he'd hugged her longer.

She'd talked about that clock ticking down to something bad? Well, it was like a hammer inside his head, ticking down to what? Why had she been targeted at all? Who was after her? His gaze caught the edge of Alex's grim scowl. What if it wasn't about her? Dunstead had been bailed out by someone. He could be going for some payback, using Hannah to side-swipe Alex. If it was that, well, it was a well-aimed low blow. Alex pretended his siblings annoyed him, but he was a fierce and protective big brother.

A rueful smile edged his mouth. He had a feeling that when things settled down, he'd find out just how protective.

Hannah stumbled over an uneven edge, and he caught her elbow. He had questions for her, too. What had she been doing with her dad? Had she seen Charlie? If she had, what had she learned? He needed time alone with the woman, time for information exchanging and time for kissing and holding. Nothing like almost losing a woman to focus your attention.

Interesting he could pick up on her relationships signals, but he had no clue what she thought about everything else. In that sense she was an enigma wrapped in a long, cool drink of water.

Alex turned and studied the layout, then said, "Sit in the meat wagon, out of sight."

Hannah made a face at him, but complied, though not with any speed. Partially hidden by the open rear doors, she stopped by her sister, Ingrid, in her CSU tech uniform.

"Fancy meeting you here," Ferris heard her say, before he

had to follow Alex up the slope to the body slumped on the bench just above them.

———

It hadn't been easy to find a spot with decent sight lines. The area was a mess of flashing lights, milling people, and Baker's crime scene up on the levee.

He'd hoped for something better when he'd begun shadowing Ingrid Baker's CSU van earlier this morning. Lots of interesting radio traffic today. She'd been on another scene when the call came through on Leblanc's murder. A pity about that one. Based on the address, it would have been ideal.

Dunstead had thought about just going for the oldest Baker, but that would be too quick. He wanted him to suffer. He wanted him to know that actions had consequences for the people you cared about.

He wanted him locked in the only jail Dunstead had the power to send him, one of guilt, grief and remorse. It wasn't enough, but it would have to do. For now. After he served his time, maybe he'd put him out of his misery.

His vantage point wasn't great. He might not make it out. That made the shot all that much more important. He'd almost taken it when she was by the body, but then he heard Baker get the call. He wanted him there. Wanted him to see it. Even if it cost him his way out, he wanted to see Baker's face when his sister went down instead of him.

So he watched and waited. Followed her with his sight, but without the targeting turned on. Not yet.

No one could say he didn't learn from his mistakes. No advance warning this time.

————

"Alex seems to have calmed down some," Ingrid observed, working on labels for a series of small evidence bags. She propped a hip against the edge of the CSU van and slanted a look over her shoulder at Hannah. "At least he hasn't killed the boy toy. Yet."

"Thanks a lot." Hannah's legs hung over the edge of the rear, swinging slightly. It was muggy hot, but it could be worse. She could be stuck in the back of the car while they worked the scene.

Since she did see dead people most every day, this was a decent change of pace. This side of the crime was also new to her, which made it interesting. And the fact that Ferris was part of the view, well, that was a bonus. And he'd managed to squeeze her hand during the walk without Alex noticing, so triple that bonus.

There were always people who hung around, unable to leave scenes of bad things until the scenes left them, but the crowd was thin. It was a weekday, not a weekend. The van was parked down by the tracks, cut off from the river by the levee, so not a lot of air movement, and the air that did move past was heavy with the smell of car exhaust. Every now and again she caught a whiff of something sweet from Café du Monde, reminding her they had yet to get lunch. She supposed she'd have to go Dutch with the guys, which meant a light lunch here at the end of the pay period.

Too bad she didn't have the temperament to be a girl toy. She'd have liked all the benefits from the girl toy part. Except the hanging with the bad boys.

"Is he as tasty as he looks?"

"If we could get time alone, I might find out," Hannah said, feeling that scrupulous honesty was not required when the subject was possible romantic entanglements, even with a sister who wouldn't tell the brothers but would totally tell the sisters. There should be such a thing as privacy, or so she'd heard. And time to change the subject.

"Anything interesting in that?" She nodded toward the vic, who was currently being fitted for a body bag.

Ingrid shook her head, accepting the change of topic, though not without shooting her sister a sister-ish look. "Bullet through the heart."

"Not the head?"

"I'd guess the perp was sitting next to him on the bench."

The other two wise geezers had been shot by someone standing behind or over them, Hannah recalled, hence the head shots.

"Boring. Glad I'm on leave. I'm tired of digging through wise geezer brains. Don't imagine a wise geezer heart would be interesting. Except for the surprise he had one."

Ingrid chuckled. "Empty coffins weren't enough of a distraction?"

Hannah laughed. "Nope. Witnesses?" More to keep the chat on the scene and off her than a real desire to know.

"Not really. Not sure how long he was here before anyone noticed he was dead."

"What?" Hannah mimicked shocked. "You don't have an exact time of death already? I'm so embarrassed for you."

"I always was a slacker—who could seriously use some lunch. Or least a *beignet*." She cast longing look toward Café du Monde.

"You can take my place for lunch and a disapproving silence with Alex."

Ingrid stowed her stuff and then turned to grin at Hannah. "I feel your pain."

Hannah saw something, like a bug dance around, then settle into a red spot on Ingrid's chest. Hannah leapt at her before her brain fully processed that it was a targeting dot.

The shot cut through the racket. They hit the pavement hard enough to knock the breath out of Hannah as two more shots hit the van.

She was distantly aware of shouts, some returned fire. She tried to cover her sister, while she groped for her neck, feeling for a pulse…

———

Dunstead tossed the gun aside and scrambled for the edge of the building, dropping down to the ground. Almost he'd aimed at the doc, but the sister gave him a clearer shot. His last look, though, he might just have gotten a twofer. They both looked like they went down. He leaned against the wall to catch his breath after the drop. Rubbed his face and straightened his clothing, then gave himself a shake and headed for the corner. Time to exit this scene—

She came round the corner before he could. Her gun was ready. It spat twice. He sagged against the wall. Shocked, but not…

She stood looking down at him for several seconds. Then she sighed and from a swiftly growing distance, he heard, "I told you I don't like failures. Or those who betray me."

With neat movements, she stowed the handgun in her

capacious purse and retreated. Glancing around, she saw some uniforms running toward her and made a *moue* of frustration. In the books, there was always time for a speedy retreat. She sighed and adjusted her face to shock and fear. She waved at them and called, "There's a man here. Looks like he's been shot!"

It's not like they'd think she did it. She glanced around and scripted her dialog while she waited.

Yes, officer, I saw a man running that way. And no, I didn't get a good look at him. I was so shocked. I've never seen anyone die, well, except my dear Harold, but he had a heart attack. But she'd never seen anyone who had been shot before....

Speaking of Harold, she hoped this didn't take too long. His funeral was set for five, and it's not like she could tell them that. It would look very odd that she'd come to the French Quarter. Though if she had to, she could come up with something clever. Something about since he'd donated his body to science, she'd come here to his favorite spot to say goodbye....

They'd believe her. She was a middle-aged woman. They'd barely remember what she looked like after she walked away.

CHAPTER 16

DIMITRI AFONIKI FOUND the note before he got the call that Aleksi was dead.

The ring is safe. Don't look for it.

He'd known and still he went. He had to admire the old goat.

He'd even planned his own exit. Dimitri frowned, wondering who had the ring? He would have to ask some questions. As far as he knew, no one but his personal bodyguard had visited his uncle in days. He'd visited him just long enough for Aleksi to suggest the meeting with Guido. Interesting timing? The old man must plot to the very end.

And really, it didn't matter, since neither Guido or Claude had a ring. It was an old symbol, as dead as the three men who'd worn them. Would he have worn it? Only out of respect, he decided. It was a hideous thing that would always have reminded him of the twisted old hand every time he looked at it.

He paced to the window of the office he'd coveted for so very long and looked out on the garden that was now his, too.

All his. Unlike his uncle, he did not think he would live here alone. Aleksi's matrimonial maneuvering had annoyed him, but now that all choices were his alone, he found the idea of a wife—and an heir—appealing.

For a few seconds, the face of Hannah Baker came into his mind. That was odd, since she wasn't his type. Now, Sarah Burland, Nell's friend and roommate, was very much his type, but she might as well be a Baker. He doubted very much she'd be open to an extramarital offer. A pity.

But he would not replicate the mistakes of Phineas or Bettino. He would not marry an iceberg or outside his…class. He did not have to settle for Cinzia or Mirabelle, but as his uncle had believed, he could see that there was merit in a local, dynastic marriage.

Mirabelle would give him an in with the St. Cyrs. He doubted Claude would or could marry, so if he couldn't eliminate the clod, well, he'd need an heir. What woman would have him, even one of their kind?

Mirabelle, unlike Helenne, was not cold. She was a blonde, his personal preference and she'd been raised to know her place. The problem? He was not sure he'd dare turn his back on her. It would not make for the most comfortable home life.

And Cinzia? Not his type, but she was dark, passionate, generously endowed. There was intelligence in her eyes, but she didn't push it in his face like Mirabelle did. She would know her place.

It was possible that Guido would marry, have an heir, but if one were close…friendly…there were ways to slowly bring the two empires together. Particularly when they shared the same goal.

They both had a deep desire to crush Claude into tiny bits of dust.

He would wait a decent interval, then let Cinzia know he'd picked her. Mirabelle would be disappointed, but one could also come to a…separate arrangement with her.

———

"You're bleeding." Ferris's voice was low, anxious, his touch light on her arm.

"Am I?" Distantly she wondered how he could tell. Her hands were covered with her sister's blood. She'd been a doctor before she became a cutter. She was still a bit surprised it had all come back to her.

She'd worked on her sister, done it automatically, her focus on stopping the bleeding and saving her sister's life. She'd only stepped back when they were ready to lift Ingrid into the ambulance.

One of the paramedics who'd worked with her looked back to say, "She'll be okay."

Hannah had nodded. The bullet hadn't found her heart. Hannah didn't know if Ingrid had moved at the last minute. Or it was her knocking her sister down that saved her. She would live. She would be okay. She knew this with her mind. But her heart was still thumping like she'd just run a marathon. Her heart was sending "might-have-beens" to her brain. Running the "not all right" scenario over and over.

She looked down at her arm, trying to stop the reel or at least change it. "It's a scratch." And then as the first shudder rattled her teeth, "I'm getting shocky."

Ferris cast a worried look around. It was a scene of chaos.

He sat beside her and pulled her close. He smelled of hot sun and comfort. She burrowed her hands in between their bodies to get them warm, too. And because the tremble was betraying. He seemed to understand she wasn't pushing him away and rubbed her back with brisk comfort.

Over his shoulder, she saw Alex talking to a woman. Hannah blinked. She must be really shocked. She looked like Miz Cookie. She closed her eyes, but the reel started to play again, so she gave up. The woman tipped her head to the side, her chin angling in a familiar way….

Hannah wanted to rub her eyes. Rub away the grit and the fear and the shock and see and think. Figure out what her brain was trying to tell her. So much noise. She missed the morgue, which was not just crazy. It was bat crap crazy.

"Do they…know who…?"

"Looks like it was Roger Dunstead." Ferris kept rubbing her back, and her shudders began to ease some. "We should get that looked at."

"You looked at it. So did I. Did they catch him?"

Ferris hesitated, so Hannah looked up.

"What?"

"He's dead. They found the gun on the roof of that building. But someone shot him. A woman saw someone running away but was too shocked to notice much. I suspect it was one of the wise boys who were tired of the heat he was bringing down on them and took him out. Not sure I mind if they did do it."

Dunstead had caused their family a lot of trouble, one way or another. "Do you think he planted the bomb in my car?"

Ferris hesitated. "It's not his MO, but he might have tried to get clever."

Or someone had given him the idea. Had he worked alone? That was what she wanted to believe. It fit most of the facts, even if her gut was uneasy. And that stupid clock was still ticking inside her head. She'd been making some thinking headway until all this. Now it felt like the bullet had shattered her thoughts, too....

"With Aleksi Afoniki dead," she lowered her voice, "does that mean Charlie and Ellie can come out of the shadows?"

Ferris stiffened. "So you did find them."

Hannah nodded, only the occasional shudder shaking her now.

"How did you end up with Zach?"

"He was there when I got there."

Ferris whistled softly. "That must have been an interesting meeting. I'm kind of glad I missed it."

She managed something that resembled a chuckle. "Oh yeah."

She watched Alex shake the woman's hand, then turn away with his usual impatience. His face looked lined, older, and his eyes were hard.

She opened her mouth to say something about him needing better closure, but the words got lost when her gaze met that woman's. It was Miz Cookie.

She stared across the gap, seeing the sweetness stripped from her like a veil pulled back, then she turned and disappeared in the crowd.

Something had just happened, and she had no clue if it was important or just weird. As if it had been waiting for just the right moment for maximum effect, the pain from the graze hit, taking her breath away.

"I probably need to get that looked at," she said, easing reluctantly out of Ferris' hold to study her arm.

"Now why didn't I think of that?"

His smile was so normal, so ordinary and so not any of those things that it took her breath away. Luckily she was still too shell-shocked—literally—to embrace the elephant-sized realization waiting for her to get a clue.

"Hannah?" The smile faded to concern.

"I'm okay." Probably. Maybe. Or not. But probably. Eventually.

———

When she went, she wanted a jazz funeral, Gladys decided. Not that she planned to die anytime soon. But it had been so emotionally satisfying. She'd truly, finally gotten closure for Harold. So much, she hadn't minded Belinda showing up. In fact, she was glad Belinda came. Gladys had enjoyed seeing her pain, now that it was certain Belinda would never get Harold.

She sighed. She'd have to do something about the business. Hopefully there would be no more unpleasant surprises when his lawyer went over Harold's will with her later.

Part of her still feared that somehow one of those donated organs would cause a heart attack, but really, bodies rejected organs, didn't they? Sometimes? It was so like Harold not to tell her something so key, so really it was his fault if one of them died.

And she could be thankful she'd had so much on her mind she hadn't had time to worry about it too much. It was one of those things that came to her when she woke in the night. And now she had a new one. That morgue doctor had been a shock *again*. Did the way she'd looked at Gladys mean something? It was too late to wish she'd stayed away from the morgue, hadn't tried to get control of Harold's body. If she could have, she'd have buried him or cremated him.

Oops.

But science had beat her to the corpse.

Science sucked. Though it had helped her ease Harold out of her life. And now she'd use his money to take what should have been hers.

And she hadn't completely given up on finding the ring. Someone was bound to flaunt it now that the old man was gone. If it had been easy to fool two wily old men, how much easier would it be to get to a green-around-the-gills wise boy.

She lifted the hat and long black veil off her head and set it on her dressing table, then headed down, confident that dear Sarah would have cleared the remains of the wake away by now. A tidy check against everything on her list, well, once she was through with the lawyer. Then her day would be complete. Not perfect, but better than expected.

At the first landing, her phone indicated a text had arrived. She almost ignored it. But the only person who would text her was her snitch. She extracted the phone and read the text.

Frank Baker requested the Zafiro file this morning.

Her hands tightened around the phone, and she had to breathe several times before she could respond.

Did he say why?

The morgue doctor asked for it.

She was about to send thanks, but the last text came:

Burning this phone.

She replaced her phone in her pocket. Was her informant

getting uneasy? Well, she'd add that to her to-do list. She wasn't done with him yet.

She frowned. Should she be worried? Even if that stupid doctor looked at the file, she couldn't know, wouldn't connect her to Zafiro. The only person who'd known was Leblanc and Afoniki and they were both dead. But just to be on the safe side, she'd look up the good doctor's credentials.

Not because she was worried, exactly. But she did look like him. For the first time, she wasn't that happy about it.

———

Hannah remembered this from her intern days, the peculiar non-silent silence of a hospital at night. The almost eerie hush.

All the sounds were distant, and nothing to look at but Zach in the other chair, or the machine monitoring Ingrid's vitals. And those were so good it was boring.

It was finally quiet. Which should have been good for contemplation and mulling, but every time her sister's heart rate did its little bump up, her thoughts did, too. She wanted to rub her face but couldn't. Not in front of Zach. He'd already ignored all suggestions that he go home, but he had the power to order her home.

"That chair extends into a bed. You should try to sleep." She got a look for her pains. "You've had a tough few days, daddy."

The word slipped out, leaving her unsure if it was for her she'd used it or a manipulation of him. His expression softened some. "What's the point of having thirteen kids if you don't let them help you every now and again?"

Instead of responding to that, he said, "Been thinking about the day she was born." He glanced around. "Spent a few hours in hospitals waiting for kids to be born."

Not to mention waiting for two wives to pass, she realized. She had a few memories of her mother, but the images were fixed, like photos, so she wasn't sure they were real memories or memories of photos. Love and loss ran through their family as sure as the river passed through New Orleans. And her dad had had more than his fair share of losing.

"I used to think I couldn't miss what I don't remember that well," she said, leaning back and keeping her voice low, "and then I get surprised when it hits me." Her gaze shifted to her sister. "Like now."

"She'd be here, that's for sure," Zach said gruffly. "Twice I married women too good for me. Still surprises me that they fell for my line of bull."

She supposed she should ask about the current lady in his life, but she couldn't quite manage it. Instead, she tried to imagine him as that young man talking her mom into taking on seven boys and him.

"She loved you," Hannah said, surprised by the intensity of this sudden memory of her mom saying, "Your dad's a good man. A real good man." She hesitated, as her brain did a bounce, wondering how to segue to Charlie and Ellie.

"I—she was a good woman."

Was it, she wondered, his fault she was almost inarticulate around Ferris? Logan. She needed to learn to call him Logan. She bit her lip, eyeing her dad uncertainly.

"Do you think it's safe for…them…to…you know. Meet the family."

He sighed and rubbed his face. "I wish I knew. Depends on

the new Calvino, I suppose. The others have no reason to care."

Hannah considered her brief encounters with Guido Calvino. "I don't think he would care. It's not like he's the abandoned son. Or the stepson." He was the guy with all the new goodies to play with.

Zach's brows shot up. "You've met him?"

Hannah stared at him. "Well…yeah…it's Alex's fault."

He half grinned, half scowled. "Those coffins. More trouble than they are worth." He was quiet for a moment, then he surprised her by asking, "Why are you interested in Zafiro?" She must have showed surprise, because he added, "I was there when you asked Frank for his file?"

"Oh, right." She tucked her hair behind her ear and considered the question. "There's been a couple of weird things that happened."

"Weird things?"

She almost told him about being with Guido when he got shot at, but she managed to catch herself in time. "Well, some strange shootings, like someone was trying to start a mob war. And there was that brick? The one Charlie didn't take?"

"The brick. I'd forgotten about that. I wonder if that's—" He stopped, clamping his lips shut like he regretted the words.

"Wonder…what? If Charlie saw something that day, I need to know."

"He said he saw a ghost."

"A ghost." Not what she expected.

"The ghost of Zafiro."

Hannah sagged back. "The ghost of Zafiro. Like a ghost ghost?"

"Of course not. It was a woman who looked like him. Shook him up."

"That would." She agreed, her thoughts spinning slowly around the idea. In the circle was the name, but all around it were the bits and pieces and some of them drifted closer, as if they wanted to connect…. "X."

It was Zach's turn to look confused. "X?"

"We…I…"

"I was there in the morgue," Zach pointed out. "So your equation wasn't just to pull Alex's chain?"

"No, it wasn't. We wondered if there wasn't an X," she stared into the circle again, "an unknown person from the past, a player that no one knew about. But I couldn't figure out how X could find out about being X until that lawyer died."

"Lawyer?"

"You probably haven't seen the news today." They were all too busy being the news. "But someone killed Raymond Leblanc last night."

"Really? Now that is interesting. And Aleksi today." He looked at her. "X."

"X." And Hannah had a very strange idea about who X was. Very strange, and yet, who better than a middle-aged woman to move around, unnoticed, unobtrusive, seemingly harmless until she wasn't harmless? She needed to talk to Ferris. Just in case. It was just possible that Dunstead wasn't behind her car blowing up. "I'm going to go get a drink. Do you want anything?"

———

Gladys managed to keep it together, though she didn't know how. Even managed to sound grateful long enough to get the lawyer out the door.

Harold had left most of his money to *charity*. A foundation in *his* name. To help her *aspirations*.

Oh, he'd left her something to live on, and she might be able to keep the house.

A foundation for Harold. Administered by his personal assistant.

All done for his wife, for Gladys, because he knew how much it all meant to her.

And if she believed that...

She hadn't expected him to get the last laugh and with such gentle irony. She remembered that about him now, his very odd sense of humor.

How Belinda must be enjoying this. And he'd made sure it wasn't worth Gladys' while to kill her. She still wouldn't get control of the Foundation.

She hadn't expected Harold to be quite so...clever. She'd always been able to control him. Until Belinda.

How she wanted to kill her. She ached to kill her. She needed to kill her. She would kill her, but...

She'd have to wait. Be patient. In time, even if she didn't get the money, she'd make sure Belinda couldn't enjoy it for long.

She paced past his chess board. It was still set up from when Harold had straightened it the other day. The same day he'd given her that odd look.

She slammed her fist down on the edge, knocking it to the floor. The pieces flew in all directions.

The white queen lay on her side by her foot. The black queen gone under a chair.

The pawns were everywhere.

As they should be.

She lifted her foot and stepped on one, crushing it, then grinding it with her foot.

Oh, how she needed to do that to Belinda. And the lawyer. And—

Her thoughts paused. She went to the computer and looked up Dr. Hannah Baker on the morgue site. For someone so young, her credentials were quite impressive. She was almost as clever as Harold…what was this facial reconstruction on her CV? Was that like facial recognition? Did that mean she might be able to recognize her? It sounded the same.

It sounded like…

She looked down and then stepped on another pawn.

Yes, it sounded like that.

———

"Why didn't you talk to me, ask me about—" Alex stopped, apparently unable to even say the words "dating my sister."

"Would you have said yes?" Ferris didn't take his eyes off the road ahead.

Long silence. "Probably not."

Ferris shot him a look then. "Probably?"

A big sigh from Alex's side of the car. "So, what—"

"I hope you're not about to ask me my intentions. I'd only answer that question for Zach. Hannah's father. I'm sure you've heard of him?"

Another long silence.

"Fair point. But if we're going to keep working together—"

Ferris stopped out front of his place and put the car in park. Only then did he look at Alex. He felt sorry for him. He really did. He didn't understand. He got that. He didn't have a sister, but if anyone messed with Hannah's heart—

"I won't poke my nose in your…deal with Nell and you do the same for me. We should be good. Right?" If he wanted to deal out advice, he shouldn't be dating the wise guy's grand-daughter, he almost added, but didn't.

Another big sigh. "Right." Alex shoved open the door, but halfway out, he looked back. "Just don't—"

"Not if I can help it." He didn't know if Hannah would give him the chance to not break her heart.

Alex clambered out and slammed the door. Stood and watched him drive away. Ferris allowed himself a sigh of relief. That had gone better than he'd expected. He sure wasn't ready to explain something when he didn't know what it was yet. Or what Hannah thought it was.

Dang. He rubbed his tired face. A relationship talk. But if he didn't man up, he might lose her. Was that why guys talked the talk? Because the fear of losing someone got bigger than the other fear? The commitment thing?

He knew he probably had some issues from growing up. Who didn't? Even knew he'd have to face them at some point, if he wanted more. And he did.

A guy didn't have to spend too much time with the Bakers to see that families could be strong. Committed to each other and better for it. That not trying to have a life with someone was a fast track to nothing at all.

Since getting to know them, yeah, he could see himself in

244 PAULINE BAIRD JONES

one of those houses with kids toys out front. Maybe not quite so many. And when he went in that back door?

His fists curled around the steering wheel as he waited in the fast food line for his turn to place an order.

Yeah, he could see Hannah there, looking up to greet him. He could see that. But could she?

He ordered enough stuff to feed half the Bakers, hoping there'd be something there that both Zach and Hannah would like, then pulled forward to pay. He was pretty sure that none of them had thought to eat or get them something to eat. He paid, stowed the bags and cup holder and headed back to the hospital. Maybe he should call and warn her?

At a stop light, he pulled out his phone. Dead. Out of battery. Crap. If he plugged it now, maybe he'd have enough charge to pop her a text by the time he'd parked.

———

Hannah could tell Ferris' phone was dead by how fast it rolled over to voicemail. She went ahead and left him a message about Gladys White. Just in case. That clock was ticking so loud, it made her head hurt.

She found a vending machine and got a couple of cans of something. Her arm throbbed a steady accompaniment to the clock, but she didn't dare take anything other than some Tylenol. She needed her head as clear as possible to finish putting her puzzle together.

Even then, her brothers might not take her seriously. As far as Hannah could tell, from the little she actually knew, Miz Cookie's only mistake to date was being at the crime scene today.

She had a thought and stopped to flip through her text messages. Yeah, there was one from Sarah about catering a wake today. It had been a general "text me back if you can" so Hannah hadn't responded. Even if she hadn't been in sort of protective custody, she'd have been on duty at the NOCC. Based on the time of the wake, Miz Cookie had come close to missing the funeral.

She didn't know enough about probable cause to know what it would take. She was pretty sure that "her skull is the same as Zafiro's" wouldn't do it. They'd want more.

She pushed open the door to Ingrid's room. Zach was sitting where she'd left him, but the look in his eyes, the peculiar stillness that managed to be hyper alert, gave her a heads up.

"Please do come in, Dr. Baker. And be sure and shut that door nice and tight behind you."

Maybe it was because she was so tired—whatever the reason, Hannah didn't flinch. Just stepped in and carefully closed the door before turning to face Miz Cookie. Though she probably shouldn't call her that. It took her a minute to pull up her real name.

"Mrs. White. I've been expecting you to drop by, but not here."

She'd picked a good spot for her ambush. She stood on the far side of Ingrid's hospital bed, so she could cover the door and Zach.

"It wasn't my first choice," Miz Cookie said, her voice still dripping sugar. "And you've been so hard to kill. I just couldn't wait any more."

It looked like her finger tightened on the trigger of the small, silenced automatic she held. The whites around her irises were disturbing. She was edging over into flat-out crazy, Hannah realized.

"But you want to talk about it first," Hannah said, with sympathy, hoping her girl-to-girl would work well enough for them to catch a break. Zach might be retired, but he was a cop to his toenails and in great shape. "It must have been so hard to keep it all to yourself, to be so alone."

The finger relaxed. So did her shoulders, just a bit. She nodded, using her free hand to brush her hair back. "You have no idea. When Leblanc told me who I was, everything suddenly made sense. I just…*knew.*"

"Zafiro obviously meant for you to have it. None of them can handle all that power. It's so obvious, once you think about it," Hannah agreed, her gaze flicking to her dad for just a second. He hadn't moved. But had Ingrid's lashes flickered? "But why did he make you wait so long?"

"I wish I knew," Miz Cookie said, her lips tightening. The hand holding the gun shifted a bit, but not enough. "If I'd been younger…there's just so much more I could have done."

The light in her eyes was definitely heading deep into the crazy zone. The lady was barely holding it together. That could be good for them. Or very bad.

"Everything would be different." Hannah nodded. "I mean, it's so obvious. You do everything so well. Your party—"

She smiled. "It was lovely, wasn't it? So bad of Sarah to put you behind the prime rib. She's lucky she's so good at what she does."

Hannah felt a chill run down her back. "Those boys sure let you down."

Her eyes lit up. "They were my first, you know."

"First?" Hannah asked, not sure she wanted to know.

"My first minions. The Red Queen needs minions."

"Who wouldn't want some minions?" Hannah managed it without a choke, but she didn't dare look at Zach. "I'm a little surprised about Leblanc, though." Hannah tried to look eager to learn.

"He was very wicked. I had two of the rings, and he wouldn't budge. Just because I hadn't got Afoniki's. He was hiding from me, you know. And then he told someone. I don't know who yet. That stupid old man gave it away. Can you believe that?"

"I never met him, but I heard he is *not* nice," Hannah said, seriously mainlining late night chats with her sisters. Apparently she'd learned more than she realized while mostly listening.

"Oh, he's not."

For just a minute, Hannah thought she'd sit down and chat, but she caught herself.

"Well, no one will be weeping for him," Hannah said, mimicking her sister, Maddy for all she was worth. She must be doing pretty good because she got a look from Zach and Ingrid's lips twitched. "And Roger Dunstead. Well, none of us are fans, that's for sure."

"Roger was such a disappointment. It was his idea to blow you up, you know. If I hadn't been so distracted by my personal loss…" She touched a finger to the corner of her eye. "Poor dear Harold."

There was a note in her voice about him that was interesting, to say the least.

"He let you down, too, didn't he?" Hannah picked Laura to

mainline now. She was really good at getting them to share things they hadn't planned.

"Bad enough him donating all his parts to science. Science," she repeated with disgust, "but he…he created a foundation. Can you believe it? He didn't even call it after me, though he claimed it was to help me with my *aspirations*. I don't even get to manage it."

And that was the trigger. Her chest heaved, and her eyes even got a little red around the edges, though that might have been a trick of the light.

"Belinda?" Hannah suggested, hoping she hadn't just dropped a match on the fire at the wrong time.

"You met her, too? Did she say—"

"Just dropped off the paperwork. For science," Hannah put in hastily as her finger tightened again.

"Little—" A most unladylike word escaped her lips. "She loved him, you know. Probably thinks he loved her."

"Having met you both, I doubt that," Hannah said, wondering if she dared move a bit closer. She shifted her weight to the left foot and the gun shifted her direction.

"You're not to move now." It was said so sweetly, it was creepy.

"My legs are just a bit tired." She pointed to the chair behind her. "Mind if I sit?"

Was it worse to wait for the nurse to come and hope that would be enough distraction or should she try to force something?

"Well, there's no reason to sit. We're leaving anyway."

"We are?" Hannah looked at her dad. *You ready*, her eyes asked. He gave a very slight nod.

"Well, I can't shoot you here, now can I?"

"I don't know, I kind of like the idea of getting shot here," Zach spoke for the first time. "Medical care close at hand."

"It does have its positives," Hannah agreed, using Miz Cookie's shift of attention to Zach to take a careful step closer.

Miz Cookie looked disgusted. "Don't be ridiculous. I'm the Red Queen. I get away with it."

"I have to try to stop you," Zach said, like he was chatting with her, too. "I am a retired cop."

"But I have the gun." She waved it a bit, but from side to side. "I shot Calvino and Afoniki. And Dunstead. And I'm the Red Queen."

Zach's eye may have twitched. But Hannah managed another step closer to her.

"That's true," Hannah agreed, "but if you're going to shoot us anyway, there's not a huge incentive for us to leave this room. From our perspective, this is just a better place to get shot."

She stared at Miz Cookie long enough for Zach to shift forward in his chair. After a period of frowning concentration while she considered this, Miz Cookie smiled with real delight, except for her eyes that showed some white around the red edges.

"I see the problem. You need incentive." She shifted the gun toward Ingrid. "How's this. You don't leave quietly with me, I shoot her."

That's when Ingrid grabbed her gun hand.

———

Ferris had trouble talking the nurse into letting him go to Ingrid's room, let alone take a pile of food in there. He juggled it all and reached for the door.

He heard the crash just as he got the door to open.

He froze at the sight of Hannah, Ingrid and Zach—stretched across the bed—wrestling with what appeared to be a crazed, middle-aged woman in black.

Then the woman took a swing at Hannah.

He tossed the food and dove into the fight.

The gun discharged once, shattering a wall clock, then Zach twisted it from her hand and climbed off his daughter, panting from the exertion.

The loss of the gun appeared to enrage her even more. First a nurse, then a security guard showed up and piled on, but she just kept twisting and screaming. They finally got her flipped over and Ferris cuffed her. Hannah sat on her shoulders, the guard on her legs as she continued to twist and moan.

Ferris, his nose about an inch from Hannah's said, conversationally, "I'm gonna go out on a limb here...X?"

She rubbed at a bloody scratch above her eye and grinned. "Don't you love it when an equation comes together?"

CHAPTER 17

IT SHOULDN'T HAVE SURPRISED Hannah how fast the Bakers could assemble—or in this case—reassemble. After the past week, nothing should surprise her. But she was still surprised. Of course, it was late. No traffic. She'd bet there'd be some red light tickets in the mail next month though.

What wasn't a surprise—after the bulk of the Bakers followed Ingrid to her new room—leaving she, Ferris and Zach alone with Alex, Ben and Frank in the mess of the old room—was that her brothers looked to Zach for an explanation. She got a kick out of their shock when Zach waved them toward her. Ferris might have hid a grin.

"I think you'll find she's the one with the answers."

Three sets of eyes regarded her skeptically.

"If you had information—" No surprise it was Frank who turned a bit pompous.

"Until tonight I mostly had guesses," Hannah admitted. She looked at Ferris. "I had a feeling something might happen, so I left a message for you, just in case. I'm surprised you got it so fast, seemed like your cell was out of battery? Your timing was perfect."

"I never got it. I came because I thought you might be hungry." He pointed at the tumbled mess of food mixed with the broken machinery.

"Oh." She studied it then smiled at him. "That's so sweet—"

Three low growls cut her off.

"Talk," Alex said.

"It's all your fault, you know."

"Mine? What did I do?"

"Your coffins. Your girlfriend."

The three brothers exchanged big brother looks, then found places to get comfortable.

"But there was nothing useful in the coffins," Alex said. "Was there?"

"Well, there was one thing I didn't tell you about," she admitted. "I found Uncle Charlie's class ring tucked down in the side after everyone left."

A long silence, then Ben broke it. "Okay, I get you might have wanted to think about it, but why not mention it later?"

"Because it disappeared. I came back from lunch, you were there, Frank."

He nodded. "The brick was missing from one of the coffins."

"Both thefts seemed to be so random, so weird, but I guess it got me thinking about the past and who would still care about it now. So—" she almost said we again. "I started digging."

"Zafiro? That's why you asked for that file?" Frank demanded. "You should have—"

"Told you what? All I had were vague ideas and this feeling that something was happening out there. A storm coming, but one that wasn't showing up on radar. And there were things."

"Things?" Alex arched his brows.

"Like that weird non-hit on Guido Calvino. And then the kids who shot at him showed up in the morgue." She didn't mention Charlie or Ellie. That was Zach's story—and theirs—to tell when they were ready, though she hoped they talked to Nell first. "And those stupid rings kind of seemed to run through it all. And your code." She hesitated there. She couldn't tell them how she knew about that without talking about Ellie and Charlie, so she skipped over that. "Miz Cookie—"

"Miz Cookie?" Ben spoke for all of them this time.

"Sorry, when she's not crazed, she kind of looks like a cookie lady." Five sets of males eyes stared at her like she was crazed. "*Gladys White* said something about the rings while we waiting for her to shoot us. You remember, Zach?"

"Would that be the 'that stupid old man gave it away' part?"

"Sounded to me like she needed them for some reason." She shrugged. So many questions and she'd probably never get all the answers. Zafiro was dead. So were the wise geezers and the lawyer. "She admitted to killing Calvino, Afoniki, Leblanc and her four minions."

"And Dunstead," Zach reminded her.

"Oh yeah." She held back a yawn. "You should be able to match her gun to the deaths. I'll go out on a limb and speculate that she killed her husband, too, though she didn't shoot him. She was seriously losing it and then when we tackled her—well, you saw it...Logan." Man, would that ever come easy?

"I caught the part about her running the world and none of us would be able to stop her," he admitted. "If she does make it to trial, do you think the wise kids will do something about her?"

No one seemed to know.

"We're already working on getting a warrant on her house." Frank gave her one of those looks that big brothers give their little sisters when they realize they've underestimated them. "You actually recognized her as a Zafiro, just by looking at those old photos?"

"If I hadn't been so distracted by almost getting blown up, I might have put it together sooner. My brain was trying to connect the dots. But maybe it's just as well I didn't. I mean, I didn't have any proof. And it's all pretty crazy."

"Not enough for a judge, that's for sure," Ben said. "But... dang. Good job. Well, except for this mess." He looked around, pushed a paper-wrapped burger with the edge of his shoe. "Pity about the food. Looks like you brought enough for everyone, Ferris."

Hannah gave it a regretful look, too. "That is a lot of food." She looked at him, finding she still had energy to enjoy the warmth in his eyes when their gazes met.

"I wasn't sure what you liked," he explained. "Or your dad."

There was a small rumble of discontent from the brothers. Hannah pushed out of the chair. "I'm tired. I'm hungry and Logan is taking me home." There'd she done it, said his name without hesitating. Score one for the tired cutter.

Ferris took her arm, but Ben's voice stopped her at the door. "Hannah?"

"What?" she gave him a suspicious look.

"You can thank us later for your wrestling skills."

Hannah laughed. "Good night, you jerks." She paused and said over her shoulder, "You know, you don't totally suck."

She blew them a kiss and left before they could respond in kind. Of course, that only postponed the day of reckoning, but she was okay with that.

———

"Thanks," Hannah said, turning in her doorway and giving him a tired smile. She wished—well, she wished a lot of things, but right now, she'd be grateful to be merely "tired."

"It was my—" he paused.

"Pleasure?" She grinned. "To roll around on the floor with a crazed middle-aged woman wearing a girdle who was trying to scratch your eyes out?"

"It's hard to get a grip on those things." He looked alarmed. "You don't—"

That made her laugh. "Not yet, but one could be in my future. I won't lie to you."

"By then I'll probably need one, too." He grinned, but his eyes were serious, intent. "I know you're tired, exhausted—"

"At least I'm not hungry, thank you for the second, and successful, attempt to feed me."

"You're welcome." His chest rose and fell in what might have been a sigh. "Will you go out with me? On a date?"

She found she had one last smile left in her. "I would love to."

He had a really good smile left in him, too. And the kiss managed to curl her really tired and trod-upon toes.

CHAPTER 18

"HE WILL WANT to marry you. Me, he will ask to be his mistress," Mirabelle said, with lazy conviction. She sipped her cocktail and exchanged an amused look with Cinzia. "I understand why Aleksi chose Dimitri. It's not like he had other options, but Bett and Phin chose poorly despite much better options."

"Do you think Phin tried to...change his choice there at the end?" Cinzia ran a finger around the rim of her glass.

"To the children's book author? No." Mirabelle shook her fair head. "If he had, he'd have changed his trust, shifted the money. Giving Nell the ring was a message to Claude that anyone was better than he was. That's all."

"You are probably right." She uncrossed, then crossed her long, bare legs and stretched a little. The water looked deliciously cool, but it was an illusion. It would be warm as a bathtub, not to mention the damage it would do to her hair. "It's been a strange week."

Who'd have thought some crazy middle-aged woman would try to pick up the long dead mantle of Zafiro? Not that she blamed her for the girl power moment, but really, it was too deliciously ironic.

She'd managed to take out two notorious mob figures and then herself. It took a peculiar level of incompetence to cause so much trouble without actually accomplishing anything significant. The two old men would have died anyway.

"We'll do it better," she said.

Cinzia nodded, not needing an explanation, as her lips curved into a smile. "Shall I marry him? Or let him think I will? And you, will you sleep with him?"

She shrugged. "Why not? I'm sure there will be benefits of some sort. And don't they say that you should keep your enemies close?"

"It's too bad Guido doesn't like women," Cinzia said, "or you could marry him and sleep with them both."

"He will still want to marry, will need to marry." Mirabelle said. "He might ask me because well, you know what would happen if that got out. The gay wise guy? He wouldn't last a week."

Cinzia chuckled. "No, he wouldn't." She sighed. "A pity we don't dare. But we need the right kind of chaos."

Mirabelle nodded. "The right kind." She paused again. "I wonder where they are?"

"The rings? Yes, it would be…useful to know that."

"But not critical."

"No," Cinzia agreed, "not critical."

———

The message was cryptic, intriguing but not enough to shift him if he hadn't known the last threat to his control of the

Calvino empire was gone. Zafiro was as crazy as the three old men, it seemed, but he and his last heir were neutralized. And eventually, she'd join her crazy grandfather in hell.

So he went back to the cemetery. Curiosity was ever his curse. And he had bodyguards to protect him from his curiosity.

At first, he thought it was Zach Baker waiting by the crypt that should have held his cousin Toni's remains. But then he turned at his approach and Guido saw his mistake. This man was a Baker, no question, but older than Zach Baker and just enough different.

"Guido Calvino?"

How did this man know him, and he did not know this man? No sign of a weapon, but that did not mean he didn't have one.

"I'm Charlie Baker. Zach's big brother."

"I didn't know he—" he frowned, a vague memory teasing at the edges of his mind. Had there been a brother?

"Zafiro, Bett, and Phin strongly suggested I leave town when I was eighteen."

Guido felt like he should know this, but he didn't. He half shrugged. "That was a long time ago."

"Yes, it was. You see, Ellie was in love with me. They didn't like it. Bett hated it in fact."

"I see." He was certainly starting to. "And now that they are gone, you've come back to…?"

"Ellie would like to meet her granddaughter. Without any complications."

He considered the man. Bett might have hoped he'd avenge his abandonment by his unruly wife, but he actually didn't much care what had happened thirty years ago. And it had resulted in his inheriting everything. So, in a way, Ellie had helped him. "You won't have trouble from me."

"Helenne?"

"Well, her activities are limited by a little tracking device on her ankle. And much of her energy is focused on hating Claude."

"And Dimitri Afoniki?"

"Why would he care who you are or why you left?"

"I have your word?" The steady gaze held his with disturbing intensity.

"Do you trust it?" Charlie didn't speak, so he added, "You have my word I have no desire to incur the enmity of the Bakers."

Charlie smiled slightly. "Then we're good."

"Are we?"

Charlie frowned. "What do you mean?"

"Are you good?"

"I was done with Bettino Calvino thirty years ago, when Ellie left with me."

"Then we are good."

Charlie nodded, turned and walked away. He didn't even look back. Not many had the guts to show him their back. Was he being disloyal?

If he was, what did it matter. This was not a man he wanted as an enemy. Not to mention all those Bakers.

———

"Are you nervous?" Ferris asked her.

"I passed nervous about six blocks back." She managed a smile though. "I mean, I think Nell'd like to meet her, but what if she doesn't? Ellie..and Charlie, they'd feel so bad. And they've waited so long."

"Do they know?"

"I told them I'd talk to her but not when. Everything's been so crazy, but I just couldn't wait. If it was me, I'd want to know —you're a brave man to go with me." She gave him a look with a little anxious in it. "You and Alex? Are you okay?"

"I think so. We had a, well, I wouldn't call it a talk." He grinned.

"Let me guess, he grunted a few times, growled some and then?"

"I pointed out that he wasn't your father."

"Brave man for sure." She tipped her head to one side. "Well, you're still breathing, and the bruises are from Miz Cookie, so you must be in the region of okay?"

He laughed. "Is Sarah going to be there?"

"I don't know. I'm not even sure Alex will be there. I only talked to Nell."

"I hope he is. I think she'll need him." He stopped, meeting her gaze outside the door. "You okay with that? With them?"

She looked a bit rueful. "We've all struggled with it, as you know, but...yeah. I am. I am little worried about Helenne and what she might do, but that's their problem. Mostly."

Ferris chuckled. "Yeah, you Bakers rally round the flag faster'n any group of people I've ever seen." He tapped lightly on the door, but before he could try the handle it opened.

Sarah stood in the opening, her eyes sober and concerned. "Well, you all look a bit banged up, but alive. I still can't believe…"

"Miz Cookie had some seriously crazy depths," Hannah said.

Sarah laughed at that. "Lucky for me she paid for the wake in advance. I thought she looked odd that day, but kind of put it down to the funeral. Did you know she had a jazz funeral for him?"

"Wow. I wonder if they'll get paid?"

She laughed again. "You don't happen to be free on Friday do you, Hannah? I've got a gig—"

"She is **not** free," Ferris said, taking her arm. "She has a date."

Sarah's brows arched. "Really? Um, does Alex know? He's in there with Nell."

"He knows," Hannah said. "He's as okay with it as he can be."

"Are they in the kitchen?" Ferris felt it time to move on from this. "You coming with?"

"Do I need to come with?" Sarah looked from him to Hannah.

"Maybe," Hannah said.

Sarah shut the door. "More bad news?"

Hannah kind of shrugged. "And no, Alex doesn't know. I'mnNot sure he knows we're coming."

"I'll come, if only to protect you from him."

———

Hannah loved Sarah's kitchen. It was like walking into a hug. Except for the space occupied by Alex. He looked suspicious and defensive. Nell looked apologetic.

"Look who stopped by," Nell said, clearly trying to let her know she hadn't brought him in.

"What's going on, Hannah?"

"It's okay, Nell, as long as you promise not to tell any of the sibs until Zach's had a chance to talk to them," she amended.

"Zach?"

"Let's sit down, shall we?" Sarah suggested, pulling out one of the stools on the work side of her big wooden table.

Still suspicious, but now also puzzled, Alex settled Nell and then sat next to her.

"Has Alex filled you in on things?" Hannah asked, wondering how she'd gotten roped into another situation requiring people skills.

"I have," he said. "What's this all about? Was there something you didn't tell us the other night?"

"Well, duh, obviously." She gave Nell an apologetic smile. "I'm better with dead people, sorry, that's wrong, too."

"It makes perfect sense," Nell said, unease turning to puzzled. "Just take your time."

"I'm better over the phone, but this isn't the kind of thing you tell someone over the phone."

Nell's color faded. "Someone…died?"

"No!" Hannah exchanged a worried look with Sarah. "At least, this is New Orleans. Someone died, but not someone—actually, just the opposite. Someone—they are both alive. Charlie and Ellie, I mean." How not to break news, she mentally castigated herself.

"Alive?" Nell started up. "Where?"

"Here. They moved here about the time things got crazy for you. They saw your picture in this online magazine. Your books…they wanted—they were afraid to make things worse. I found them by, well, kind of by accident." No need to mention she'd worried they turned into geriatric murderers.

"You've talked to them?" Alex said, a bit grimly. "Zach? Zach knows?"

Hannah gave him a look and turned back to Nell. "They'd like to, you know, meet you. If you'd like to meet them?"

Her eyes filled with tears. She covered her mouth with her hand. Sniffed. "If? Oh my gosh. When? How? Where? They've been together? Please tell me they at least had each other…."

Hannah nodded, her eyes pricking with tears. "They are living at the Happy Endings Retirement Center."

Nell laughed, a laugh that broke on a sob. She looked at Alex. "I have a grandmother that doesn't suck."

"And she has a wicked sense of humor," Sarah said, wiping tears from her eyes, too.

Alex folded Nell into his arms, holding her tight as her shoulders shook. He looked at his little sister over her head. Hannah held up a hand. "Save it for Zach. I'm just a bit part in that story. An accidental walk on."

Nell pulled back, wiping at her face with her fists. "I want to see them, talk to them…"

Hannah pulled out her cell and handed it to Nell. "Just punch that number."

Nell looked at her, then looked at the phone, hesitated, then pressed it and held the phone to her ear. It only had time to ring once.

"H-hello? Grandma? It's Nell."

CHAPTER 19

HANNAH TRIED to recall her last date. It had been a while. Quite a while. This was not a happy thought. It was also not a good time to remember that relationships that start under intense circumstances never last. Was it even a relationship? Just because it felt like one, and also felt kind of, well, huge, didn't make it so.

It was too soon to have **the** talk, but she kind of wanted the talk before **the** talk. Even though it was too early. Way too early. A little over a week, a few kisses—really nice kisses—didn't add up to **the** talk. Not even the prelude to **the** talk.

Okay, she was a scientist. Time to act like one while she waited for the knock on the door. Instead of wishing she'd spent more time digging through her meagre wardrobe. What were the facts in evidence?

Were kisses facts?

They felt like facts, or possibly evidence.

What about warmth in a guy's eyes? What did that add up to? And the hug. The hug had been right there in front of Zach and Alex, though it kind of felt unpremeditated, so maybe it didn't count.

But he'd faced down her dad and her entire family. The guy had staying power.

Did he want to stay?

Did she want him to stay?

That was the heart of the problem.

She did.

It didn't seem to matter that he was younger and might weigh less than her. Or at least wear the same size pants.

On the upside, he didn't seem to fear her brain. Or think she was a dumb blonde. She'd had *that* date back in college. More than once.

The truly terrifying part? When she'd peeked into the future, well, the dream future? She'd seen him there, throwing a ball to a couple of kids. With no evidence at all, she thought, he'd be a good dad.

What else did she have? Well, Alex trusted him with everything but a sister and he wouldn't have trusted anyone, okay, he might trust his sisters with God. But that was it. And because you kind of had to do that. But if he hadn't trusted Ferris on the job, he would be long gone. And possibly dead for pressing lips to his sister.

She rubbed a finger across the lips in question and smiled.

Did they have enough for the long haul? How could she know? She just knew she'd like to try. If he did. But what if he didn't? She would turn every epic age before him. Forty. Fifty. Sixty. Unless she died first. Odds were she wouldn't. Women tended to live longer—she rubbed her head. It felt like a squirrel got loose in there. With some reluctance, she met her own gaze in the mirror again.

She couldn't fall in…love that fast, could she? If she had… she rubbed the place where her heart beat. It might get broken.

A scientist shouldn't be afraid of learning new things, but they also didn't run into a wall on purpose.

A knock sounded, making her jump higher than science decreed she should. She stared at it. She'd have to open it. She couldn't run now. And if she did? She'd never know.

Whatever she was, woman, scientist, or crazy. She needed to know.

She opened the door. "Hi."

———

Hannah had seemed a bit tense when he picked her up, but then so was he.

He'd gotten himself all ginned up to have **the** talk with her, had even practiced the words and now they seemed, either wrong or stuck in his throat. He wasn't sure, but he knew they weren't coming out of his mouth.

To have the **talk**, he needed *to* talk. With words and every-thing. Mostly words. He frowned. Not mostly. Talking needed words. Jeez his head was all messed up. He could punt. He knew, not sure how, but he knew Hannah wouldn't say anything.

But he'd seen what happened when she wasn't sure.

Distance.

He wanted to close the distance, not increase it.

She wasn't easy to get close to, but he managed it. It felt the most natural thing ever, getting close to her. It was as if they had always been, always would be. He wished he knew how to tell her that.

He glanced at her. It looked like she was focused on her food, but then she looked up and smiled. That smile almost stopped his heart. How did she do that? And why her? Why that smile?

"I—" Dang that was close. He'd almost used the l-word. Way too soon. How could she trust the words now? "This is nice."

She glanced around. "It is."

"I meant…" He pointed to her and then him.

She smiled again. "That's nice, too."

The distance eased some. That hadn't been that hard. He wished he didn't have to talk. He could sit here looking at her and be happy. Of course, he'd like to kiss her again, too. He finally rubbed the back of his head and chuckled.

"What?" Hannah asked, her eyes wide and curious.

A guy could get so lost in those eyes. "What color are they?"

"Excuse me?" She shook her head.

"Your eyes. It seems like every time I look, they are different."

"Oh." Color ran up under her skin. "It says blue on my driver's license."

"Yes, but they're more than blue." He leaned in, but the light wasn't good enough.

"Are you flirting with me, Ferris?"

He went from looking at her eyes to meeting her gaze. "Yes. Problem?"

"No. Give it your best shot." She leaned her elbows on the table, rested her chin in her palms and looked at him.

He swallowed. "I want to," he swallowed again, took a

drink of water, and then went on, "have the talk, but I don't know how."

"To talk?"

He took one of her hands and cradled it in his. "To have **the** *talk*."

"Oh."

Her lips pursed around the single word. If the table hadn't been between them…then he realized she wasn't saying more. Just as the panic started, she spoke.

"That talk." She looked down, then slowly looked up. "I don't know how either. I've never actually had it with anyone."

"Seriously? I mean I haven't but you—" He gestured with one hand. She was so…everything. He couldn't believe she was free enough to be sitting here holding hands with him.

"Mostly guys have been afraid of my brothers. Or my brains."

"Now, see that's just crazy, well, not the brothers. They're pretty scary. But your brains. I mean, I was like guys like that until I read *Pride & Prejudice*—"

Her lower jaw slackened in a really cute way. "You read *Pride & Prejudice*?"

"Well, there was this girl." He grinned.

"Of course there was. How old were you?"

"Sixteen."

"Okay, I might be a little impressed."

"As you should be. Anyway, that book, well, I hadn't really thought about, you know, about wives and the future and stuff."

"Most of us don't at that age."

"I mean the romance stuff, I was like, boring, but that dad and the mom. And that sister? The one who ran off with the jerk and was happy about it? Who does that? That's horror story stuff."

"*Pride & Prejudice* as a horror story?"

"Exactly. Started me thinking what it would be like to live years with one of them. Well, that's when it happened."

Hannah blinked a couple of times. "What happened?"

"Well, I decided to only date smart girls. It was tough, because the smart ones were sometimes too smart to waste time with me."

Hannah laughed, a rich throaty sound that kind of scrambled his brains for a minute.

He grabbed her other hand, raised one to his mouth and held it there until the laughter faded from her face and small flames flickered in her eyes. Oh those eyes.

"Now see, if I hadn't learned a few things, one of them being that it takes time to woo a smart woman, I'd l-word you right now." He kissed the other hand. "I'd say some other things, too, but I know they wouldn't mean much. Not yet. You're smart. I'll save the l-word for when it'll mean something. But I'm..." He considered for a minute. "...putting you on notice. I may not be the smartest man to come along, but I'm smart enough to know when a woman is too good for me. And dumb enough to hope she'll still have me. Because I want the best. For me. And for my kids."

"Your...your kids?"

Her hands trembled a bit in his and she licked her lips, her eyes so big he could fall in there and never find his way out.

"Well, the ones we'd have—if you want them. I mean, I can see why you might want to think about that, and if you didn't —both parents should want kids. They should **both** want them." He stopped, aware he'd lost track of his point. And strayed into a place he tried not to go.

Something changed in her eyes. She freed one hand, but only to touch his cheek, smoothing his hair back from his face. He must have said something right, because she felt closer.

"If we got to the l-word—and the m-word—"

She paused, but he didn't flinch, which made him kind of proud.

"—then I promise you that any kids would be very wanted. Very. And—" her gaze flicked away, then came back to him, and her smile deepened until it was mysterious and filled with promise. "I think you are much smarter than you realize."

He took a deep breath and let it out in a relieved sigh. His first time with **the** talk and he had apparently nailed it. This relationship stuff wasn't as hard as all the brothers kept saying it was.

"So, we're, you know, in it, in one of those…"

She giggled. "Apparently. And you know what is even more amazing?"

"What?" Apparently he knew her well enough to be wary.

"No one died."

"That is amazing." He gave an uneasy look around and while he was looking the wrong way…

"Fancy meeting you two here."

"Zach." Hannah's voice sounded a bit strangled.

They both dropped all contact, almost slamming them-selves against the back of their chairs. His even rocked a bit. A bit symbolic that. He'd never liked symbolism. Ever.

"And Felicity." Hannah stood up. Her smile looked stiff, but she shook hands with her dad's date.

Ferris studied Felicity, mostly so he wouldn't have to look

at Zach. She was younger than Zach, though still older. He could see why Zach liked her. Some gray in her hair, kind eyes, nice smile.

Hannah was a bit stiff introducing them. He tried to imagine one of his parents dating someone else and decided he might find it a bit awkward, too. The dogs wouldn't like it either, which for his parents would be the bigger problem.

"So you're out for dinner?" Oh, yeah, state the obvious. Well, he had warned Hannah she was smarter than he was.

"Just finished."

No one could say Zach talked too much.

"We're thinking of going to a movie," Felicity said, brightly.

"That sounds fun," Hannah said, dropping the words into the silence that had formed.

It might have been funny if it hadn't been his date's dad out on a date, too.

"We'd better get going, hon-Zach. We'll miss the credits."

"Be a pity to miss the credits," Ferris agreed. Was that his voice that sounded so hearty?

"Have fun," Hannah said.

Zach started to go, then stopped and said, "I'll be home tomorrow, Ferris."

"Oh." He blinked. "Okay."

"You're off, right?"

"Yeah…" It didn't help that you could see trouble coming if you had no clue what kind. But he knew something was coming.

"Stop by anytime."

"Stop…by?"

He couldn't see it, but he sensed a trap closing around him.

"Alex said you had something to talk to me about." Zach's grin was toothy. And feral. Then he turned, took Felicity's arm and walked away.

Ferris tugged at the neck of his shirt. Wasn't the tee shirt choking him though. No, that was fear.

"Talk?" Hannah turned from watching him leave. "What do you have to talk to him about?"

"Your brother is evil."

"I know that—oh." A pause. "You could always tell him about *Pride & Prejudice*. He might like it if you make it sound like a Western."

He grabbed her hand and pulled her close. "Let's get out of here. If I'm going to do the time, might as well do the crime, er, the kissing."

"I might be willing to be an accomplice in that. But then you have to tell me what other books you've read to get girls."

––––––––

Thank you for reading

I hope you enjoyed it! While you're waiting for my next book, I hope you'll check out some of my backlist books by visiting my website

To find out about all my releases, be sure to sign up for my New Release eZine and get a free eBook by visiting my website.

If you enjoyed this book, I hope you'll consider leaving a review. It's not just because I'm needy (even though I try not to be!). Reviews help other readers decide which books to buy. :-)

––––––––

Louisiana Lagniappe Excerpt

Louisiana Lagniappe: The Big Uneasy 4

A Reunion, a murder, and a wedding... What's next?

Becca Smith Poole should have known her fiftieth high school reunion would be anything but normal - especially when a dead body turns up! Renowned for her problem-solving skills, Becca is determined to discover who the murderer is - and if her former high school crush is still as handsome as he was in their younger days. The first will take some time to solve, the second one took her breath away.

Retired detective Zach Baker has been lonely since the last of his Baker's Dozen moved out. When he sees Becca Smith's picture in the "where are they now" brochure, he wonders if this might be a first chance for him with the gal he could never connect with in high school. But before he can ask her out, a murder breaks up the party.

Lucky for him, his son's upcoming wedding is full of problems requiring Becca's professional problem-solving touch. Can a retired cop and a mystery reading problem solver unmask a killer before the wedding? Even more challenging, can Zach convince Becca that there is no end date for falling in love?

Dive into the next installment of the Big Uneasy series that reviewers have said "will make the reader feel as if they've been plopped down right in the middle of the Big Easy." Get *Louisiana Lagniappe*: The Big Uneasy 3.0 now!

———

Fifty years.

It had been fifty years since Rebecca Smith Poole had graduated from high school.

Dang.

When Becca got the email from Lisa Linda Bailly, their senior class president, she'd had to do the math twice because it couldn't have been *that* long.

Only it had been that long. Every minute of that long.

So much for the class that was going to beat old, who would live forever. With very few (possibly chemical and/or medically induced) exceptions, they'd become gray hairs, or no hairs, the oldsters that back then they'd thought had one foot in the grave.

Anyone looking into the room would see a bunch of candidates for Senior Discount Day at just about anywhere. Lots of shoulders bent by gravity—not to mention other bits sagging from its evil grip. Here and there she caught glimpses of the young people they'd been in the septuagenarians they were now.

They were here because fifty years ago they'd shared four years in the same high school, a lot of it spent in this gymnasium. It was kind of shocking that such a slender connection, that something that—with the hindsight of years—was so fleeting, had gathered their class's survivors in from all over the country.

In high school, they'd been divided into small clusters based on reasons that made no sense now. What would they even talk about, she'd wondered, as she'd hesitated over her RSVP. She was glad she'd come though. They might have more in common now than they'd had back in high school.

They were all old.

They were the ones who weren't dead.

And they were more or less variations of the same shape.

Time had erased the other stuff, all the who-liked-who, and who-didn't-like-whom. The dividing lines had dissolved because what life they had left was too short. The theme of how freaking old they were was pretty much the go-to conversation that had started during the mixer—where they'd actually mixed—after a brief period of "do you remember?" The only other digression from the main theme of the night was those who had grandchildren to brag about.

Becca smiled as Mary Joanne who-used-to-be-Rivet shared a story on the theme of the night.

"I swear she was fifteen or something and she's putting the blood pressure cuff on my arm, and she says to me, she actually says to me," Mary Joanne switched to a high-pitched falsetto, "Isn't seventy the new sixty?"

"She did*n't*." Bettina Bailey would have gasped it in the old days, but now all she could manage was a distressed murmur.

"Oh yes, she did. And I told her, no, sugar, the new seventy is still the old seventy."

And some days, Becca thought, it was the new eighty.

"She's squeezing my arm and having to tuck the saggy bits

into a tube, and she says to me, well, you're only as old as you feel."

"I would have slapped her..." muttered Dot, who used to be Becca's best friend in the way back when. Her family had moved away about a week after graduation—it had felt like the end of the world at the time.

"...but who has energy for that?" Daisy Dixie finished.

They all chuckled because they were all out past their bedtimes.

As more oh-my-gosh-we're-old stories flowed past her, Becca pushed aside her paper plate. She'd eaten as much as she could of the catered meal—there was something to be said for those senior servings, even if the idea had annoyed her at first—and looked around.

The gymnasium had seen as much wear as her class. The dispirited school hangings looked the same, though they must have changed them out once or twice. Behind the lackluster food smells lingered the scent of dirty shoes and perspiration, and mixed with the smells their class had brought, it all of it now being pushed around by a desultory and probably ancient air conditioner.

She smiled at the sight of Georgy Guidry snoozing in his chair. Just like old times. His wife, Barbara Betty, had her back to him while she caught up with—well, Becca needed to get closer with her cheaters on to see the name tag.

The tags had been Becca's contribution to the effort. Lisa Linda had initially been a little annoyed at the font size Becca had chosen—it made the tags take up about half a chest—but everyone loved them, and the high school pictures Becca had added below the names.

Becca had needed the name tag to recognize Dot who had

apparently recognized Becca without a problem. Or she had been more farsighted than Becca. Upon a closer look, the remains of the girl she'd been were still very much there. And her voice sounded the same, both plaintive and resigned as she somehow managed to cut Becca out of the herd so she could catch her up on the past fifty years in the Life of Dot.

Becca kept her smile in place, nodding occasionally as the big clock over Dot's shoulder tracked how far past her bedtime it was. When Dot paused to take a breath, Becca pushed her chair back.

Pale eyes blinked. "Are you leaving?" Her tone quivered as if she might cry.

Becca lifted her empty cup. "I need more punch." Her gaze did another sweep, but she knew he hadn't come, even though he'd RSVP'd an acceptance.

Her secret crush—one so secret she hadn't shared it with her best friend. Or her diary. If her heart could have kept it from her brain, it would have. She couldn't remember now why it had been imperative to hide it, but whatever the reason was, it still had her in its grip.

"I thought someone said Zach Baker was coming," Dot complained.

Becca may have twitched.

"I used to have the worst crush on him," Dot continued.

"All the girls had a crush on Zach," said Daisy Dixie from Dot's other side. "He didn't come to the last one either." She and Bettina sighed in unison. "I heard he's still a dish. And a widower."

"With *thirteen* kids," Bettina pointed out, with a slight shudder, though she added, "They must all be grown though?" She cast a languishing glance toward the entrance and sighed again. "Donna May says that Zach could give Harrison Ford a run for his money in the looks department."

As she moved away, Becca wondered, had all the girls Zach hadn't dated in high school been hoping for a reunion movie moment tonight? After fifty years? Becca examined her hopes critically. No, she was long past hoping for movie moments, but it would have been nice to see him. Still a dish, aye?

And then, as if her thoughts—or their talk—had summoned him, he appeared in the doorway. She gave him a critical once over. Yep. Still a dish who could give Harrison Ford a run for his money. And he had enough of "it" left to make her heart skip a beat.

Maturity had somehow made his lined face handsome and his gray hair distinguished. She'd been a widow longer than she'd been married, but she could honestly say she hadn't thought about Zach, hadn't wondered "what might have been" until the reunion planning began.

He'd married twice, lost both wives, and there were those thirteen kids, she reminded herself—like the others her information had been culled from the "where are they now" booklet that Lisa Linda had compiled. This was the moment she should be grateful for unanswered prayers.

Women did not age as well as men, and she couldn't imagine the kind of damage thirteen kids would have done if she'd been on the delivering end. She did know the damage her three had done and that was plenty.

As he hesitated in the double doorway, she might have sighed. It would have been nice to have one of those, we-went-out-a-little, lost-love, might-have-been memories from high school. She'd mostly been invisible for the four years. Of the very few guys who'd paid her brief notice, two hadn't survived and the others, to her relief, had declined to come. She'd read where they were now, and it wasn't pretty.

When Zach's gaze started to scan her direction, Becca changed course. The punch bowl would take her toward Zach, who had been spotted and hailed with delight by his old friends—the gals and guys he'd actually shared high school memories with.

It wasn't because she was afraid to talk to him that she slipped between two tables without attracting the notice of the occupants. She just wanted to see the notable events of the past fifty years table. Lisa Linda, Mary Magdalene, and Donna May had gone to a lot of trouble to put it together.

Wow, seen this way, the years seemed even longer. While she'd been living her life wars and walks on the moon, all kinds of technology, and a new millennium had happened. With each step, each event she felt older, so she moved on to the memorial display. Because looking at who had died would make her feel younger. Not. But it was better than going back to the Life of Dot, Part Two.

Like the last display, this one was chronological, starting with Michael David Lorante, who had died a couple of weeks after graduation.

Forever young, she thought, staring at the dimly remembered face. She moved slowly down the line. The time gaps were big at first, then started to close as their class aged and the years racked up. At the end, she stopped, a frown forming between her brows. John James Normand and Larry Garry Olivier had both died within the last two weeks. That was sad. And odd. She did a minor double take to check the dates. They died exactly a week apart. She took the small step to the last memorial picture and did more than a double take.

Georgy Guidry? Born nineteen fifty-three and died...today?

She glanced back at his slumped figure. It was just a bad joke, she assured herself, and Lisa Linda would not be happy about it. They were all supposed to be grownups now. Georgy might think it was funny...

"Becca?"

Becca stiffened. That sounded like Zach. How did she know how he sounded after all this time? She turned around. It was Zach. Zach Baker looking at her, apparently wanting to talk to her. Wow. He looked better up close, which was not fair since she knew she didn't.

He smelled good, too. Nice for her—time had been kind to him. Not so nice for him, since time had been a meanie dancing all over her face. The gymnasium's A/C wasn't up to the job, and she wished she had a fan. Not that it could wave away the wrinkles and sags. She reminded herself how old she was and her lips curved up as her sense of humor returned.

"Hi, Zach. You're late."

It had to be her imagination that he seemed pleased to see her. Which was, she reminded herself, because they were class-mates and they weren't dead. This made her glance at Georgy again, but her gaze refused to stay there. Not when Zach Baker was a few inches away from her *by choice*. All her dreams come true—fifty years too late.

He grinned, and her heart might have skipped. Because it was old and not quite up to the trip down memory lane.

"I saw the menu."

"Our budget gets smaller every reunion," she pointed out, without rancor. Mary Magdalene had been in charge of the food. For someone who'd grown up in New Orleans, her palate was not great. "As the class gets smaller."

He nodded as if she'd made a good point. His gaze moved briefly along the memorial row. "The attrition rate is for sure getting higher."

It didn't seem to worry him. It didn't worry her that much. She wouldn't open the door and invite Death in, but she knew now that no one got out of this life alive. Her smile turned wry.

"Weren't we the class that was going to live forever? How delusional was that?"

"Everyone is delusional in high school," Zach pointed out. "We all thought we were invincible." A hint of sad entered his gaze, which felt like headlights beamed on her face.

Becca knew how to hold a gaze. She had to in her business, but it was the first time she felt like, well, a girl. With a guy. Almost young again. Like they had been an item way back when and now they were having a moment.

And then, because fate was mean, over Zach's shoulder Becca saw Bubba Pascal approach Georgy and give him a shake.

"Wake up, dude, and join the party," he said it loud enough for the words to echo around the gym, causing conversations to break off as everyone turned to look.

Just in time to see Georgy slide sideways off the chair and face plant on the gymnasium floor.

Get *Louisiana Lagniappe* !

Also by Pauline Baird Jones

Romantic Suspense

The Big Uneasy Series:

Relatively Risky (1)

Family Treed (A Big Uneasy Short Story)

Dead Spaces (2.0)

Louisiana Lagniappe (3.0)

Worry Beads (4.0)

Fais Do Do Die (5.0)

Beaucoup Fracas (6.0)

The Big Uneasy Bundle

An Uneasy Collection: The Big Uneasy Books 3-5

Lonesome Lawmen Series:

The Last Enemy

Byte Me

Missing You

Lonesome Mama (Bonus short story)

(The *Lonesome Lawmen* is also available as a digital bundle)

Do Wah Diddy Die

The Spy Who Kissed Me

Perilously Fun Fiction Bundle (includes *The Spy Who Kissed Me* and *Do Wah Diddy Die*. Bonus: *Do Wah Diddy Delete Short Story Collection)*

Dangerous Dance

A Dangerous Duet - 2020

Science Fiction Romance/Paranormal

Project Universe Series:

The Key (book 1)

Girl Gone Nova (book 2)

Tangled in Time (book 3)

Steamrolled (book 4)

Kicking Ashe (book 5)

Found Girl (book 6)

Lost Valyr (book 7)

Maestra Rising (book 8)

Cosmic Boom (book 9)

Project Enterprise: The Short Stories

Time Trap: A Project Enterprise Series Short Story

Operation Ark: A Project Enterprise Story

Cyborg's Revenge: A Project Enterprise Series Short Story.

General's Holiday: A Project Enterprise Story

The Real Dragon

Nebula Nine (time travel adventure)

Open With Care (Christmas collection that includes, "Riding For Christmas" and "Up on the House Top"

Specters in the Storm: A paranormal / steampunk / science fiction romance novella

Out of Time (World War II Time Travel Romance)

Just in Time (An Out of Time Story)

An Uneasy Future

(A science fiction romance mystery series set in future New Orleans)

Core Punch (1.0)

Sucker Punch (2.0)

One Two Punch: An Uneasy Future Bundle

Short Story Collections

Project Enterprise: The Short Stories

Do Wah Diddy Delete

Let's Fall in Love

The Real Dragon and other short stories

About the Author

Award-winning, *USA Today* Bestselling author Pauline never liked reality, so she writes books. She likes to wander among the genres, rampaging like Godzilla, because she does love peril mixed in her romance.

To find out more about Pauline or her books:
http://paulinebjones.com
pauline@paulinebjones.com